GORILLA PACKAGE

BOOK TWO: in the CHRONICLES of the
DARK ILLUMINATE
By: Dick Owens

Published by Newlight Company

ISBN: 978-0-9855120-0-2

Acknowledgments
EDITOR: Kim G. Mc Knight from Shropshire
England
PROOFREAD: Amy Lucas
PHOTOS: European Space Agency, Google
Earth, NASA
SPECIAL THANKS: to Kovien Z. Owens

PROLOGUE
Moscow, Russia December 4, 2021:

From the moment he looked into her eyes he wanted to have his way with her, deep inside her. She was the most powerful woman the modern world had seen, at least in the public eye. Vladimir Peter Chuikov had to make the decision of his life. Groomed to make this decision all his life, Vladimir Peter grew up in Moscow a member of one of the rich families who helped bring down the Soviet Union and opened Russia up to international trade. Coming from a rich and powerful family that somehow owned thousands of acres of land along with many buildings as soon as the Berlin wall came down, he would say he made his fortune building Western-style food chains such as Burger Max, Lil Mama's Pizza, and Taco Man in former Eastern Bloc countries. His critics say otherwise, using Vladimir Peter as a poster child for the former Communist Party - bosses who abused their positions of power by dividing the huge country amongst themselves and a few aristocrats. They then voted amongst themselves to place someone in a position of Prime Minister. Regardless of how he ascended to the position of Prime Minister, Vladimir Peter Chuikov had managed to bring Mother Russia to the prominence of being the largest economy in Europe, causing the European Union to beg Russia to join. He brought prosperity to millions of Russians as well as other Europeans using 1980 style United States political and economic strategies some termed "Peternomics."

Prologue

He moved Russia to the far right, initiating a war, first on drugs in the year 2014, then in 2016, as part of a campaign promise from both he and his then-biggest rival, entered Russia into a "War on Terror." Several new laws signed into effect took Russia back to 1949 style human rights conditions for the targeted groups deemed "enemies of the state", but for the fast-growing middle class and the rich, life was greater than ever. The Russian war on drugs, with penalties almost as harsh as some of the States in the United States, instantly created millions of criminals who needed to be kept in prison. The Russian prison system had been deteriorating since the end of the 80s, so several hundred new prisons were built, creating jobs. Next, following the lead of the United States and India, corporations were allowed to contract labor from the prisons that were mostly privately owned. This created even more jobs and wealth for the middle-class and the rich, as they had over two million free laborers in prison growing at a rate of 4.2% annually. The astonishing economic prosperity of Russia benefited the European Union as millions of rich Russians would travel to Western Europe to spend their hard-earned money on drugs and prostitution, which were expensive but legal. Now, this was all threatened, by whom he could not imagine.

Rather short and a little overweight with a boyish face, his deep strong voice and thoughtful blue eyes were his best attributes as they made him a great public speaker. Women commented on how sexy his voice was. It was so good he could sing rather well. In a beautiful baritone voice with an occasional tenor and bass note, he moved a nation to tears while singing the Russian National Anthem once before a debate in which he thoroughly destroyed his opponents. As a young boy, his grandfather would take him alone when he would meet with powerful men since he was seven years old. He would always remember this one particular old man. His grandfather called him Sir. Rothschild, but told young Peter to

Prologue

simply call him Uncle Rothy. Once, after he had met with Grandpa and Uncle Rothy for the third time in four years, Uncle Rothy spoke to young Peter. It was something small, minor.

"Young man, I see you've grown much since the last time I have seen you. How old are you now?" Young Peter's voice cracked and squeaked out a stuttered,

"E..l…even." Young Peter tried to put as much bass as possible in his reply; what came out impressed even himself. After all, this was the first time any of his grandfather's friends spoke directly to him. He would never forget that meeting because it was the last time Grandpa took him to a meeting. Later in life, his grandfather called Peter to his deathbed took his hand and said,

"I taught you all I know but one thing which is probably most important…but, I… I did not teach you… humility. I am sorry I did not teach you… only because, I did not know what it was then…I am sorry." Grandpa Chuikov coughed and strained to get out his words. "Now I know what it is…You should have said 'Eleven, Sir!' to Uncle Rothy with less bass in your voice way back then. You see I never did business with Uncle Rothy after that day and it caused me nearly everything." He coughed a few times and then died. Now before Vladimir Peter made a big decision, he always thought about humility. He had to unleash the Russian armed forces on one of the greatest military forces the world had known — the United States of America. His decision was unlike any other scenario played out over the years in common folklore. He would not have the combined might of the Soviet Union backing him. Although it had a population of 150 million and vast resources, Russia itself would have to bare the brunt of the casualties. Russia would not have to go at it alone, an Asian coalition led by China would be attacking the West and India, with the help of a few African troops and South American forces would be attempting to take the Gulf States

Prologue

to open the interior of the United States. Prime Minister Peter's decision would set the tone, as Russia would be sending troops in coordination with the European Union to secure the East Coast. In accordance with the United Nations resolutions 2665, 2666, 2667, and 2668, Russia was to be the first country to give a number on how many troops it would commit to the invasion. Prime Minister Peter sent the number "1.6 million men." He would tell Parliament.

"It is critical to show the world who we are," and, "everything our brothers and sisters die for on foreign soil we will want to keep so their death will not be in vain."

Prime Minister Peter's tone set the mood and the bar high in two ways. First, all the invading countries committed larger numbers of military forces to show their prowess; China's President Wu Ho Ning committed 3.9 million men, India 2.6 million, and the European Union mustered nearly 2 million men. Another 2.3 million troops came from African and South American and a few other countries, notably North Korea, who alone committed 122,081 women, soldiers, and 316,078 male troops.

By the end of the day, it would be nearly 15 million people attacking the United States from three borders. Canada was to be neutral in accordance with U.N. resolutions. The second effect Russia's Prime Minister Peter's gestures had was governments began to explain to their citizens that they would be protecting their assets inside the United States. This soon turned into the conquering countries plotting to divide the United States up like a fat turkey.

The European Union nations went back to old maps from the 1600s and 1700s to decide which States originally belonged to what country. Certain countries such as Ireland and Switzerland stood to gain more land than their current size. Of course, Russia always felt it had gotten the short end of the stick on the whole "New World Discovery" thing. Now Prime Minister Peter was getting a quarter of Alaska back and

Prologue

a third of the original Louisiana Purchase. China was going to take most of the West Coast with a few concessions to India, Saudi Arabia, and North Korea.

All the cybervisions in the world tuned in as President of the United States, Mary Lee, addressed the world with all the leaders of the world at her side. She pleaded with the American people to cooperate with the United Nations, NATO, and other International Organizations entities such as Federal Reserves. She told the American people that a massive international force would be coming to liberate them and they would be free again. Her speech ended with "God bless America." Behind closed doors; President Mary Lee look-alike was in communication with resistance forces inside the US, mostly made up of former State Employees.

China suggested a President Mary Lee look-alike be used to organize a resistance inside the United States. This proved to be a brilliant ideal as millions of former Federal and State Employees were willing to fight alongside them to bring back the old system where they were paid to tax, police, and govern. For the first time in history, every single country leader set down as allies to re-forge a new world governing body some dubbed as UN 2.0. After all the meetings and celebrations of peace and prosperity amongst Nations, it was time to get down to the business of planning the war.

For China it was simple, they were going to coordinate with resistance on the ground, then send massive waves, rather it be land, sea, or air. Once the military goals were accomplished, assimilation would be the number one priority. China planned to build a Great Wall of Defense at the Rocky Mountains, unlike anything the world had seen. Saudi Arabia coveted land from West Texas to Arizona and thus hired several hundred thousand Islamic mercenaries to go and carve out the stretch. Hardened from years of actual brutal combat in which they were usually technologically inferior, these were some of the toughest soldiers in the world. Their

Prologue

objective was to seize their goals and objectives, then set up defensive perimeters against the Chinese to the West.

The Sino Pact to the North was to be a coalition of smaller States occupied by the Koreans, Thais, and a few other Southeast Asian countries to act as a buffer with China. Then there would be the Indians to the east. They had a huge army amassed and said "all" of Texas to the Mississippi River "will be taken" for India. They said it was ordained in all of their holy writings and that the original inhabitants were from India and so on and so on.

For Russia, everything had worked out better than Prime Minister Chuikov could have ever imagined; he could not believe his fortunes. Just a few days ago, he was worried about an American-like civil war coming to Russia. It appeared all the Governments of the world had the same fear as him of the "awakening movement" sweeping the so-called "world citizens." *"It would be crushed and go down in history as a simple anarchist uprising easily shrugged away,"* Prime Minister Peter thought to himself. He called in his top aide and made sure the 1200 lb. and 1400 lb. Siberian wild boars were shipped to his old friend Fiske Braun. Fiske's intelligence work had helped Peter in many ways. Fiske wanted Prime Minister Peter to meet someone from the former United States Defense Department who survived the Washington DC bombing and had insight on whom or what they would be facing when attacking the rogue nation. Peter was hesitant, but he really wanted to do whatever he personally could to lower the estimated casualty numbers of invading a country with armed citizens.

The meeting took place in a private building in Moscow. Prime Minister Peter, Fiske Braun, and Preston Ross set down to lunch and discussed the upcoming war that was on everyone's minds. Preston gave the Prime Minister a small book entitled "The Gorilla Package." He told him,

Prologue

"Read it and it will explain what happened in the United States to bring the world to this stage. Take everything you read literally regardless of how strange or far-fetched it may seem. This is the only way you can truly calculate the proper way of approaching the United States militarily."

"What do the people really want? Are they going to fight us tooth and nail?" Prime Minister Peter Chuikov asked Preston Ross with sincerity in his eyes that let Preston know maybe Vladimir Peter was ready to do more than lip service on keeping casualty numbers minimal.

"They are willing to try the new system. China says millions of former State and Federal employees are willing to fight with them, but also millions more are willing to fight against them. This is the nature of the American people. There is no homogenous mind."

"Tell him about the hi-tech weapons", Fiske Braun interrupted.

"Well, yes, they do have a few unconventional weapons which could pose a significant threat to unprepared forces… they are detailed in the brief I gave you." Prime Minister Peter looked at the journal Preston had handed him. It was about 200 or 300 pages, like a book.

"It's quite long. I…"

"Peter, we have been friends for decades. You have always said you trusted me… please take the time to read it," Fiske said to him in a whisper of a tone.

"It's translated into Russian. It is the best I can do. I am moving my family to Europe. I included some notes in the journal. I was going to give it to a Col. Brett but maybe he already has a copy. I am honored to be able to meet the Prime Minister of Russia, but I must excuse myself." Preston said as he stood up while looking for the exit. Bodyguards escorted Preston out as Russian Secret Service types were investigating Preston's background in real time from his fingerprints to his

Prologue

DNA samples left in various areas. It came back he was the real deal. He knew what he said he knew.

The rhetoric was passed back and forth as the United States proclaimed itself to be the only free country on the planet where the people actually did run the government instead of the other way around. In the year 2020, they chose the President of the United States by popular vote via cybervision and unemployment was soon close to zero.

The problem was this experiment in freedom was a serious threat to the social structure and fabric of other nations. These other nations claimed, "an illegal" and "an evil régime" had seized control of the Presidency of the United States and had "weapons of mass destruction" under their control causing the United States of America to be a threat to world security.

One of the greatest wonders of the 21st century will be how The Day was kept secrct. It was called "The Day" because it was to be on that date 15 million men, the largest known invading army in history, descended on the United States of America. Its goal was to decapitate the Government and seize control of all the ballistic missiles, command and control, and other key military facilities within 24 hours. Within the next 48 hours, State and local strategic objectives were to be taken.

Prime Minister Vladimir Peter Chuikov gave his fieriest speech, which was cybervisionized at the same time China was having huge military parades celebrating some obscure Chinese tradition. The evening news broke as tensions went high along the Indian border when India moved many troops in response to China's military parades. Indian officials said, "China's actions appeared threatening from satellite images."

After his speech Prime Minister Peter could not sleep, being one of a few people in the world who knew what tomorrow would bring. All the military parades and false alarms were deceptions to cover actual military movement for

Prologue

"The Day." There was something he just could not put his finger on, something important, a last-minute detail he had forgotten. Then it hit him like a ton of bricks. The document Fiske Braun gave him from the rude American named Preston Ross or something of the sort… *Vital information he thought to himself*." He found it and started to read. There was a letter, then several chapters with strange titles. It appeared to span several decades. Prime Minister Peter started to read. He read from cover to cover using his trained speed-reading techniques. Not believing what he had read, because, for one, his name was in it, he went back slowly and reread it page by page. This is what he read:

TABEL OF CONTENTS

Chapter 0

NO VASLINE

Sir Mighty Ant greetings,

It is for Summer I finally finished the most powerful of all my devices. She was the woman who had my heart. Her spirit was enduring like mine, but a female version. There was no man in his right mind who would not want to be loved by her. Even though I have not touched her and she claimed she is a virgin (of which I am most certain is not true) our spirits have connected on deeper levels than my prior lovers Grace and Honor. Maybe after losing both of them, I've learned a valuable lesson since now I can love a woman's spirit and other characteristics besides physical love expressed by having to have sex with her at least three times a week.

Grace, who was my number one girl, was heaven sent. I prayed to God one day to send me a woman, then that night, at some hole in the wall nightclub, I met my soul mate Grace. For three years, I destroyed the greatest love God had on Earth at the time because I could not accept her imperfection even though I was not perfect. Once I met Honor, I had the courage to leave my Gracie, my Pooki Pooh, my Pookimus.

Honor was a virgin, giving Grace one flaw, plus she had more money. She also seemed more caring than Grace. I was not fair to her as I took her love for granted, also losing Honor as completely as I lost Grace. Anyway, to put things into perspective, it is after Summer I named our major campaign to dominate the Western hemisphere before the leaders of the old-world order cause it to collapse into chaos. This would be bad for both our family and friends if millions of US citizens' lives were wasted just to prove a point.

I have motivated Mr. Lion by way of a parking ticket to stand up and take action. I am sure his brother and cousin will back him to the end. A stupid parking ticket was all it took; now I have five votes. My vote and of course the most Honorable Gorilla's who, because of his unfortunate living conditions, is 100% behind the Summer Offensive as we will come to call the next series of predictable events that will take place for the benefit of the human race.

After you read this letter, I want you to be sure to destroy it. In the past week, police officers have harassed me twice while I was walking down the street. The first time, while in Hollywood, I was stopped, then handcuffed. Once my hands were hogtied behind my back, the police officers ran through my pockets. The second time I was walking alone to go across the street to a friend's house when a police car passed by me and then turned around. The police flashed their lights on me to get some reaction and institute fear in me. I ignored them, so they just drove on by. Because of these two provocative encounters, history will show who fired the first shot and I have been assured it's time to finish the device because I refuse to be their slave physically or mentally. I want you to document everything and put into a form easily understood by the masses. Make sure to include the stories I told you about the Shindinki and you must include the Theories of the Great Nothing. So, my friend, the Summer Offensive has begun, and its ultimate success will depend on you.

- The Great Elephant
Letter to the Mighty Ant, March 20, 2020

No Vaseline

Although the Great Elephant's genius seemed to border on insanity sometimes because he had seen so much further than any man before him, often I wondered if he was even human. After I read the letter from one of the only men I can honestly say I ever admired it became decisively evident it was time to tell the world the truth.

I have known for many years of plots and conspiracies to control and manipulate the masses caused by greed and lust. I have seen the billionaires and millionaires prey on the less fortunate with the same depravity as that of a child molester who harms a defenseless victim. Like Jesus kicking over the table in the temple, I am forced to exist in a state of war with a group of people who are in the business of depriving people of their God-given rights. Throughout history, these people have been seen and in all circumstances; they were either a kingdom or the Church. When these two works together, they are called a State. Once you have a few States gathered then you have a Country.

For the purpose of this book, you will understand that even the mightiest Country is no more than a few thousand key men and women who have positioned themselves high above the rest of the citizen in the nation. They control all the land and they have their own money with military and police to enforce what they will. These government States always rule ruthlessly since they have all the power and can make changes for a greater society but choose to only drain the life force from their fellow human beings.

It is a phenomenon how millions, and now even billions, of people let only a few thousand people control their lives. It shows the power of collective stupidity. I think the best example of collective stupidity in most recent history would be World War I. Here we have about 30 or 40 people in the countries Italy and Russia who had ties with a few hundred people in England and France. These may be 200 people from these four countries had a rivalry over oil and resource-rich lands in Africa and Asia with a couple hundred people from Germany, Hungary, and The Ottoman Empire. The Ottoman Empire was the closest thing you would have to a United Arab and Persian Empire, which would've been seen as just as formidable as the Soviet Union did after World War I to other countries in their respective eras. Neither of these groups of people had any legitimate rights to any resources or lands they were coveting. They had Treaties saying they would all aid each other in battle if something happened. One guy got killed in a parade. As a result, these three or four hundred men from these countries, through chain of command, forced millions of citizens from their countries to die on the battlefield. The Taghuts, as they are called from ancient times, are the men who are controlling the countries.

Before World War I, the Taghuts could be easily distinguished by their unmitigated effrontery, as they actually called themselves Kings, Queens, Czars, Emperors, Popes, and Kalifs. Most did not sit on thrones, only gathered, and controlled resources, the root of their power.

They own all the land in their respective countries, so all the citizens of that country were indebted to them through property tax. Taghuts would have been large industrial owners who were integrated with the politicians, so they could make policy which benefited only themselves.

The people who were dying in the trenches were the everyday people. Most met their terrible fate starting with a whistle blow to "go over the top." This meant the soldier would climb a ladder to go into no man's land where he either would be hit by machine-gun fire or blasted by cannon shrapnel. The only other option after the whistle was blown was to be shot in the back by his commanding officer for treason on the battlefield.

Because neither their lives nor the lives of any of their immediate loved ones were at stake, Taghuts continued this war of attrition in the hopes the other side would run out of men or bullets. More than 35 million died or were injured beyond recognition because of a decision of a few hundred. You could make the argument that the soldiers were all fools for allowing themselves to be used as pawns of the Taghut. However, if you look at it from a different perspective, many of the soldiers were either drafted, which means they were forced into military services, or they were duped by the press and other propaganda tools of the Taghut. Now the accountability swings to those who were in charge and the criminality of World War I comes into focus. Another member of the Taghut may be the media mogul.

I sat watching the cybervision; or rather, the cybervision was watching me. The first thing that comes to my mind is that here lies a very small group of people who are controlling what millions of people think by manipulating what they see and hear through the media. This has to be a very powerful form of mind control. It is probably essential to controlling the people inside a country.

If a person reads what I have written logically you would have to consider what I have written to be at least as true, if not more correct, than what you would get through your cybervision since I only write to achieve my destiny in heaven.

In America, it would seem one group of people has disproportionate control of the film and television industry. This group of people learned their trade from the Nazis during the 1930s and Communist of the 1950s. The Nazi is a study in human psychology. What I've seen in the Nazis was being repeated inside the United States in the form of the Patriot Party and other far-right political parties. As with the Nazis, the Patriot Party members have to have a similar régime in which all members share the same type of ideology in order for them to exist.

In the first part of the 21st Century, the far right found their allies in every country; the most important the United

States, British, Russian, and Indian governments which were totally dominated by covert entities comprised of only a few like-minded individuals who controlled the government with absolutely no say so by the people.

These governments supported wars first in Columbia than in Iraq, Afghanistan, and later Mexico. The crimes they committed against humanity included killing hundreds and incarcerating thousands daily without due process. This has not gone unnoticed and is well recorded. The prevailing belief that the average citizen can do nothing about the problems of the world is a false belief perpetuated by the media to benefit the proprietors of the wars, famines, and preventable death.

The media will show you, to entertain you, the novelty of an African American President of the United States of America interviewed by a famous talk show host who is hostile to the President's policies during the Super Bowl! It is an interview high in drama and informative, "must see C.V." What you really got was proof racism still dominated the United States of America way of thinking in 2011 and the media and the political establishment was the same just as they were in Nazi Germany or Communist Soviet Union.

The audacity of arrogance never ceases to amaze me as if it was possible to separate them. I have actually once known a man who was arrogant but at the same time humble. Maybe to be a Black President of the United States of America one would have to have such special abilities such as being both arrogant and humble, to say the least. This in the interview with the Black President at the Super Bowl I did not see. Instead, I saw the hand of a racist nation scripting an arrogant reporter and a humble Black President. Quickly I will reveal the United States intentions. It was to show the world a good face in the form of a Black President after the dastardly preempted Nazi-style wars of the United States.

The Black President was to serve not only as a healer to the rest of the world but as retribution for the slavery. After his four years, a new American savior was to take the stage and another Black President was not to be seen for another 400 years. The script called for first a woman, then a Latino. Maybe they will condense all of this into a gay Republican Latino woman as a super candidate.

Chapter 1

ANTEBELLUM

December 21, 2012:

There will be two new High Schools built in the good ol' USA in the future. The first will be called Adolf Hitler High School. I am not a Nazi and I do not sympathize with all the murder and mayhem they caused. To demonstrate a point, I feel one of the two schools should be named after Adolf Hitler. It would most likely be called just Hitler High. Kind of has a ring to it, huh? Which State in the Union do you think would most likely have a Hitler High? I can see several thousand like-minded idiots all gathered first in Alaska and then Texas— several other States would soon follow the largest lead. After about 20 or 30 years there wouldn't even be any complaints about the name anymore, after all it's just a name and from day one they would have established they only named the school after Adolf Hitler because it was unique.

The question I ask now is, could government officials force Jewish kids to attend these schools? Well, hell yea! If a poor Jewish family moved to Alaska, Texas, and probably by now, Florida where some good ol' folks from the private sector put up funds for an Adolph Hitler School of Arts, kids would have to go to the public Hitler schools. If not, the parents would be placed in jail and the kids separated from their families if the

State Family Laws and Codes are not complied with as long as,

"…the students at Hitler High have the same curriculum as every High School in the State," State Supreme Court Judges would most likely rule. The racial makeup of the student body would most likely be majority White kids and then Native Americans (a.k.a Mexicans), followed by Blacks, Mulattos, mixed breeds, then others—Asians, Jews, and

Antebellum

Arabs —in that order. It seems the majority of these groups would not be too offended by the school's name. The majority must always rule. One has to wonder if the name of a building one attends eight hours a day for four years could influence one's perspective on life. The school colors of black and red and the mascot being The Tigers for the football team and Panthers for the basketball team would go unnoted by most. If ask the athletic director would explain,

"The tiger is a big powerful cat while the panther is agile and that's the difference in the two sports so this is how we want our players to think on the field and court." It will go unnoticed that every athletic director, no matter the year or even decade, would give you the exact same explanation for the two-mascot system. The inside joke in the town was the basketball team was made up of mostly Black kids, so they called them the Panthers. Everyone would giggle equally at the joke—Blacks, Whites, and Mexicans making it a cool joke. What would not be funny was all the State championships in both football and basketball Hitler High racked up. Even more impressive in honors would be the marching band who goose-step up and down the field with fire in perfect unison being acknowledged as the best in the State because of the unique "goose-step style" no other band can quite duplicate.

My grandson would have trouble attending Adolf Hitler High School. Because of the way he was raised if he met Adolf Hitler in person, he would wait until Hitler was giving a big speech or doing something very important in front of many people. Then run full speed at him, jump, and deliver a flying one-foot dropkick to the side of Hitler's rib cage, probably breaking his ribs. The kick would send Hitler flying to the ground. After that, he would just kick him in the rear like a dog then walk away since; he knows Hitler did not like people of color because he felt they were inferior. Also, I have instilled into his conscious and soul the lessons of Isa Ben

David that state no man has the right to take another man's life, no matter the reason although true self-defense is a natural reflex such as to regurgitate or a cough. The consequences of this violent disrespect of Der Fuehrer would not matter because he would know in his heart he got the right one. My Grandson would not understand the actions of the old Jewish man who would want to start with wire pliers and for a couple hours just pull flesh and meat off Hitler's body while he screams in agony. My Grandson may try to restrain the old Jewish man long before he put down the bloody wire pliers and picked up the billy club and then proceed to beat Hitler's shredded body in an invigorating excited bloodlust. The old Jewish man would start at the feet working his way up to the head for the next hour followed by the old Jew slitting Hitler's throat with a slow slice taking 20 minutes as he whispers in Hitler's ear.

The next school to make all things fair and equal will be named Nat Turner High School. Nat Turner is by far the greatest African-American Civil Rights worker besides Harriet Tubman—far ahead of Malcolm X and Martin Luther King Jr.. Here is a man who was uneducated and had absolutely no financial backing yet, he started a revolution. It is safe to say that if it was not for Nat Turner, all African-Americans would still be slaves today.

It is unfortunate to have to put a more than likely decent man beside a perceived evil person such as Adolf Hitler to prove the point. A lot of good ol White folks would just as vehemently object to a school named after "The Nat Turner" paid for with their tax money as a Jewish family would object to the Adolf Hitler High School. I do not think Jewish or Latino people would mind a Nat Turner High School as much, although both their ancestors owned slaves thus Nat Turner and his men would have beheaded and chopped them up too.

After a few years, White families would not complain about the name, as most would not even know who he was,

Antebellum

because his legacy is long forgotten. I wonder if a White man, such as the ones who represented the political parties GOP or their children who were calling themselves "The Tea Party", ever-met Nat Turner in person would they be willing to issue out some retribution such as my grandson and the old Jewish man did to Hitler? Or would they just allow the Nat Turner High School to rise? I could see some GOP and their kids in the "Tea Party" who seem to have represented everything detrimental to the so-called African-Americans, going to go get some more people, some rope, and a branding iron. They would probably tell someone to bring some kerosene and a sharp knife because someone is going to want to cut off Nat's balls while he is alive... poor Nat. So it should be expected for there to be problems with Adolf Hitler High Schools and Nat Turner High Schools because of what they represent.

One would think this is not even a subject to be pondering in the 21st Century; but at last, are the White kids, whether they be Jew or Gentile, more precious than the colored ones if there exist Robert E. Lee High Schools in the United States? Public schools were Black and Latino kids are forced to attend. This is like forcing Jews to attend Adolf Hitler High. Robert E. Lee considered Mexicans an inferior race to be either exterminated are used as slave labor if they would not bow down to the "superiority" of the great White race. Of course, he would have been a crusader against Muslims and hated all Arabs. He considered Asians a "nasty and inferior race" and not to be trusted. They would have gotten nothing but hard times and slavery in the United Confederate States of America. Robert E. Lee was more than likely an anti-Semitic who believed "the dirty Jews killed the Christ", and he for sure felt the great White race should enslave Black people who were nothing but talking animals in his mind. He even fought a war against his own country to uphold the institution of slavery of which some would agree will always stain the American image as the symbol of freedom American kids are taught to see the United States as in elementary school. Robert E. Lee more realistically represents the imperialistic, murdering oppressor of the poor and people of color image displayed by United States foreign policy, which is racist. Maybe this is why despite the fact that Robert E. Lee's name represents racism and discrimination just as much as Adolf Hitler and more so than Nat Turner's there are still Robert E. Lee High Schools in the United States. Students along with the entire community around these beacons of hate seem to be stuck in the 1850s or no more than 1950s. Towns with Robert E. Lee and other major Confederate landmarks tend to behave exactly how a Confederate racist White man is supposed to act. Their actions are evident in the deliberate mis-education of the colored kids and their overt racist justice system.

Robert E. Lee High School and Adolf Hitler High School both maintain the status quo for the higher education colleges and universities of the State and separate the students into three groups based on arbitrary tests usually based on vocabulary only.

Group 1: The "smart" kids who are children of the elite and have the broadest vocabulary are educated.

Group 2: The "average kids" consisting of regular White kids, preferred minorities, and Black athletes who behave like good house niggas are taught the basics to survive.

The third group,

Group 3: are students who usually speak ethnic slang, consist of people who do not speak English well, poor White kids who will drop out, and defiant Black kids, all labeled, and excluded from extra curriculum activities such as sports so they will not have any incentive to participate. It is important to label the delinquent kids early so no resources are spent on these kids. Because they have been classified as smart, most of the wealthier kids are placed in "advanced classes" or "honor classes" and given the best- qualified teachers. Coaches and other unqualified teachers teach the Black kids,

Antebellum

along with Mexicans and poor White folk kids. Often, they are just suspended or expelled from school.

The delinquent youth's files are shared with the local authorities and they start to prepare the prison cells for them. This is where the prejudice justice system kicks in. Two kids could do the exact same thing yet a "Group 1" White kid, gets talked to about his dad's antics back in the day, by a police officer and not even arrested, while another kid, the Black kid, goes to jail, thus receiving a criminal record. Immediately, doors start to shut such as getting licenses for high paying professions barred by felony convictions resulting in the best jobs becoming out of reach. The prison doors open wider due to the enhancement laws and the illegal handling of trials by Judges, prosecutors, and court-appointed defense attorneys who all socialize together with the majority being bigots. They have to be because they are all proud alumni of Robert E. Lee and Adolf Hitler type schools taught through custom to be prejudice. If there were Adolf Hitler schools in America, I can assure you, Jewish kids would be placed in concentration camps because African-American kids are being held in slavery just as you would expect.

In these States, the Black residents have absolutely no political power and are constantly harassed and intimidated by the police and sheriffs so consistently, it is nothing less than herding tactics. Once in court, on often frivolous or trumped-up charges, people of color are exposed to arbitrary court proceedings and often held in harsh illegal confinement in county jails for years against their liberty. This incarceration comes after they have been deliberately mis-educated. This is done to forcefully extract involuntary pleas from people by torturing them with time and fear of the unknown. Prejudiced Judges consistently make prejudiced rulings and allow prosecutors and defense attorneys to not follow rules, laws, or procedures when it comes to dealing with Blacks, African Americans, "darkies", and "niggers." Once they got away with doing it to Blacks, then the Mexicans "Latinos" were next, and now it's time for the Arabs.

There exists a dual justice system where the same crime can give one-man probation and the other, because of the color of his skin, a life sentence. The whole time "They" (being the ones who honor Robert E. Lee in public and Adolf Hitler in private) are holding these miseducated young men and women of color in their penitentiaries, county jails, and prisons without law libraries or even one law book, thereby turning prisons into concentration camps. Slavery took place in several States after Texas led the way sanctioned by the United States since they had knowledge of the enslavement of millions of "African-Americans" and Latinos. The State houses them with the criminals to disguise their true social status. A person is unjustly incarcerated if there are no victims or damages resulting from the actions the person is accused of, bottom line. As far as the State or government being the victim, it is impossible, as they are both inanimate objects. Only the people representing those entities could be a victim or suffer damages, thus only a crime directly against them could be considered a crime.

A good example is The Hippie who is caught growing pot in a National Park. His indictment will have him named as the Defendant and the United States of America or possibly a State named as the plaintiff. This indictment makes no sense. First, the Plaintiff is an inanimate object. Second, since the park was public lands, the Hippie actually had ownership rights to the land since he was a United States citizen. He would have the right to work the land if he was not harming anyone and another citizen was not using the land he used. This is the way of freethinking groups of oppressive "leaders" do not want you to think like. Can the average United States citizen grasp the reality of there being millions of acres of "public land" yet millions of homeless Americans who do not

Antebellum

own even one square millimeter of this land? Unfortunately, the United States Constitution as written in the

13th amendment condones slavery. After the Civil War, the 13th amendment was a compromise with the 14th amendment for the former slave owners. The wording in the 13th amendment states:

- "Neither slavery nor involuntary servitude, except as a punishment for a crime whereof the party shall have been duly convicted, shall exist within the United States."

This dubious wording created the blueprint for the former Confederate   slave States to legally run their operation presently in the 21st. Century. The key is to convict as many African-Americans and Latinos along with any other undesirables of crimes no matter the nature and regardless if there was any intent to commit a crime, any victims involved, or damages for anyone other than State officials to collect.

To better put it into perspective, there were States in the U.S. that legalized marijuana, however, the use of that same substance, which was named medical and useful by some, was causing others to be imprisoned for many years in other States. Logically, both States cannot be wrong and right at the same time and this fact proves both the hypocrisy and the illegality of the disguise of slavery which was perpetrated upon African-Americans as a final solution by the White Establishment in the form of a War on Drugs. This is also why when the same White Establishment wanted to go the war with the Arabs and Persians, they had to first wage a war on Terrorism to change all the Laws and Rules to accommodate a new enemy which the crack cocaine laws couldn't stop.

In the year 2012, about 95% of minorities were convicted without jury trials, and despite the façade of being innocent until proven guilty. These victims are always in jail for months with extravagant bonds before their trial to soften them up, aiding the prosecution in coercing them to plead guilty. After over a century of this practice being passed down from one generation to the next, it has created a group of people who have come to believe they are the Law, and the incarceration of African- Americans and Latinos is not only their job but a duty for there to be peace and order. It is the most insulting to African-Americans, Latinos, and descendants of American Indians to hear people in the United States Congress say they want to change the 14th Amendment, which guarantees citizenships to these groups' ancestors without referring to the 13th amendment that officially legalizes modern-day slavery as long as the proper procedures are followed.

When it became publicly known there was a private penitentiary opening in the United States. Starting in States federal troops had to be sent into several months after the end of the Civil War to finally free all slaves. In these prisons, the same descendants of Africans are being herded by White men, dressed in blue and grey uniforms (the colors of the Confederacy) after being auctioned off by other White men in suits posing as the Prosecutor and the Judge who said it is legal. On that day, America entered into a new antebellum which it would not return. Maybe, they were inevitably more captivated by the illusion of ineptness portrayed by the Black rappers and athletes who were the voice in the Black community because of the true ineptness of the African American leaders—the Uncle Tom politicians who do not represent their constituents in the government but are only there to sell them out officially. Minorities must think of their politicians as court-appointed attorneys.

What group of people in the world has more rappers and convicts then all other professions combined? The American Negro is the answer. There is no other group in the world like the American Negro. The Justice System is totally set up against the African-American male because first they are arrested more. Most prosecutors are White and there are few Black defense attorneys and fewer Black judges. These are the three biggest factors in the continued increased incarceration

Antebellum

of Black men in the U.S. and this is why I, The Mighty Ant, write to prepare them for the future revealed by The Great Elephant using principles of the Great Nothing to thought travel making time and distance one.

Chapter 2

BAMBOOZLED

I should just be blunt and to the point, as it may be appreciated later. In the year 2012, it will start with the disputed 2012 Presidential Election in first the United States and then France, Brazil, and India. In the U.S. and E.U., the media will have a field day with Israel benefiting the most, as Jewish candidates are involved in the disputed French and Brazilian elections at the top level. In the United States, Vice-Presidential nominee and member for the Patriot Party, Dr. Samuel Goldstein (the certified descendant of a slave on the ticket), was a 3rd generation mixed breed that looked white but whose father was the son of a Holocaust survivor and could actually sport a Jew-fro. His running mate, Presidential nominee and self-proclaimed incumbent, Mary Lee, was the only so-called true American on the ticket because she was a White, brunette, and plain-looking Christian. The Patriot Party, via Mary Lee, seized control of the office of the President of the United State against the majority of the people's will, losing by more than 6 million votes via what was considered a coup d'état in the Electoral College.

Several months of news spin and television networks charging Super Bowl and World Cup prices for advertising slots on news talk shows featuring celebrities and past politicians, all weighed in on the controversy to follow. The Peter O' Keith Show had nearly 300 million viewers worldwide when he aired a special two-hour open debate section with the guests being an ex-President, the biggest

Bamboozled

Hollywood comedian/actor, the 2012 NHL MVP, a porn starlet, a US Supreme Court Judge and Leroy the Dump Truck Driver. One day the media blitz all stopped and turned its attention to the nomination of the first female President of the United States, a historic event. After just three months of propaganda with exhilarating stories about both the lives of the nominated President and the accomplishments of Dr. Goldstein; America accepted the election of President Lee with open arms. Well, at least this is how it appeared to the world through the eyes of the media with friends and foes alike embracing in tears.

It was in India where Bollywood's media machine similar attempts to put a favorable face on the landslide defeated nominee failed leading to violence. Thousands were shot dead in the streets by the new far-right regimes claiming terrorists were causing the unrest. At first, the World fell for it until violence erupted in Brazil and then France. These rebels fought with the reasoning they were not a small minority of troublemakers as the Government and media were portraying them to be, but indeed the majority who were betrayed at the polls. After several arrests and a few deaths, protesters calmed down. In the United States, President Lee signed several new Bills into law in her first few months in office giving the Patriot Party nearly total control of all three branches of the government by placing all major congressional and judicial committees under Patriot Party member's oversight. The reasoning was the U.S. Government needed more

"coherency" as outlined in Presidents Lee's book *What if the South Won*. Some political analysts suggested these moves were designed to protect the White House as well as insured the Patriot Party would be around for a long time. All electronic media was wiretapped, and law enforcement and other Homeland Defense workers were given separate citizenship classification, which enhanced any offense committed against them while at the same time protecting them from liability in case of accidental injury or death in the act of performing their public duty.

The first new laws were designed to help United States companies compete with "overseas." welfare was eliminated, and the Federal minimum wage fell to first $5.00 an hour and then $4.00 and finally, $2.75 to encourage corporations from all around the world to come to the U.S. The Supreme Court of the United States ruled that the Federal government could not set minimum wage guidelines for the States. This meant States could set any minimum wage or have no minimum wage at all.   With the high inflation caused by the panic of 2012, the world was finally getting American made quality goods at Third World prices by the year 2015.

The year 2016 was the same old story—the Patriot Party focused on local elections, passing many new laws disqualifying many voters. A "grandfather's clause" for Social Security benefits was made into law and a new provision allowing private corporations more control over prisons and police forces, and, for the first time, the courts. It was not unusual for a Patriot Party member to postpone a trial at which he was a sitting Judge because he had a dinner appointment with a CEO from the E.U. or Asia for some goods his company, a private penitentiary, was manufacturing; using the free slave labor of the inmates he was sentencing to his own penitentiary.

By 2017, with more than 28.6 million Americans incarcerated in some form of free labor situation, the United States was starting to rebound from its economic crisis. The cities of the U.S. were all full of rich foreigners feasting on Black and Latina girls prostituting themselves for $200 on the streets and $600 in the clubs—the White ones from the country towns could get up to $1,000 but wanted drugs also. They all would give up all three holes for €50 euro as the dollar had lost some value. The Patriot party had to work hard to eliminate the poor White trash image by giving away nice

Bamboozled

two-story FEMA trailer homes to mostly poor White families for one reason or another in a move which did a lot to divide the country but gain many votes. President Lee stated at a big party meeting in Nebraska,

"Millions of dollars are being spent to house criminals and terrorists. This should be offset with the housing of America's good citizens." She received a standing ovation. The Patriotic American Housing Program (PHAP), created fast-growing rural areas with picturesque countryside full of good ol' American industry with all majority White American schools competing against the mixed-race urban schools.

Again, America had a strong army after initiating the Hoodlum to Heroes program in which some troubled youth could go to the military instead of prison. Despite all the tests and stipulations, the only way a youth who committed a felony could be assured he would be sent to a boot camp instead of a prison camp was if he was Caucasian. The U.S. military doubled in size and claimed to be "smarter" with 62% of the teens who "enlisted" being of Caucasian descendant from juvenile delinquent programs. It was something to think about though, as some 30% of those Caucasian descendent had some other race listed on previous applications.

By 2018 most of the developing countries from Asia, Africa, and the EU invested as much, if not more, into their corporation's assets inside the United States than in their own countries. They were manufacturing products with the free slave labor of the private penitentiaries and then stamped the good ol' "MADE IN THE USA" on the products to sell them for premium market prices worldwide. The corporation set up their own towns. Corporations in the United States were given the ability to pay their employees with Company Credit$. When written the Company Credit$ only had to have a money sign at the end, regardless of the language, to make it legal. This was done simply by an interpretation of a law that deemed corporations were only responsible for paying their taxes in U.S. dollars, not their employees. Thus came the Company Credit$ System, which allowed corporations to sell their produced goods on the world market for federal currencies such as dollars, euro, and yen, but paid their employees with Company Credit$ allowing the employees to purchase almost anything inside the micro city with them. The employees were paid in such a way as they believed the Company Credit$ were more valuable than other forms of currency. In return for the much larger profits for the corporation, the local, State, and Federal governments received more tax money from them.

Every business inside of the micro cities accepts the Company Credit$ as if it were cash for the exchange of goods and services, including the hospitals. It started out with only a fraction of the salary was Company Credit$, such as bonuses. Once corporations made medical benefits part of the

Company Credit$ system it quickly went to 100% Company Credit$ for salary. The Company Credit$ system could be accessed through fingerprints or DNA, but older people wanted the Company credit$ on cards with numbers. Several modern micro-cities, holding up to several hundred thousand people sprung up in Alaska and desert of the western U.S.

In 2019, with the US dollar worth 10 % of the Euro, India becomes the 4th richest country ahead of Brazil with

China in first, followed closely by the E.U. which included Russia and Britain's economies. The United African Union was third far ahead of the United States sixth place economy that boosted the most billionaires and the most homeless people along with one of the worst healthcare systems in the world since only the wealthy could afford real treatment. The corporation's HMO, PPO, IMO, TERRA, MDT, CDC and every other medical benefits program always found everyone healthy and do not believe in preventive healthcare. The Patriot Party used the threat of a possible

Bamboozled

United Arab Nation forming as a threat to national security to persuade the U.S. Supreme Court to clear the way for President Mary Lee to run for office a third time.

On January 1, 2020, the theme for the New Year Celebration for the nation is "America is Back!!!" citing how for the first time in 50 years the United States took jobs from overseas by producing everything from corkscrews to computers.

Now to the reality of the rest of the world in 2020: Iran has several nukes. Britain and all of its Isles decided to become members of the E.U. with rumors of Russia joining in the experiment. The victory of the Republican Party who favors the Nation States sovereignty rights over the Union's dominance opens the door for Russia and Britain to enter the E.U. Their opponents in the Social Party argued the weakening of the Union's dominance over the Nation States will inevitably undermine the Union. Israel and Iran may just become the best allies. They only need for a United Arab Nation to form in order to have a mutual enemy.

Documents revealed that since 1973 China has officially concluded by analyzing all scenarios that it could defeat the United States in a conventional war and only with the use of nuclear weapons could China lose because it has a larger population to sustain catastrophic casualties. The same was true for the Soviet Union but in their simulations, the most brutal battles would occur in Siberia instead of Canada after a nuclear exchange. Wu Ho Ning, one of China's premier thinkers and politicians wrote a book in 1971 espousing the philosophy that China would have to govern itself with a wartime economy to keep pace with the Soviet Union and the Americans. Many of China's most prominent men -- using Ning's book as a blueprint -- positioned China in 1996 to surpass both Russia and the United States economically. In 2000, after the shenanigans of the Presidential elections in the United States, proving once and for all, there was no true democracy, only greedy men, and deception, China put all its efforts into its national defense. The 2000 elections in the United States also added to Wu Ho Ning's mystique as he predicted in his writings from the 1970s, *"Given the right opportunity the American elitists would use force to commandeer elections showing their true self."* His foresight gave him sway over China's largest political party, The Nationalist-Communist Workers Party, making him their leader.

By the year 2016, China had an effective ballistic missile defense shield in place using satellites and land-based rockets positioned around its cities and military facilities. More than 280,000 stationary and mobile Multiple Headed Mini Smart Rockets Launchers (M.H.M.S.R.L.) units capable of striking a dime moving at mach six from 80,000 feet were inconspicuously set everywhere from behind billboards, to along the countryside, to atop skyscrapers, and bridges. The old KGB network in China convinced Russian leaders to follow suit, but by the year 2018, the Russian elite had decided to join the E.U. to compete with the world's largest economy. England, as well as the rest of the E.U., was horrified when they discovered Russia's 6,000 Multi-Head Mini-Smart Rocket Launchers. As a secret term of Russian membership into the E.U., Russia was to share its technology. Thus by the year 2020, most of the EU nations had some sort of M.H.M.S.R.L. units in place around important locations.

The 100-year-old Wu Ho Ning was still one of the most powerful men in China as leader of the largest political party, the Nationalist Workers Party. In a fiery speech, he was translated as saying,

"The situations in the United States, with its history of military aggression against States, were Asian or other persons of color set as head of State, is dangerous to China's national security. But that threat is far behind our greatest threat being India who has a billion more people along with

Bamboozled

20,000 Chinese top-secret weapons." Wu Ho Ning was referring to the M.H.M.S.R. L.—highest-ranking Chinese officials until then believed China had a technological monopoly on. Political analysts from around the world took this speech as a sign of a shift in China's policy concerning the West, in particular, the United States. Top-ranking U.S. officials had no idea what Wu Ho Ning was referring to in regards to "secret Chinese weapons." President Lee made an assertive effort to appear on live television within a few days after Ning's speech. In a State of the Union Address, she warned China and the rest of the world of America's and its allies' prowess with the most formidable being the EU and India military. President Lee was seen as a strong, assertive leader in the eyes of the Western media but foolish in the eyes of the East.

China, along with the African Union, demanded the United Nations condemn the United States for its involvement in the Mexican Drug Wars that had killed over 1,800,000, people and human rights allegations regarding the private penitentiaries that the African Union claimed was nothing more than modern slavery. The United Nations refused to place any sanctions on the United States citing China and the African Union of Sovereign Nations had just as many documented human rights violations. Once the prospect of Brazil emerging as the largest economy in the Western Hemisphere became apparent, China and the African Union, along with several other South American countries, including Brazil, threatened to withdraw their membership from the United Nations. They planned to form a similar organization but with the focus on protecting trade. This organization was set to form officially on January 1, 2022, unless there could be some form of agreement.

Chapter 3

I SEE YOU

Club Katrina River Boat Hotel and Casino Shreveport, Louisiana August 16, 2019:

"Now we can get down to the business we have gathered here today to conduct." Jacob Honeycutt growled. "I can assure you neither group wants to be here, and I want to let you know of all my men, I disagree the most about dealing with you. Allow me to introduce myself. I am..."

"I don't care who you are!" Clark Johnson snarled as he rose from his seat and slowly backed away from Jacob. His cold gray eyes focused directly on Jacob as if Jacob was some savage animal that could attack at any moment. Clark Johnson never weighed more than 165 pounds in his life. He looked to be in his early 70s with a full head of grey hair and an older body that still looked like that of an army lightweight boxing champion of 1974. Clark's directness got a snicker from Bubba Moody Jr. when he looked at Kerry Price who had a sheepish grin and let out a barely audible chuckle. A southern inside joke that Jacob Honeycutt had to restrain himself from addressing. "Now, what is it exactly you have us here for? I mean this is some strange shit," Bubba Moody Jr. said. He was looking around at Jacob Honeycutt's entourage with wide eyes now. Being kind of a celebrity, Bubba Moody Jr. dressed the part. Even with the inflated U.S. economy of the year 2019, Bubba Wear was still expensive for casual clothes. His fancy shredded uniquely painted designer jeans cost $800.00 a pair and his T-shirts start at $300.00 for one. A nice button-down shirt on top, considered a classy upgrade, came in at $550.00 but since they had the Bubba Wear logo, he didn't have to pay for it. A large diamond- studded necklace hung to his belly with a compact disc sized solid gold medallion laden with diamonds, rubies, pearls and whatever other colored gem was needed to make his logo. The Bubba Wear logo was the Confederate flag, a guitar, a rifle, and a heart combined. Before Bubba could get an answer, Kerry Price moved toward him with his hand out.

"I haven't seen you in a while Mr. Moody... I'd like to shake your hand for your courage and hard work in the face of the assault on our great White race." Bubba Moody was well known since there had been several documentaries and a few movies made about his life. He was only 46 years old but worth about 12.5 billion. He was the guy that made being an Arian Skinhead cool and sexy. He was CEO of the Corporation that owned several clothing lines, three heavy-metal and hard rock groups, an entertainment network along with the newest major league baseball team The Mississippi or Jackson Rebels. Depending on where you were inside the State of Mississippi, you had better call them the Mississippi Rebels. Also, he was co-owner of the number one hockey team, the Anchorage Vikings, who were known for their violence, the key to their success. Clark Johnson paused and looked directly at Bubba Moody Jr.

"Mr. Moody you know who I am and what I represent. We were to meet in private and discuss some sensitive issues... if this is the company you keep, then I have nothing to discuss with you."

"Indeed Mr. Johnson you are the Grand Dragon himself. The most powerful man in the United States, lord of the triple K and protector of the Circle... Uncomfortable as this might be for you, this is who you have to buy the Areocar from, and not only do you have to have money, apparently... ughum... apparently, the four-hour interactive training virtual reality video wasn't a joke. You might want to have all maneuvers memorized before you are 40,000 feet above a suburb," Bubba Moody Jr. said looking serious though trying to hold back laughter.

"I can see you still have your sense of humor Mr. Moody. May I ask what the training video consists of?" Clark mumbled as he slowed his march toward the door.

"It is psycho interactive. You know, where they put headphones and goggles on you so they can simulate the experience and you get used to it. You wouldn't want to be 40,000 feet and…"

"I heard you but…"

"Most of the instructions come in subliminally, so you will learn quickly." Big Bubba had a way of looking at you in a way in which demanded trust. Clark kind of relaxed and turned away from the door.

"What's up partner? As I was saying, you can just call me Snake. That will be 4.5 million euro, please," Jacob Honeycutt said as he pulled out the money-processing device connected to his phone. Clark came forward, reached inside his wallet and pulled out a credit card then swiped it. After a few seconds, a green light appeared approving the transaction starting the process of 4.5 million euro in gold and silver coins being physically transferred from Clark's account to Jacob's. Kerry Price then came and asked Clark to follow him to a couch.

Clark sat on the couch with another tall, light-skinned man with shades and a thick gold necklace which caught Clark's attention. It had a huge medallion with the exact same symbol as the one the Snake dude had on. The one last thing Clark remembered seeing before the man placed some headphones and goggles over his eyes was the man's pinky ring which had a gold eagle with its talons stretched out as if reaching for its prey. Finally, after a few seconds some type of breathing apparatus, similar to the kind dentists use, was placed over Clark's nose. Lights started flickering inside the goggles and a slightly muffled beat could be heard from under the headphones as the unorthodox Areocar how-to video started to play. A strange smell of blueberries, chocolate, grapes and a sweaty gas station attendant began to stream through Clark's nostrils while his whole body relaxed. He noticed his favorite songs were playing in the background. After a few minutes into the middle of the third song, Clark started to sing along then colored lights started to flicker in patterns. Clark did not notice the visuals, sounds, and smells all blurred into one as he enters a dream-like state. Someone who seems familiar was telling him something of the uttermost importance and what he must do.

January 11, 2020 Thawada, Texas 8 A.M:

The tall redheaded man, with what appeared to be either a bad rash or sunburn, carrying a large toolbox and wearing work overalls walked past the security desk of the Federated National Bank Building, the tallest building in Thawada, and did not stop. His badge read "Sterns Air Condition and Refrigeration", but no one noticed the name; they only see a name badge. He reached the top floor, the 49th; no one seemed to have noticed or said a word to the redhead man as he gained access to the rooftop. After a few minutes, a security guard arrived at the rooftop since the alarm had sounded in the security booth notifying him the rooftop exit had been opened.

"What's going on up here?" the old silver-headed guard said as he stepped onto the roof.

"It is just a scheduled inspection… I have to check the coolant levels and the thermostat. "It'll only take about 20 minutes and I'm out of here," the redheaded man said as he started to remove a panel on the huge chiller.

"Oh. You should've checked in its..."

"Next year I'll stop by, I am almost finished now."

"Well um okay. Let me know when you are done." The old guard ducked back inside the door and left. The red-headed man checked his watch and then opened his large toolbox. He pulled out a triggering device and screwed on a barrel and then a scope, and then texted ready on his phone.

8:10 A.M.

As soon as he received the text from the redheaded man, the tall Hispanic looking man in the dark blue suit (as he was later described) started for the rooftop of the Douglas Building, the second tallest building in Thawada. It was 35 stories and had a restaurant on the top floor. It was not secured like the bank building so after he was on the roof he placed a lock on the door. He had to hold that rooftop for the next 15 minutes. The tall Hispanic man reached into his pocket and texted the word go.

8:15 A.M.

The day started out like any other Monday in the 395th District Court of Thawada, Texas. Known as the Texas Hanging Judge, Judge Murphy had been on the bench for 30 years and was now rumored he would begin a position in the Federal Courts next spring, as he was nominated by President Lee. Insiders could tell something was different about the old judge. He was not passing down long sentences like he used to. He always gave Black defendants the very long prison sentences regardless of the crime, and any White defendants accused of committing heinous crimes were treated as bad as the Black defendants in his court. The White ones had to be subjected to a 30-minute sermon. He often tended to show mercy on White kids accused of small infractions by always giving them probation and the long speeches he was known for. Black kids would get the maximum and Latino kids somewhere in the middle depending on whether they looked Spanish or Indian, spoke good English or not.

For the past few months, he had broken with his traditions and started giving everyone similar sentences to appear fairer before the Senate Confirmation Hearing

I See You

Committee. One case even surprised the District Attorney Kevin Harper Sr. who usually asked for the large sentences on all cases in an attempt to intimidate criminals. About a year ago, he asked Judge Murphy to sentence a pretty little White girl named Gloria Price to 10 years on a drug possession case in which officers found some weed and cocaine in her car. Gloria had taken her father's car to the store without his knowledge, and it had been his ounce of pot and 5 grams of coke in the car. Gloria took the charge because she had never been in any kind of trouble and expected to get probation she could have completed, whereas her father would get 40 to 60 years because he would have been a repeat offender. Judge Murphy gave her 12 years hard time and no speech. Mr. Harper Sr. would never forget the Price case since Mr. Price got a "Contempt of Court" charge for talking very bad to both him and Judge Murphy staying just short of threatening their lives. Since that day his job had been a lot more interesting since he never knew what to expect from his old friend.

"All rise!" echoed off the walls from a heavy bass authoritative voice coming from the large lumberjack looking bailiff. District Attorney Kevin Harper Sr. rises and smiles at his long-time colleague, Judge Howard Edmond Murphy.

"Now comes the Honorable Judge Howard Murphy to the bench of the 395th District Court of …, Court is now in session. You may all be seated," boomed the Bailiff. The judge took his seat behind his tall podium. He looked down and stared over some documents before him. As soon as he looked up a strange sound was heard somewhat similar to a sewing machine but louder. Then across the Judge's face appeared what first looked like stitches, running in a straight line diagonally across the Judge's face, from above his right eye to his lower left jaw between his ear and chin. This stitch- looking lines then immediately started to open into large lacerations and the upper left side of the

Judge's head began to slide away as his body fell forward and the rest of his brains rolled over the front of his podium onto the clerk and minutes keeper's desk. At first, the two women just stared at the yucky pink and yellow material on them and their desk in disgust, as they did not know what it was and they had not yet figured out what was happening. It was then that an albino looking man with an afro, glasses, and beard, who was standing up, took one-step and aimed what appeared to be a gun at District Attorney Kevin Harper Senior. The same sewing machine sound was heard again then Mr. Harper Sr.'s blood and guts began to fly. The women figured out what was on them and started screaming. About this time, another guy in a suit with glasses, a big fake nose, and mustache stood up and threw a golf ball-sized, spiked ball at the bailiff, but he missed. The bailiff then reached for his gun as his eyes were still on the albino guy with the afro. The second man in the suit with the big fake nose then fired the same type weapon the albino had at the bailiff but at his thighs. The bailiff dropped his gun as he screamed in pain when his legs were cut from under him. The albino with the afro ran and picked up the bailiff's gun and headed for the exit as the suited, big nosed person followed. Right before they got on the elevator, and just as the screams were starting to gather more attention to the courtroom, the albino with the afro fired five shots into the air with the bailiff's gun then started to smile as he ran down the hall.

8:18 A.M.

Sheriff King heard the shots fired. The Sheriff's Department was right across the street from the courthouse.

The call came in approximately 32 seconds later.

"Shots fired at the courthouse! Shots fired at the courthouse!" There was really no need for him to "go across the yard" as he called it whenever he went to the courthouse. Even something as serious as this rank and file could handle. A shooting inside the courthouse means the captains and police department would handle it. What did matter to him was there was a breach of the security, so someone had to be fired for it.

There were three ways for Sheriff King to get to the courthouse. The first was for him to use the underground tunnel connecting the Sheriff Department with the courthouse. The second way was to use the front door and just walk across the street above ground. He ruled out the first because he did not know how dangerous the shooters inside the court building were and the second way seemed too cheap. Once he heard the distinctive sound of the news chopper that was newer and smoother sounding than the police bird, he knew he would use his third option and drive across the street. After all his squad car was the new Cadillac truck distinctively painted with the city colors of blue and grey and the County Seal and Thawada Sheriff's Department printed in big gold letters. This would be the only fitting way for the cavalry to arrive he thought to himself. Sheriff King, being a rather short man, made up for his size by being very muscular and having a loud mouth. Once he made it to his squad car, he called Lt. Neils to get an update.

"People are fleeing the court, Sir. It happened in Judge Murphy's court." Lt. Neil huffed over the walkie-talkie. He was overweight and probably out of breath from running through the tunnel.

"Set up a perimeter around the courthouse and let no one leave! I will be at the bottom of the stairs by the main entrance in two minutes. Don't let anyone outside that perimeter!" Sheriff King barked with a now more determined demeanor. He and Judge Murphy divided Thawada up between themselves years ago and controlled everyone around them with an iron fist. It was even said that Sheriff King brought all the dope into town from the evidence confiscated by his deputies. District Attorney Harper Sr. did whatever Sheriff King told him to do as long as he was paid in what the DA called "favor points"—one favor point equaled $500.00. Sheriff King stepped out of his car with a megaphone barking orders to sheriff and police officers alike. The officers had stopped eight people at the exit as they were leaving. Two of the people were the albino and the big-nosed man in the suit. Now in the sunlight, they appeared to be in costumes and makeup. Two police officers pointed at them and started to move toward them. Both suspects put their hands in their pockets when they noticed the two officers coming toward them.

"Take your hands out your pockets!" a deputy sheriff demanded as he started running down the hall from inside the court building. An old Black janitor could be seen pointing at the two gunmen as he talked to another deputy who had just come from the basement where the underground tunnel was. This deputy holsters his gun and started to run toward the two disguised gunmen.

8:28 A.M.:

The tall red headed man could see the police cars pull up in the parking lot of the Federated Bank Building. Their reaction was a lot quicker than he had calculated. He figured he had about three and half more minutes before they would try to put a sniper team on the roof. This meant he had just three minutes to get his shot off. He looked through his binoculars but his target was nowhere to be found.

The tall Mexican looking man on top of the Douglas building was relieved to see the sniper team go to the Bank building instead of choosing his building. This meant he could focus on protecting his comrades who appeared cornered. He opened his briefcase and pulled out a softball-sized spike ball similar to the smaller one the big-nosed person had thrown at the bailiff. He dropped it over the side of the building, when it landed, thousands of small spikes exploded in every direction. They seemed to have no effect on his comrades but when the spikes struck other people they would immediately fall to the ground, some paralyzed, others having powerful muscle spasms and cramps, and then some clutched at their stomach as the feeling of uncontrollable laughter took their breath away causing them to feel as though they were going to die. The stomach and respiratory effects were accompanied with the most intense orgasms, several times more powerful than normal and uncontrollable, lasting for several minutes. Most of the law enforcement and news crew, along with some bystanders, were on the ground screaming and shaking. Some police officers who had their guns drawn, fired off shots when the spikes struck them, hitting two officers and three bystanders. One sheriff accidentally shot himself when he started convulsing.

A second ball dropped, and it started to make massive amounts of smoke. It was about the time the smoke was starting when Sheriff King's car pulled up and he hopped out to take control. One loud rifle shot rang out as Sheriff King's brains landed on the ground beside a newswoman and police officer locked in violent convulsions. One last text was sent by the redheaded man on the Federated Bank Building— "done." He then tossed the gun he had fired over the side of the building watching it shatter like glass when it hit the ground.

The redheaded man quickly hurried from the roof to the elevator. He passed Thawada Special Tactics sniper team on his way down. He put on some dark shades similar to the ones the other three men were wearing. A thick black smoke as intense as the smoke released from a burning oil well had risen to the 20th floor of the building making visibility absolutely zero yet, the four men wearing shades could see clearly. All four men who had done the assault made their way to their cars and left in four different directions as explosions echoed through the courthouse setting it ablaze.

Chapter 4

TOP OF THE PYRAMID

Getty was somewhat amazed at who all was present. It kind of made him feel special for an instant. They were all grouped in a large room with about 100 seats. Since the meeting was not at the Capitol, he did not think it would be this important, but then he realized he was called to meet at an undisclosed location as close to the center of the country as possible, instead of D.C. There was the President, some Congress party leaders, a few Governors, and two high Court Judges whom Getty could recognize, although it was quite dark. The other 80 or so people, Getty could not get a good look at nor could he recognize their voices. After only a few seconds and before Getty could grasp who exactly he was in the company of, a large 10' X 10' flat screen slowly lowered in front of the powerful audience and started playing. There was a person in what appeared to be a mirror-plated space suit costume that looked like an inflated bodysuit with a perfectly round fish tank for a head. The costume appeared to be one piece. The mirror plating made the suit appear to blend in with the environment since the footage had been shot in a forest setting. Getty could even see the video camera reflected in the chest of the suit. The camera then zoomed into the super polished metallic bubble helmet, or at least head segment. The camera looked like a canon through the reflection. After a few awkward seconds, a voice blasted over the speaker. The image on the screen did not change so Getty could not tell if the voice was coming from the costumed character or if it was a voice- over. The voice was unlike anything Getty had ever heard. It sounded digitally manipulated morphing several people's voices into one. It boomed over the surround sound.

"It is a fact that if a one megaton or more hydrogen bomb hit any metropolitan area in the world it would kill all humans within 90 miles of Ground Zero in every direction within 14 days. Thus far, this has been the only reason why there has not been a nuclear war. However, there are other weapons with just as much power! In 1933, once this power was discovered, there became a mad rush for it. Men undertook every conceivable plan, plot, and scheme, which led to just as large a physical reality being created to control nuclear power. Only nations of millions with unlimited resources due to unlimited paper money could accomplish the goal." Getty closes his eyes and starts to doze off as the voice drags on.

"...The United States government poses itself as the most powerful entity on Earth. It is composed of 100 men in the upper house called the Senate, and some nearly 500 men in the lower house, nine judges, plus a President, Vice President, and some 10 Cabinet Members, or so. It would appear that some 650 men and women run the entire Country, but because of State rights, there appear to be 50 states with 50 governors, whose powers are divided among State courts and the State senators. These 15,000 people or so, plus a few other powerful people throughout the States, come from families of the "industrialists" or "aristocrats." What the people of the United States and the world are led to believe is this division of power and States' rights are the reason nothing is ever accomplished. The first problem is that these government officials are not representative of the American people. Americans are given a choice of whom to vote for, but all the choices, all two of them, come from only one place— the existing establishment.

The "Industrialist" and "the Aristocrats" or you can call them "Democrats" and "Republicans", although from time to time they change their name when their agenda changes, such as now, we have a Patriot Party. Once they even had a "Tea

Party" in which members from both parties could attend and be openly racist. Either way, we the people of the United States of America have been subjected to "their" will since the days of the slave owning George Washington, and phony elections to follow, in which Electoral Colleges choose the President in public and all other offices in private on the Federal level.

Rich property owners divide the state and local offices amongst themselves as they were forming "their" counties. Never has a leader risen from the people! It is always someone who is put in front of the people. Never has anyone who performed great acts of justice or showed great wisdom been elected for the benefit of society. These American aristocrats use a few hundred other men and women who control TV stations and newspapers called "The Media" throughout the United States to control the masses through propaganda. This propaganda is the single most important component of civil control. The greatest weapon these aristocrats have is fear.

I use the United States to show how 15,000 people or so can be used to control the so-called most powerful entity on Earth. Every country throughout Earth is run pretty much the same way. A small group of people whom we call Taghuts control these 15,000 people or so. Only what the Taghuts want to accomplish is accomplished. Each European nation has maybe one Taghut. Most nations do not have any Taghuts, just agents who do their bidding. I could not personally identify even one Taghut, but what I do know is that our goal is to take the power of the world from a few and give it to the people so they can choose their own leaders, and only then will there be an advancement of society as a whole. I will say the model of government the United States Constitution provided is one of the greatest endeavors conceived by men. The greatest fault in this endeavor is the unlimited power given to the Government, which was to be limited by a Constitution that could be amended, suspended, and even

Top of the Pyramid

arbitrarily interpreted, thus giving the American citizens only hope for mercy from the people who were to call themselves Government. The greatest endeavor by men in governing failed because it was of men and not God. This endeavor was to satisfy the will of a few men and make a few richer. Nevertheless, even with these major faults of the United States Government, they did at least have some due process. Now, indeed this is gone!"

The abrupt change in the speaker's monotone speech was loud enough to awake Getty. He immediately wiped his mouth to be sure no drool had slipped out. He looked around the room to see if he had been caught dozing then noticed half of the old men over age 60 were nodding, but Getty was only 47. The strange video was still playing. All the people in uniform looked very attentive and serious. The strange voice continued with the character stepping up the tone of his rhetoric.

"…There are places in the world with less justice, and this too is also unacceptable. Therefore, we are proposing a World Constitution that is not to be amended, with very few points and only created to protect humans from any entities created in the name of Government or God.

•A World Constitution is written and every Country, Nation, and State on Earth is to follow it. Every human being born on planet Earth is an Earth Citizen and possesses at least equal rights to every other citizen.

•All weapons of mass destruction are to be under international control of a single entity for the protection of Earth and cannot be used against its citizens.

•Every human has the right to vote on any matter concerning their well-being regardless of their social status or situation. The vote is to be free and non-secretive. Everybody will get one vote, and the one vote will count for one vote.

•No human can be punished with any physical punishment, neither pain nor incarceration, for crimes that have no human victims or damages.

•Every Earth citizen is to be given some piece of land or shelter. It is understood this planet belongs equally to all those born upon it, equally.

•Every Earth citizen is to be provided the full extent of health care and education as can be given, without any distinction or prejudice.

•All Governments on Earth must reflect the actual demographical make-up of the areas governed, if possible, unless this is not the will of the governed.

•No human is allowed to kill another human regardless of their position in society, either directly or through policies set by officials.

•No individual or entity will have the power to override, change, or alter the meaning or the intent of any of the laws, rules, and procedures set out by the World Constitution.

•All Countries, States, cities, or any other social established entity, considering themselves a government, can make their own rules and regulations that do not conflict with the World Constitution."

The voice or recording paused then continued.

"With this outline, the United States of America will lead the way into a new world society ruled by reason instead of human lust. It will be most difficult for those countries such as China, India, Switzerland, Nigeria, and Mexico to give up their sovereign rights to a World Constitution. It must be understood the exact proportion of the social economic or racial class will only govern a region. This means China will have mostly Chinese representatives and India mostly Indian representatives but as the barriers of invisible borders caused by racism are torn down by the World Constitution established today, millions of new people from all different races and backgrounds will replace those Chinese and Indians who have traveled abroad. To have the minority represented is the right thing to do. The people of China and India must remember their sons and daughters who travel

Top of the Pyramid

abroad could hold powerful positions in the future in far off places, and the Chinese and Indian spirit will be represented. Although they are minorities in a faraway place, they will be guaranteed to be treated fairly and impartially.

To the people of the world, the biggest resistance to this World Constitution are those individual governments who want to hold power. The few hundred politicians, kings, and queens from the old era along with the dictators and those corrupt régimes with only a few hundred leaders who desire to hold millions of world citizens in slavery. These are the people who have ruled the world for thousands of years, and there has been nothing but, war, famine, and slavery. These people have kept you in the dark. It is to this point, I will let you people of the world know, your leaders have actually compared how advanced their society is by the gap in their knowledge to the common person's knowledge. At this time in history, the gap is larger than ever before. The average human cannot even grow their own food, make their own clothing, or provide shelter for himself or herself. Most humans do not have the knowledge they need to survive. You are totally dependent on the system set forth upon you. There is no general education policy for the advancement of humans as a species. The present leaders only goal is to capitalize on the world citizens. They have created a monetary system, where they can say the American dollar or the British pound is worth 100 times as much as a Third World country's money. The leaders of the Third World are wealthy so they go along with this scheme; because they feel they are not robbing their citizens any worse than the citizens of the rich countries are being robbed by their governments. 'Our citizens pay almost no taxes,' they say. The leaders of China and Russia, England, Pakistan, Nigeria, and Brazil all set at the top, as do all government officials of the world, while millions of people in their countries are without food and shelter. This phenomenon is caused by the misuse of power and does not have to be accepted. With the current world society, if you do not accept the unjust government, you're persecuted and killed. Thus, the law, 'no government can kill a human' takes away the most powerful tool these people use other than propaganda."

The screen went blank and the flat screen monitor started to rise. The lights did not brighten. It was not totally dark just dim. Getty could see the people in the room but if you did not know them then you most likely wouldn't remember them.

"What the hell was that?" President Lee said to her right-hand man Don Abernethy loud enough for everyone to hear. There was intensity in her voice that sounded mean and nasty. From the look in Lee's eyes, the pure expression of hate, and the thick vein across the Presidents forehead that split in what appeared to be a pitchfork all of which most had never seen.

"*Quite frightening,*" Getty thought to himself. *Only the closest to the president would dare speak so I should just keep quiet, wait and play Yes man.* Then a tall blonde headed man in his 50's appeared at the front of the crowd. He stood under were the flat screen had been on a raised section of the floor.

"Is it Larry Feingold the genius of Wall Street? He's worth billions but I never knew him to be the political type." Getty heard a woman behind him say. He thought to himself "*she would probably let ol' Larry bang for sure now that she knows he is multitalented.*" Getty felt like he was watching a golf player quarterback the Redskins. Larry started with a soft sophisticated New England accent.

"Most of you are wandering why you are here. This strange broadcast appeared on four major networks in the United States, as well as three international ones making this an international broadcast. Because of the content and the fact that possibly a billion people around the world viewed it, it is cause for alarm. We had absolutely no control of it..." Larry threw his hands up in a very feminine manner and then looked over towards the President, rolled his eyes and continued,

Top of the Pyramid

"This is the most serious threat to our national security. Every country is having this same meeting right now. We need to figure out who this is and how they did it. The people in this room are the select few who have been chosen to be briefed and to react to this threat." Larry took a deep breath and his voice became more solemn. "There was more to this broadcast, much more…" his voice cracked at a higher octave. "but we managed to stop the broadcast." An older man then took the stage. To Getty's surprise, it was the old Retired Judge who sat in on some of his briefings. This was the first time Getty heard him say more than hello and goodbye. He started with a kind of old wise guy from the Bronx accent in which Getty did not expect.

"We have been in contact with our friends around the world and they all agree this originated inside the United States, so we have chosen the most intelligent and talented special agents to get to the bottom of this. We want to inform you that the networks are cleaning this up as a prank but there are sure to be some who would care to follow-up on this idiot's suggestions. So we called you here to prepare you. I would like to introduce to you Mr. Serwin Getty, the Chief Deputy of CIA Special X UNIT, who has single-handedly prevented some big crimes from happening before they occurred. He will be leading this investigation." The old gentleman then went back to his seat by the military brass in the room. Getty was shocked by this announcement. Getty was head of a CIA department that dealt with nontraditional threats. He was in command of 20 agents and reported only to a secret committee of three Congressmen and two military officers; one a three-star General, the other a Colonel who was 15 years the General's senior and seemed to call the shots. Also, the old Retired Judge who was close friends of the Colonel would attend some of the meetings, but never said anything, just listened. Getty served as the inside intelligence guy for the cases no other agent could handle. The cases highly educated whitewashed agents who attended the top Ivy League schools in the country or their affirmative action minority counterparts could not grasp. Getty was not from either of these classes. Because Getty was so valuable, the wise commission tended to keep Getty on missions close to home in order to keep things smooth. He had thwarted many plots and saved many American lives. The only thing he ever demanded in return was a very high salary and privacy. His seniors figured he had a weird fetish like most other geniuses had.

Chapter 5

NEUTRALITY

Seven days later:

Scheduled for over a year now, the meeting between two top world dignitaries was set to be held high on a Mountain in Switzerland at a very large, old castle. When President Lee and her staff arrived, one of her aids suggested the castle looked like the ones you see on the postcard, appearing as if there was no way to reach the entrance. Beautiful paintings covered the walls; most were stolen by German troops from "enemies of the state" during World War II. There were stunning sculptures from the Renaissance, along with large magnificent gardens that surrounded the entire castle inside the outer walls. Four towers housing two guards with high-powered assault rifles overlooked the moat around the castle. They heated the moat in order to keep the piranha alive—Fiske Braun's idea.

Fiske was the premier architect of impregnable security. His tall ideal Aryan look of blonde hair and blue eyes contrasted his burly upkeep and the large scar across his cheek.

Fiske looked as though he lived in a secluded castle. He put piranha in the moat because he felt they would be the only sure way to stop a human. He made sure to schedule a diet that starved the fish to the extent that if an 800lb. cow was dropped into the moat it would be eaten to the bone within 120 seconds or less. It would be highly unlikely that any mere mortal would even make it to the moat. The castle sat on top of a hill about a half-mile from the road. Around the hill stood a 15foot wall with four sharpshooters camouflaged to assure lethality so they were not there for intimidation. Two of these guards are armed with the M.60, the one with the grenade launchers. Since the wall was beneath the castle, the guards had a clear view of everything between the wall and the moat. The grounds were roamed by six watchdogs; two large solid black Italian mastiffs known as cane corsos, two white Argentina dogos, and two Turkish kangals. Fiske would give the history of the dogs while giving the personal tour of the castle.

"These wonderful animals were trained from birth together so all six of the dogs have known each other since they were puppies and mainly they are brothers within the bloodlines." Fiske would start as the dogs appeared.

"The dogs are trained to attack. Cane corso running the intruders down and the dogos get there next and lock on, breaking bones and snatching flesh off by the chunks. Once the 200 pounds kangals gets there, they usually eat what is left," Fiske would add, matter-of-factly. The dogs were extremely vicious and love no one except their master. The trainers used a special chemical that secrets a smell the dogs recognize as a friend. When dignitaries came and wanted to move around the yard, they would put small sacks in their pocket that were soaked in the chemical, so it secreted the smell the dogs loved and would protect. It was hard for leaders to believe the big friendly pooches were trained to kill.

When the dignitaries first arrived at the castle, they would meet its proprietor, Fiske Braun. He would give them the grand tour in his German/Swiss accent in seven different languages. The elite from around the world would get to meet an international staff, most of whom have been in servitude to the Braun family since they were children, the castle being the only thing they knew. All of the staff's parents had worked at the castle and so had their parents. Some visitors were most impressed by the natural beauty of the premises, others by the lavish extravagance such as the 32 different ethnic specialized chefs on call.

What visitors never forgot about their visit to the castle was Fiske Braun demonstration of what happened if you go into a restricted area requiring you to have the chemical-soaked beanbag sacks in your pocket. At the end of the tour, the guests are taken to a second-floor balcony overlooking an open area where two 600-pound hogs are released into the yard. Within a few seconds, two of the large playful pooches appeared running full speed toward the pigs with their tongues hanging out. It was the cane corsos. One of the hogs ran and the other, obviously, a large male, lowered his head showing his tusk preparing to charge the dogs. One cane corso ran around the entrenched boar in pursuit of the fleeing pig. The second corso   jumped to the side of the charging boar nearly avoiding its tusk and bites the tenacious pig on the hind leg. At this time, a solid white giant pit bull looking beast hit the aggressive boar at full speed, knocking it to the ground. It was the Argentina dogo. A second dogo arrived grabbing the pig by the nose and started shaking his giant head viciously from left to right. Because he had the boar by the snout not even a squeal was heard. They then see the cane corso release the boar's foot and then bite the pig in the neck on the main artery as blood squirted as far as the balcony.

At this same time, a loud squeal was heard as they saw a large Turkish kangal jump out of the bushes ambushing the fleeing pig. The large dog, nearly the size of the pig it seems, bites it on top of the head and peeled back some of the pig's scalp. The coal black cane corso pursues biting the pig in the side of the stomach exposing its guts. The cane corso proceeded to disembowel the pig along with the other large Turkish kangal which causally strolled up. This one, being the largest dog, paused and looked up toward the balcony before he started to eat. Fiske never understood why he got an erection watching the dogs eat the pigs. He takes a deep breath and smiles,

"As you can see, it's very important to wear the treated clothes or place a scent ball in your pocket when outdoors in the red areas."

The Braun Castle was known as Castle Neutrality because of all the international diplomats that were always present. On this day there was no one else present; the staff, interpreter, and all the media had stepped out. This was the big event—everyone had waited for the private meeting between the two most powerful people in the world at the infamous Castle Neutrality. Both rehearsed well on what to say. Every move, every gesture made, they had envisioned years before. Since the two leaders had met before, they had become quite familiar with each other. They both understood that they shared more in common than anyone else did in the world. Therefore, they decided to just make each other's job easier for the other by trying to cooperate, just like ol' Reagan and Gorbachev. There they sat. President Lee and Vladimir Peter, Russia's President. The United States had invaded Iran, searching for weapons of mass destruction, and had found nothing. Akbar Mohamed, the Iranian dictator, was then in U.S. custody, along with thousands of other terrorists. Russia was having an all out war with several of its breakaway states.

"So Vladimir, you're giving me your personal word... if we go into Iraq there will be nothing," Lee asks Vladimir Peter directly in a Southern-accented Latin.

"I will only say as many words, or act as hostile as you act when we go into the Ukraine, Armenia, and Uzbekistan." Vladimir Peter replied bluntly with a Russian accent, but more proper Latin.

"Yes, we both understand how important it is to have the power centralized. As for the treaty Syria signed with Iraq, this could be quite a problem. Those Russian anti-tank guns

can just about cut through anything from what I hear. And…"
Lee said with a sad expression on her face as she was not
supposed to know about these weapons someone in Russia
had obviously received oil or gold in exchanged for. She
paused to eat a pastry accompanied with fruit and cheeses,

"Hunf… we will supply troops, just as you will supply
weapons to fight the Terrorist," Vladimir interrupted. He
continued, "You must remember China is going to help with
the Terrorist in North Korea as long as your guys do the right
thing with the Taiwan issue."

"You don't have to worry about that. The cheapest labor
in the world is in China, and they have a billion people to
work," Lee said with a smile coming to her face.

"Can't beat that with the stick," Vladimir said in a heavily
accented Russian English.

"Oh, on the World Constitution matter…" President Lee
asked as she was rising from her seat.

"Niet such thing! There is no need to discuss," Vladimir
said aggravatingly.

President Lee and Premier Peter shook hands. The
camera took the picture of the first handshake from outside of
the room.

The next day there was little in the papers about the big
meeting between the two world leaders. Where it was
mentioned it was on the second page or as an after note. What
made the front page was a letter from the fools behind what
was being dubbed, the "Cable Network Jacking" incident that
had occurred seven days earlier. The letter went out to several
of the world's largest newspapers, then reprinted in some of
the major editorials. Here is what the letter said,

"We are not an Islamic movement; we are a mixed
   race of people; Mexicans, Mulattos, Arabs, Indians, and
Jews. We are called Black or brown, even yellow, but never
White and never accepted by either. We are a pure Human
being who believes that a higher power created humans to be

free and master of their own land. We recognize that man has created Countries to suit his need for power. Each country has its own money with the most powerful country's money being the most powerful. We can accept this, but we cannot accept these Countries' inexhaustible appetite for human life. We are here to report these Countries have put themselves above the higher power, which created all men and maybe women too, to be free and to have land. This higher power gave us the Earth, and these Countries have taken the Earth from humankind. It is our goal to take Earth back and give it to the people. Right now, we believe less than a 100 people are in control of the Earth, but they hide behind armies of millions of brainwashed idiots. It is hypocritical for Countries to have laws and rules forbidding murder, rape, and reckless destruction and then send armies of troops to other countries to carry out such atrocities. This can be termed as terrorism by Governments against their citizens. These Countries will go to war because of disagreements among a few men over issues that do not concern the majority of the population's well-being, using weapons and tactics causing massive human carnage tantamount to human slaughter. They are able to do this because they say they are the only ones who can govern. The ones who now govern are ones who have governed throughout history, and throughout history, humans have been slaughtered. The number one thing we are fighting for is a law banning the murder of any human life by any entity. So, if there must be a binding World Constitution that cannot be amended, changed, altered, or construed in any way, and this document is agreed upon by all humans, or vast majority, to be fair, that is just and a guarantee of life and liberty, then this is what it must be for humans to be free. A decent human should not want murder, rape, theft, and poverty, or unjust and unfair laws forced upon them by a private individual or groups of individuals representing themselves as any entity such as a

Government, State, or Country, nor anything smaller, such as a police force.

We have decided to take the first step in producing this document. Any person who opposes this World Constitution will be deemed as not decent and does not deserve to hold any formal power. This is only reasonable by their own reasoning since a person convicted of any felony could not vote regardless, if the crime has any victims are damages, or if there was a trial by 12 peers. A person who is deemed not decent is a person who is barbaric. There will be no place for barbaric people to hold power in this new world. Those politicians will be of the past such as the pharaohs, czars, furors, emperors, and all other false human deities. We feel it is only natural that Government takes a position against religion, since they both worship Gods, which could come at odds with each other, and are both in the business of reaping souls by controlling lives. What is so great about our movement is that any person, regardless if they represent a Jihad or a National military; they will be held accountable for even one murder on that day at that time. The people will not be able to kill the murderer, but the murderer may have to leave Earth, and after some years in a prison camp on a moon or another planet working to pay back their victim's family, they may get a second chance in space or at an oceanic sea-floor colony, but never back on the Earth's surface. This applies to murders after conviction by jury trial and appeals to a council of 144 people who will ultimately decide guilt and punishment. Never again will one judge decide the fate of a human. It is going to take many years, but we're going to break the circle of ignorance and slavery which has been forced upon us by a certain group of people we have identified as Taghuts."

Signed, THE NETWORK HIJACKERS

One Day Later:

Vladimir Peter left his office and had his driver drive him some 500 miles southeast of the capital to a small town which did not appear on most maps. "Welcome to Svteitchnozn" an old sign read in Russian which was the only real clue you had when arriving in the town. He ate at his favorite restaurant then went outside to a pay phone and made one call to Switzerland—Fiske Braun answered. Vladimir Peter directed him to go to the U.S. and terminate whoever was behind the "Cybervision Network Hijacking" incident regardless who it was and by any means necessary. A group of private individuals and members of his Russian Government would pay one billion euro and arrange for some very rare large 1,200 lb. Siberian wild boars to be delivered to castle Neutrality upon completion of the task. Fiske's heart was racing as he thanked his new best friend in the world. He felt a stiff, hard erection coming on just thinking about the 1,200 lb. wild boars and his puppies. After a few days of research, which entailed some internet searches and a few phone calls, Fiske caught a flight to America—his destination Thawada, Texas, United States of America.

Chapter 6

COLLEAGUES

It didn't take long for law enforcement to figure out whoever was behind the "Cyber Network Jacking" incident was somehow connected with the assassination of the Judge, District Attorney, and Sheriff down in Texas that by now was getting just as much media coverage, as there had been no arrest in either incident. The biggest clue to the crime's connection was a small ball of spikes that detonated sending one hundred spikes in all directions. The spikes incapacitated victims for an hour or two with a toxic solution mixture comprised of synthesized centipede venom, poison oak tree sap, and concentrated rat piss. The spike balls were used at all four cybervision networks to gain access to the central broadcast booth in order to send the unauthorized broadcast. The material of the ball was somewhat fire resistant, as it survived the fire at the courthouse. It was only at the CBC network hundreds of wooden toothpick-sized projectiles were found buried in the wall as if a tornado had placed them there. The same projectiles were found splintered in the deceased bodies of District Attorney Harper Sr. and Judge Murphy. Getty wrote in his report to his superiors he believed the wooden bullets were fired from a plastic gun, which explains how the perpetrators were able to walk right past security. This was the most well-organized assassination Getty had seen on domestic soil.

Being extremely clever, Getty believed he knew who was behind the courthouse massacre. He traveled to Texas to see if he could find some more evidence. Upon arriving at the Shreveport, Louisiana Municipal Airport, he was greeted by none other than Preston Ross reminding him just how quickly events could change the world. A few months ago, Getty was in front of a Senate Hearing committee facing possible indictment on one of the many Patriot and Home Land Security laws that gave certain government officials absolute dictatorial power over U.S. citizens and everyone else in the world. The only check to this absolute power wielded by these government officials was when another government official also had absolute power rather it be real or assumed. Getty was to be Preston Ross's victim because of an incident at a government barbecue where Preston felt Getty got out of line.

August 16, 2019, Washington DC:

"It was quite remarkable how the idea just came to me—it just popped into my head, although I had smoked a lot of bud that day." Most of them laughed but a few gasped. After all, this was the Dr. Serwin Getty talking. He was said to be one of the most brilliant men of the 21st century. With one invention, he had changed the world, yet he had just contributed his genius to an intoxicating plant. He continued, "I am sure it helps you elevate to higher or lower states of consciousness. I was of course in a higher state when I thought of the Areocar." Again, Dr. Getty paused, showing he had a sense of comedic timing. Gathering laughter as the group understood him now to be serious.

"Dr. Getty this is a serious matter, don't you understand? Senators of the United States Congress are questioning you. You have caused widespread unrest with some of your antics and we have the power to recommend that a host of Federal Charges be filed against you," rumbled Senator Gomez, the old Republican from Nevada who oversaw the Committee for Internal Security.

"I agree," Vice President David Goldstein shouted as he banged his gavel several times.

"This is neither the time nor place for pot jokes Dr. Getty, as it is a distraction," added Senator Kim from

Colleagues

Nebraska, the youngest and sexiest Congresswoman on the Hill. She was said to be very conservative although she did not look it.

"If there aren't any more jokes, we can end this and make our recommendations," drawled Senator Ambrose Phillips, the infamous "Black redneck" from Florida who was only there to add diversity to the committee, since Senator Philips was sure to be voted out when he was up for reelection After a speech at the University of Miami, Senator Phillips was caught on video at a party with a lot of young White sorority girls, saying he hated all niggers, especially very light skinned ones.

"I did not personally manufacture 1,643 Areocars and 5 Areosport 3000s. As for the fools who want to spend 300.5 million euro or more to buy the Areosport 3000 and fly at 1,000 mph, 300 feet above the ground, I cannot be responsible for them." Getty was referring to the incident that got him in the hot seat in the first place. The Senators whispered amongst each other. Senator Kim then took off her glasses and looked at Getty with as much authority a beautiful, sexy 32-year Asian lady could muster and started to read from the report.

"On June 15, 2019, U.S. Navy's early detection sonar equipment began to pick up several rhythmic sonic booms which seemed to be moving fast toward the United States. Neither the U.S. Navy nor the U.S. Air force could pick anything up on radar, so planes were sent from the USS Ford. A visual was made at 0900 hours of what appeared to be a supped up Areocar quote 'swanging lane to lane on an imaginary freeway at 893 mph, 250 feet over the Atlantic Ocean." They seemed to be peddling vigorously'. Close quote."

Setting the tone for the rest of the Getty hearings was Senator Phillips chuckling to himself over the thought of "they seemed to be peddling vigorously" to get away. This was caught on tape and aired on the evening news. The image of

12 heavily armed fighter jets chasing a drunken dude that was none other than Vasquez "Eagle" Williams in an Areosport 3000 was only increasing the demand for the new machine. Especially since the chase lasted from the middle of the Atlantic until the craft landed safely at Club Katrina in Shreveport, Louisiana .

Congress decided to let Getty and IST Corp. off the hook if Getty supplied blueprints and IST Corp. stuck to manufacturing clothing and running restaurants.

Dr. Serwin Getty became known in elite circles as the man who made the flying car. Even though there had been others before him, and the patent belonged to International

Standard Trading Cooperation owned by the Honeycutt family. Dr. Serwin Getty, or Getty as he preferred to be called, designed the first version that was both practical and safe.

IST Corp. was a small, minority-owned company that owned clothing manufacturing plants and a barbecue fast food chain with no vehicle manufacturing experience. They built nearly 700 of these magnificent vehicles in 18 months, shocking the entire world. Legend has it, IST Corp.

purchased the patent from Dr. Getty for $7.5 million dollars at the time when the Areocar was still only a dream on paper. Somehow IST Corp. not only produced it but also made it affordable at only 100 million in the ultra-inflation of 2016.

The Areocar used the highly efficient IST. Corp's Honeycutt C.V.E.G. Motor® also called the Constant Velocity Electromagnetic Gravitation engine. A motor capable of almost perpetual energy only requiring the occasional non- tedious peddling of any one of four bicycle-style cranks located in hidden compartments in the floorboards of the vehicles. The outer skin of the Areocar was covered with colored solar panels, allowing customization while keeping a highly efficient battery charged which helped start the engine and backed up the entire system. The Honeycutt Motor® was really 36 smaller motors packed into

Colleagues

less than a cubic meter on one block in a honeycomb pattern. If all 36 of the engines stopped running, the battery could power the propulsion system for 30 hours under optimal conditions. Tuned for maximum efficiency, it reached a comfortable cursing speed of 450 mph, making travel over large bodies of water safe. Even if the battery also ran out of energy or malfunctioned, a person could peddle his way to safety, (in theory, only because no one has had all systems malfunction without complete destruction of the craft). The Honeycutt C.V.E.G. Motor® could, in theory, run indefinitely, but after about 20 or 30 hours of constant running, or on cloudy days, pilots may need to peddle 10 to 20 revolutions with the bicycle style peddles which rise up from a discreet compartment in the floorboard. The peddling increased the speed of the Honeycutt C.V.E.G. motor and also added to the confidence of the passengers since they know it could never run out of fuel because absolutely none is needed. The motor design was kept secret by elaborate booby traps that destroyed the working parts inside the motor case if any outer pressures seal were broken. Even a camera the size of a particle, inserted into the motor case would rupture the electronic pressure seal destroying the inner workings. In addition, if only one motor of the 36 was tampered with. A chemical reaction would be triggered in all the motors leaving nothing but ashes.

As a gift to society, IST Corp. released some drawings of the C.V.E.G. motor that showed much of its efficiency came from the fact that absolutely no moving parts made contact with each other. Getty was let off the hook with only a slap on the wrist. Not because there was a public outcry caused by all the Hollywood superstars and billionaires who supported him because they felt Areocars were the hottest toy ever. Nor was it IST Corp. cooperating with the government by releasing the useless blueprints. It was his high-security clearance and knowledge of many government secrets that kept them from coming down on him hard. Getty had no political power and seemed to have no ambitions, so he did not matter to them. After a week of paid leave, he returned to work only to be greeted by Preston Ross, the "underboss" of the Defense Department—the one person who Getty for sure knew wanted him dead. The prick he had to give his C.V.E.G. motor blueprints to. Thus far, the surrender of his blueprints had been Getty's biggest defeat Preston had in their rivalry. Preston's roots run deep in the "good ol' boy network." So much so, he was rumored to be moving over to the executive side as either the Secretary of Defense or Secretary of State in President Lee's third administration. He would then be either Vice President or maybe groomed to precede President Lee, if the rumors were true.

"So, Mr. Getty you have pushed with all your might to get the contract for IST Corp," Preston Ross stated in the most sarcastic voice he could muster. He had long ago decided it was not worth the energy to pretend to like somebody he really did not like. He was blond-headed with blue eyes, bout 6'2, middle-aged, with a Midwestern dialect. What made Preston so distinct was his bushy goatee, giving him the look of a biker. If he would have been bald, it would have fit, but he kept a traditional clean-cut, making the style goatee he had seem not to fit. He wore the new "suit-a-form", a hybrid of a civilian suit and military uniform, every day.

Every Sunday you could find Mr. Ross at church service with his wife and grankids. Both he and his wife could trace their bloodlines back to the Mayflower and had U.S. Presidents on both sides of the family as ancestors. He was like a government hustler, moving billions in the name of national defense. Getty always found it odd how people such as Preston Ross could spend billions of taxpayers' money by sending most of the money overseas to friends with international companies and not a whimper is made, yet he does something beneficial only to receive a Senate Hearing.

Colleagues

"You have never seen a President or have stepped foot on Capitol Hill, yet it seems as you are making policy." Preston continued with his whining which Getty knew was a ploy to get some type of reaction from him —some hint to who Getty was as a man, maybe a hint to what his weakness was. Up until now, Preston had been giving nothing. Getty's office in the Pentagon was totally plain. He was only there when he was required which was about 25 days a year, with the rest of his time being spent in the field—the exact opposite of Preston. It was accepted that Field Agents such as Getty, no matter how high-ranking, cannot accomplish much in their dungeons, as the small offices appropriated to them are called.

"What are you talking about?" Getty countered with the most baffled look on his face.

"You sent your pimp around the Secretary and made… you… I just don't like you because you are too radical. You just don't understand the old saying "if it is not broken don't fix it.""

"You are just upset because the Areocar takes money out of the hands of your fat, greedy friends, the oil companies. Anyway, I sold the patent; I am no longer responsible for the procreation of energy efficient vehicles, so it is my only job now to protect this country."

"Listen you faggot! It's about to get geopolitical on your ass if you don't slow your road!" Preston exploded. Getty stood and looked Preston in the eyes. They were about the same height. He pauses to remind himself to keep with tradition and not let him have anything.

"Yo mama's a faggot… Please leave my office…" Preston was shocked by the "Yo Mama!" reply. He was far down the hall and two floors up in his large office before he realized Getty won the exchange by making him lose his cool, then softening him with the "Yo Mama" comeback when a lesser man would have lost his cool and thrown it all away for one swing.

Getty was a good ol' boy it would seem since his great-grandfather, Dorian Getty once owned one of the largest mineral mining and shipping companies in the world. During both World Wars, his small fly-by-night companies supplied both sides by shipping small amounts of the highest demanded minerals to the safest port of importation. Being a great speculator, Great Grandpa Getty used the hysteria of the Atlantic unrestricted U-Boat war against merchant vessels to his advantage by literally having the ports of the competing side's bid for his precious cargo. As he was well aware, the loser of the bid would attempt to sink his ships, as they would be full of the winner's and now 'enemies' goods. Old Great Grand Pa Dorian Getty would just send a telegraph to release the goods from any one of many warehouses located throughout several countries; as he had brought in the goods weeks before guaranteeing the goods would not be lost at sea. Once both sides caught on to what Great Grand Pa Getty was doing, they were both hesitant to sink his ships as they could have been carrying their country or its allies much needed raw materials instead of the enemies for the next month.

Dorian Getty III only slept with Getty's mother twice and then never spoke to her again, yet his surname and the blood test allowed Getty's admittance to anywhere Preston Ross's "pure" unbroken lineage allowed him, and Preston hated him the more for it. It only took one of the two multi-trillion-dollar oil companies to openly declare war on the True Alternative Energy Program initiated by the Honeycutt Foundation— the so-called charity organization established by IST Corp. After Getty gave them the C.V.E.G. engine, they created a larger version about three times the size, which could power a four-bedroom house indefinitely with absolutely no waste and only five minutes of pedaling a week. They did not sell the generators but instead accepted million-dollar donations for them and gave two away free, every day, so the company paid no taxes.

Colleagues

Preston whispered Getty's whole name to himself. He sat in his office where four 52" thin 3D Cybervision screens broadcasted the world's news, stock markets, and other updates. To think all this started at a 4th of July party thrown by the Retired Judge three years ago.

Getty being "Mr. Perfect" was working the huge smoker, teaching five college interns how to barbeque using the Texas dry rub style, and how to make deviled eggs. One of the female coeds, enjoying the show, arrived with Preston Jr. who attended the University of Notre Dame. Preston rudely interrupted, wanting to change the recipe to South Carolina-style while protecting the Ross family name. Getty proceeded to make Preston the object of ridicule while simultaneously coasting to a threesome with the lovely female students.

Preston was with his wife of 30 years and was red hot. "Getty had been a wonderful adversary, but his time had come. Rule one in the art of war… know thy enemy," Preston mumbled out loud as he opened and thumbed through a file entitled "The Getty File", which he had spent lots of time and money on, and now owed some favors for

DICK OWENS

Chapter 7

RAIL GUN

July 4, 1992 Boondocks of Texas:

Young Serwin was washing his car when he heard the explosion. It was the loudest and strangest sound he had ever heard. It sounded like a large rifle had fired with the echo continuing to ring for several seconds after the sound of the big blast. He heard glass shattering then smiled when he was sure his precious car's tinted windows did not shatter. It was in the evening, right at dusk. A few stars in the sky were visible but it was not fully dark. It was a warm summer evening in Thawada, Texas. The explosion had been so loud it got the attention of everyone in the city. It seemed everyone had stopped to look around and see what had caused such a sound. Serwin's heart was racing as the thought of Gabriel blowing his horn and the skies opening crossed his mind when he saw a thin dark line descend from the sky and lead to the old oil 2. He started to say first, to himself, and then again aloud, "No way!" He hopped in his car and started to drive toward the abandoned oil field where he and his friends attended a party a year ago. On that night, his cousin Harold, after smoking with a friend Mach Brown, got so high he thought he had a scientific breakthrough in astrophysics. From that day forward Harold kept returning to the oil wells with Mach to build some kind of machine or something.

For a while, Serwin thought maybe Harold had been given some bad drugs but Harold excelled in College courses, even making the honor roll He was so good in science he became a lab assistant and had access to most of the College equipment. Serwin looked at the sky again but it had gotten too dark for him to see the thin dark streak he had seen a few minutes earlier. Serwin's phone starts to ring and it was Harold.

"Where you at?" Serwin starts, still taking some deep breaths from being rattled.

"I am at the laboratory at the school! Did you see… well um hear my probe?" Harold always sounded excited and, in a rush, but much more so when he was at the college.

"You mean the explosion?"

"That was the probe being fired from the 2,843-foot launching tube I built. Look, you know we cannot talk on the phone. Meet me at the optics lab on the third floor of the science building ASAP! I really need you man." Harold hung up. Serwin thought he had seen it all since he moved to Texas from back East. On his first day in Thawada, when he was 14 years old, he had seen a huge gang fight, which ended with some kid named Prometheus Green receiving an attempted murder charge. Since then, he only hung around his cousin. Serwin walked into the lab after passing a sedated security guard and a broken lock.

"This time I got it!" Harold said aloud to himself as he nudged the joystick slightly to the right

"Ughhh!! Damn it… I lost it… auh, auhhg... There… there!" Harold ever so slightly moved his finger up the beam of light that represented the zoom wheel on the computer interface in front of him. The computer screen zoomed in on what appears to be a monument of a face, a giant face. Harold was amazed at the detail of the headdress that is adorned by the giant monument. "What is so special about today is that in 30 seconds the satellite view is going to switch from the overhead view to a never before seen side view of what appears to besides of a plateau in which the face sat…" Harold mumbled to himself. He couldn't possibly have expected to see what he was witnessing. NASA had said that the 'Face-looking rock structure' on Mars was about one or two miles wide and long, but from Harold's calculations, the face was at

Rail Gun

least twice that size. This discrepancy was easy to verify, since the camera was descending at a set rate of fall. The reflection rate of a beam of light measures its distance from the surface. These measurements are crosschecked with sound, radio, and microwaves and are also reflected back. Once this distance was determined, objects on the ground size can then be easily calculated. This four-tiered way of measuring large objects from space has proven to be 99.9% accurate with only black holes and other strange anomalies causing inaccurate readings. *Of course, there are no black holes this close to earth,* Harold thinks. The next set of numbers caused Harold to get nauseous. Harold had the type of mind which could really picture things in perspective. The walls of the seven-mile-long structure were two miles in height! He pictured himself standing at the base of the structure and looking up at walls that appeared to travel all the way to heaven. The descending camera was not only using a parachute to slow its descent, it also has a small fan and heater, which blew warm air into the parachute, causing it to fall as slow as six feet per minute. He focused in on the sides. He wanted to measure the angles of the curves around the structure to prove if it was indeed designed or just a natural rock surface. Serwin walked into the computer lab.

"Is the camera getting anything?" Serwin said with his weird European like accent.

"The fact that eyes, nose, and a mouth with teeth are clearly identifiable is not enough since many people see a man in the moon... I need you to keep watch; if we get caught in here, I will be kicked out of school and probably go to prison for a long time." Harold whispers back. Serwin glances over Harold's shoulder to look down at the 52-inch high-definition plasma display as the screen focused in on what appears to be hieroglyphic symbols all along a huge wall with some monuments on top.

"Looks like your rocket went to Egypt," Sherwin said, looking past Harold. Harold turns to look at the screen as it focused in even more.

"Oh Shit! This is the greatest discovery in the history of man!" Harold shouts well above a whisper, as the screen focused in on hieroglyphic symbols all along the mile-high walls.

"shh.sh,shh,ssssh!"

"Don't fucking shh me! This is now about science and the further development of society. "Harold shot back in a louder than normal speaking tone.

"OK, OK. You don't have to convince me about the ramifications of this, but a jury might find the sedated security officer a victim. Also, I've told you because of the high-level security in this area, any unauthorized trespassing is a Federal offense... "Serwin whispered.

"I get the picture. Do you have the HD data disc, so we can start saving?" Harold replies in his normal tone.

"You fuckin ass hole... you left out some of the details about this little mission of ours... like the security officers are authorized to shoot intruders," Serwin whispered as he reached into his pack and handed Harold an HD data disc.

"I've done my research on this and the fact we're breaking into this area is probably a minimal 10 years. I am well aware of the consequences," Harold jabbed back as he placed the HD Data disc into the laptop computer connected to the university's mainframe computer. Harold moves the camera to record as much of the wall as he could. He then focused on the top of the monument and recorded around the eyes and around the headdress of the object. From the microwaves and other waves, it indicated that the headdress was made of a metallic material—gold and platinum. As if the hieroglyphic symbols on the walls was not enough. The headdress was also covered in elaborate pictures, symbols, and drawings. Measurements of the eyes, nose, and mouth area proved to be in symmetry with a human face. All of a sudden, everything shut down and the room was totally dark.

"What the fu..." Harold reached for his cell phone to get some light.

"Listen...   you hear that..."   as they both got totally quiet, they heard footsteps approaching sounding like more than one person.

"OK, let's get out of here now," Serwin said as he fumbled on the ground for the laptops to disconnect them from the mainframe.

Harold reached down to stop him,

"Maybe if we just be quiet they will just go away," Harold whispered.

"It's too late," Serwin said as he disconnected both laptops. They heard walkie-talkies now. "We have to make a break for it. I am going to run out and go down the stairs, here is your copy." Serwin handed Harold a laptop. "You are on your own." He grabbed the other laptop and put it in his backpack. "Meet me at Bear's house in two days." Serwin then stood up and went to the door.

"This is Detail One... looks like we have a man down. Send up some backup, over..." One of the guards was heard speaking into his walkie-talkie.

"Central reads you... check, we're sending back up, over..." A woman's static voice responded back over the walkie-talkie. Right as two figures appeared in front of the door through the stained glass, Serwin slams the door open into the men shattering glass on one and knocking the other to the ground. One screams as shattered glass cut deep into his hands and chest. Serwin had his plan of escape in mind. He had to escape down the stairs. Once downstairs there was a 100 feet long hallway with two exits at the end. One was to the gymnasium and the other way goes into the cafeteria. Serwin thought if he could make it to the gymnasium, he would be home free. By knocking the guys down, it brought him a few seconds. If he could get to the end of that hall, they couldn't see which direction he went. Once he got into the gymnasium, he could get out back to the locker rooms and then exit to the dormitories where he'll be able to blend in long enough to get a ride out of there. The officer that had fallen to the floor reached for his gun then fired three rapid shots in Serwin's direction.

The three shots exploded throughout the laboratory and echoed off the walls causing Harold's ears to ring. His heart skipped a beat then started to race, beating so hard it felt like it was going to explode out of his chest. He immediately squatted down out of instinct to avoid the bullets. He saw one of the officers holding his hand and bleeding profusely screaming,

"I'm cut! I'm cut!" Harold then saw the other officer run past the door before it slammed back closed. Since the frosted glass was now broken out of the door, light from the hall was shining into the laboratory. The bloody officer looked up, and right into Harold's bulged eyes.

"Freeze ass hole!" the officer shouted, but instead of reaching for his gun, he gently slid his uncut arm through the broken glass and begun to unlock the laboratory's door. Harold turned and ran toward the back of the laboratory. The front part of the laboratory was well lit from the hall light, but the rear of the room was very dark causing him to stumble over the student's desk as he tried to make his way to the back of the room. Harold heard the door slam behind him, but he did not look back. He knew the guard was through the door and was anticipating a bullet to the back of the head at any moment. Instead, he heard the guard stumbling over a desk and coming toward him—he was grunting like a savage animal. Finally, Harold made it to the Professor's office. He went inside and locked the door. Only a second later, he heard a violent slam against the door. Then the officer started to kick the door. It would only be a matter of seconds before either the door was off the hinges or the lock was smashed in. Harold heard his heart beating in his ears. He looked around the room and spotted a small window that was more for ventilation than anything else, but because of Harold's small size, he might be able to squeeze through. He pushed the Professor's large desk over to the window. He hopped on top of the desk, opened the window and pushed the screen out, looked down at the 20-foot drop.

"Damn we are on the third floor," he thinks. It was at this time he thought about Serwin for the first time since the shots were fired. *"Damn this is my fault,"* he thought as he started to tear up. Then a loud bang came from the door, and he turned to see that the deadbolt on the door was pushing through the doorframe. A few more kicks and that door would be open. He could hear ferocity in the grunts and growls as the officer kicks the door. No matter what, he was not going to be in a room with this guy, Harold decided. He thinks that if he can get out feet first, he could hang from the window. His drop would only be about 13 feet or so. There was soft grass and bushes below, so he would probably be okay. He got one leg out the window but could not work his body to get the other leg through. He decided he has to get both legs out at the same time, so he got in a handstand, walked his feet up the wall, and then put both feet out the window. The edge of the window scraped and hurt like hell against his shinbones. As Harold pushes himself up to his knees a loud crashing sound came from the door.

"I gotch yo ass now!" the deep voice roars from the big six-foot-five Black man as he started toward Harold holding his bloody arm. Harold turned his head to see a big upside-down monster coming toward him, all bloody. He screamed while walking his body up the wall when his belt buckle gets caught on the window frame. He started to worm his body frantically to give his belt buckle some clearance over the window frame. Harold dared not look back because it would waste too much time. It was about this time he heard the security guard let out his final battle cry. Harold cringed as he thought at any moment he was going to be grabbed and slung to the floor. He heard a loud crashing sound and grunt as the security guard bumped into another desk, giving Harold one more second. This was it. Harold pushed and wiggled at the same time with all his might, flinging himself feet first out the window. He reaches for the window frame to try to catch it, so he could suspend a little bit to slow his fall. However, he misses. Harold was lucky there were a lot of bushes to break his fall. He got some scrapes and cuts but was okay. He looked up and saw the security guard looking out the window at him and talking on his walkie-talkie. He could hear sirens in the background. He crawled out the bushes and ran behind one of the buildings out of the security guard's line of sight.

The campus was well lit, and from the commotion, he was sure students and teachers would start coming around and they would definitely point him out. Behind one building, he hears people talking on walkie-talkies coming toward him. In front of them, through a gate, he hears others shouting orders and a dog barking. He always thought if he were ever in this situation, he would keep running so he would not be caught inside a containment circle. However, Harold gave into basic animal instincts and started to look for a place, to hide. He squeezed through the door of a metal shed that had a chain and lock but could be opened enough for a small human such as Harold, who weighed only 155 lbs. to squeeze through. Once inside he realized he was in the ground keepers shed from the smell of gasoline along with several lawnmowers, weed-eaters, and trashcans full of leaves. He can hear dogs barking which made him nervous because maybe they could track him down. He quickly rigged up a domino effect, "better mousetrap" type scheme, where he got inside one of the trashcans then used a rake to set off a chain reaction of things falling on top of him. Starting with a bag of leaves to protect

Rail Gun

him from the heavier metal items such as the shears and gas-powered weed-eater. When it was all done, it looked like it would have taken a second person to get him in his hiding place.

Chapter 8

THE FOX

July 1992 Washington DC:
Lieutenant Haraesio Martin sat in the cheap, uncomfortable plastic chair he hated more than anything in the world. The chair was so cheap and flimsy; it felt like the legs were going to buckle. It had a spring or something that would sometimes poke him and worst of all it made strange and inappropriate sounds every time he moved so he was never in a comfortable position while sitting in Colonel Lenard Brett's office. Despite the accommodations, Lt. Martin could not help but appreciate the artwork decorating the office. The walls were adorned with portraits of military men, all direct descendants of Col. Brett going back to the 1600s. Some of the oldest paintings were of Bavarian officers. Col. Brett also went out of his way to make sure that each frame was made of different wood. He walked in, dressed in his usual dark blue suit and one of the 365 different ties in his collection.

"Lt. Martin, good morning. I'm sure you've seen this morning's newspapers."

"No sir, I usually catch the news late at night..."

"How can you be a top agent if you don't stay informed?" Col. Brett interrupted with a look of disgust on his face.

"I've had a large caseload as of late. Not much time for the morning paper."

Col. Brett flipped through a large folder he had on his desk with Lt. Martin's name on the tab.

"I can see you have had twice the caseload and twice the success of most agents. Here, read this and tell me what

The Fox

you think." Col. Brett handed Lt. Martin the "Daily Post." The

headline was Terrorist Attack on College Campus.

"No one was killed," Lt. Martin replied after he speeds-read the article in a few seconds.

"It doesn't matter if anyone was killed! Whoever is behind this is attacking the foundation our nation was built on. We believe there has already been some bloodshed. This case is definitely in line with what our agency was set up to do, although it's going to be a little stickier than previous operations we've been involved in," Col. Brett gruffed from under his silver Kaiser mustache as he stood up and started to pace the mirror-polished hardwood floor of his extremely large office. Col. Brett stood six- foot, six inches, weighing in at 280 lbs., and was in his early fifties. You would think his silver blond hair, ice-cold blue eyes, and dimples moved him up the military ladder more than his battlefield tactics, as he had never seen a battlefield... His position was only recently created after the terrorist attacks and was a high- paying, coveted one.   He was the boss of thousands of people, both military and civilian, of which Lt. Martin was one. He also sat on various Senate Committees, but he could only make recommendations, whereas here, he was the boss.

Lt. Martin was also tall, with an athletic build and dark features. In his early thirties, he earned over six figures a year, along with full benefits, such as travel expenses and a company car. Even his meals were paid for. He really loved his job, so he put up with anything from his superiors. Col. Brett knew this, thus Lt. Martin was his favorite crash-test dummy.

"After looking over the files, I see two, Level 5, native U.S. born citizens that we're possibly dealing with. Up unto now, I can recall only a few Level 3s, and they were all military. How did we go so far, so quickly? To be honest with you Lt. Martin..." Col. Brett pauses as he pulled out a small and skinny Cuban cigar. "I believe it's a test from above," Col. Brett gruffed as he walked towards the large custom hand carved cherry oak wood Civil War era fireplace mantle—his favorite spot to give his big speeches. "Few men in our time earn the legal right to take upon the missions we are indebted to our great nation to partake. Do you feel privileged to be here?"

"Yes Sir… I'm ready to give my life serving my country, Sir."

"Humph… apparently according to the new Federal Military Civilian Code, page 97, outlining the handling of Level 5 civilians requires immediate termination." Col. Brett walked over to his desk and stood in front of Lt. Martin. He reached under some papers on his desk and pulled out a dark blue leather covered book with a big United States of America Presidential seal and "Federal Military Civilian Code" in big, gold letters written on it, Lt. Martin could detect the smell of money on Col. Brett. Only 217 pages long, the Federal Military Civilian Code is a secret field manual and the bible for the field agents. Agents are given one copy when they are hired into the covert Departments of Homeland and Security Agency and are told they will be terminated immediately if they lose it, as it was a top-secret document. So secret, only high-ranking military agents are given the document on a disposable micro-disc only readable on a special government-issued decoder device. Col. Brett opened the book and pointed as Lt. Martin read the words to himself.

"Level 5 threats must be terminated immediately." Col. Brett then handed Lt. Martin a file on his desk. There were two folders inside and a paper outlining his objectives. Lt. Martin placed the documents in his briefcase as he stood to shake Col. Brett's hand with a firm grip. He turned, smiled and added,

"Thank you, sir, for this opportunity."

The Fox

"We have a lot younger men whom are qualified Lt. Martin," Col. Brett said, as he walked toward his closet. Lt. Martin always wondered what was inside Col. Brett's closet literally. Col. Brett sensed this, so he always waited for the door to close behind Lt. Martin. He would then reach into his closet and roll out a lavish, ostrich-skin covered, fully adjustable with massage features office chair that was almost as expensive as his own. He then slowly rolled the cheap ugly torn plastic chair back into the rear of his closet.

Lt. Martin flew to Thawada the same day. He recovered the HD disc Harold had dropped in the lab. After observing surveillance video, he walked the campus until he came upon the locked shed. He had a groundskeeper unlock the shed.

Harold awoke when he heard the chain being removed from the shed door. His heart started to race. Lt. Martin searched but did not see anyone hiding. He initially left the shed to go look at more video when he realized how small the person would have had to have been to fit through the window. He quickly headed back to the shed.

Harold heard the voices of the people poking around walk away. He felt now was his chance to make a break for it.

He started to push some of the objects off him. Right as he poked his head out, a gun barrel was pointed at his head. It was Lt. Martin.

"What is the name of the man who was with you?" Lt. Martin demanded.

"Am I under arrest? What did I do?" Lt. Martin hit Harold in the top of the head with the butt of the gun. Harold's skull cracked, and a stream of blood streamed down his face.

Before he blacked out he said,

"Serwin had nothing to do with…" This was all Lt. Martin needed. He proceeded to splatter gasoline and set the shed on fire. Local authorities pulled out Harold's charred body a few hours later. There was nothing his family could do but bury him.

Once Serwin heard what had happened to Harold, he could not believe what was happening. He did not know what to do. He received a call from Mach Brown asking him to meet him at the old oil field. When Serwin arrived, he saw Mach Brown, his childhood nemesis, standing on top an old oil derrick with tears in his eyes. Beneath him were Harold's cousins on his mother's side, the Honeycutt brothers, along with his best friends, Vasquez, Hawk, and Bear. Mach Said,

"The government murdered Harold because he had successfully launched a probe made from a rather expensive alloy of mostly copper, but also some silver and a fraction of a percent of gold was needed to get it right. This probe, the size of a baseball, had an optical system to take pictures and video. It did not store the data but beamed it back from space. Certain equipment found only at the University was needed to put the data into pictures. This is why Harold broke into the lab," Mach went on to say, "The baseball- sized probe was launched from a 2,843-foot launching tube converted from an old oil well's shaft by pouring melted aluminum down it. This metallic shaft was rifled and magnetized with 2,000,000 volts stolen by way of the city supply and then frozen with liquid nitrogen." Power lines from a telephone pole could be seen going to the shaft. "This probe launched at more than a million miles per hour because the magnetic field of the probe was manipulated to repel against the magnetic force of the launching tube. Once the switch turned on, the probe attempted to eject from the underground shaft and was hindered only by its own mass vs. the magnetic repulsion force. It reached the planet Mars very quickly—like within a hour or so. Serwin has the proof." Serwin took the HD disk out and placed it into Jacob Honeycutt's laptop. After a few seconds, images of the Cydonia region of Mars appeared in High Definition. There was a giant face monument as well three large Pyramids, and a city of windows and streets were all fascinatingly crystal clear. The hieroglyphs were so clear on the giant face and the Pyramids' individual characters could be made out. A fortress with what appeared to be some type of ancient alien weapon was still intact, and several other buildings could be made out. Mach then buried the disc and destroyed the computer as well as the launching shaft by pouring acid down it.   He gave everyone present another copy of his "Theories of the Great Nothing" which he said Harold used to build his space probe. Serwin read the manuscript this time. He enlisted in the military and did not leave the base the next day, which saved his life as Lt. Martin could not get to him. Once Lt. Martin's superiors viewed the other HD disc Lt. Martin had taken from Harold, he was removed from Serwin's case and no further official record existed for Serwin except a stellar military career in Special Ops unit for five years. He was then moved to the CIA's Special X Unit.

January 31, 2020 Washington DC:

For Preston Ross, there were only two things of interest he may be able to use from the Getty Report his new-found, powerful friend, Mr. Fiske Braun, had generously provided him in exchange for all he knew and a copy of the undisclosed official record of the Television Station Hijacking. First, Lt. Martin may be a guy he could use to destroy Getty, and second, he needed to gather some big guns if Getty had anything to do with both IST Corp. (which appeared to be obvious as he virtually gave the Areocar to them), and the infamous nightclub owner Vasquez Williams or Eagle, as he was called.

He started with Lt. Martin, who turned out to be the ultimate yes man. He would not make any moves on anyone unless Col. Brett gave the word. It was obvious he had to speak to Colonel Brett. The problem with this was Col. Brett was over a department which positions were created after the terrorist attacks. They were looked upon as the other guys who were trying to take over the system from the "real good ol'

Boys." They were mostly second-generation immigrants from Europe and the Middle East who looked White, but also a lot of half breeds and the tricky Chicano who also tried to pass for good ol' boys. There were also far too many women in positions of authority than there should have been according to Preston's way of thinking. There were even the unthinkable, openly gay males and females, prancing around as if they were in California or something. Since the suspension of the U.S. Constitution, the United States Government was split in two, hence Preston had absolutely no rank or file with Col. Brett. This, in itself, would be hard for Preston, as he always has to be the Boss. He decided to attempt to barter Lt. Martin's services for a few weeks. Preston figured even if Getty discovered someone from his past was snooping around; it would at least unnerve him enough to make a mistake.

Preston first attempted to set up a dinner meeting with Col. Brett through a mutual associate named Willoford, one of Preston's senior golfing buddies. Willoford, who plays with Col. Brett several times a year, informed Preston of Col. Brett's background. He was a second-generation immigrant from Germany. His family on his mother's side was into sausage production and beer breweries on his father's side. Col. Brett was a career military man and had been married three times. Preston being a big family man, found fault in Col. Brett.

At first, Col. Brett accepted, then, at the last minute, he canceled. To Preston's surprise, he never called back or apologized. Preston figured the Colonel's ego was too big for his own good, so he decided to pay him a visit. "He *could well be my next victim if the old fool wasn't careful.*" Preston thought to himself. Again, Preston did not get to meet with him because his secretary said he was in important meetings all day. Later that day, to Preston's amazement, one of his largest civilian defense contractor's CEO called him asking

The Fox

why a Lt. Martin from Homeland Defense had just left his office requesting documents he should not have been asking for. Preston then realized that maybe Col. Brett thought he was coming after him somehow, which was why he was stonewalling. Col. Brett's audacity impressed Preston, so he decided to just send a nice email, on the record, briefly explaining what he was after. He used no incriminating language. The next day he was invited to Col. Brett's office.

Preston was certainly impressed with Col. Brett's office. It was one of the most lavish he had seen, and he had been in some lavish offices. The ostrich skin office chair he was sitting in was so firm and comfortable; it almost put him to sleep. When he felt the heat and gentle massage actions, it was almost difficult for him to focus. Col. Brett, being about 9 years Preston's senior, after greeting him started to look through a folder with Preston Nathanial Ross written in big red letters across the top. Preston thought it was funny someone had a file on him. He knew so much dirt on all the most important people... he was always safe.

"Hmmm... Mr. Ross, you feel Serwin Getty is a threat to national security because of his connections to IST Corp. and the infamous Vasquez "the Eagle" Williams. I see here you have actually offered some information I did not have— this changes some things."

"I must be honest with you Mr. Ross..." Col. Brett lit a skinny Cuban cigar, then walked over to the fireplace and took up his speech position.

"I hate Vasquez Williams and all he represents. I ran him out the country several years ago. Then the bastard opened 100 more clubs internationally."

"Last I heard, closer to 200," Preston remarked. Col. Brett stared at Preston Ross for a few seconds then took a puff of his cigar, the smell of which Preston recognized as an expensive robust cherry Cuban Muduro, Col. Brett continued.

"Have you ever witnessed the debauchery which takes place in these houses of sin?"

"No, I have never been to one of the so-called Black Triad clubs"

"Humph...The Black Triad... according to the info you provided me, Eagle is really a three-headed monster with Vasquez being the face and someone named Hawk and Bear being the brains and muscle-controlling operations inside the US. Thanks to you, I have some new targets." A slight smile crossed Col. Brett's face.

"Well since I got you something will you fire Dr. Serwin Getty?" Col. Brett looked at Preston as if to study him.

"I will be honest with you. You are right to believe the Eagle is a danger to national security for the fact that every week his clubs blast every negative and rebellious song you can think of to at least a quarter of a million people, and maybe many more. As for Getty, he is one of the few people on this side I cannot touch, well at least not alone. You see, I sit on the committee which could get rid of him, but, to be honest with you, I am not finished with Getty myself." Preston, being the professional salesman, saw his opportunity to close a deal for what he really wanted after swinging for the fences.

"How about Lt. Martin... could I use him for a few weeks to see if he can find anything?"

"Lt. Martin is busy with a very important case involving national security."

"Did the case just start today, because two days ago he was in Pittsburg creeping around Tritek Securities corporate office?" Col. Brett was impressed by Preston's network. It must be nice if he discovered Lt. Martin's little investigation. Lt. Martin had a special knack to be able to see beneath the surface. After studying Preston's affairs for a few days, he went straight to the most unsavory defense contractor Preston had ever dealt with. This was why Preston wanted him. Col.

The Fox

Brett put out his cigar and walked back to his desk. He shuffled through some files. He then looked Preston square in the eyes.

"Despite our ancestors probably being on opposite sides of two Great Wars, we have a lot in common. Getty is the least of your problems, as well as the damn Eagle,   is the least of mine now. Col Brett handed Preston a folder with Ralph De' Shawn Honeycutt written in big red letters.

"Did you know this guy was running for President?" Preston's jaw dropped—he was speechless.

"With IST Corp's money behind him, he could theoretically win… This is what Lt. Martin is on. Help me get Ralph Honeycutt and I will have Getty fired and stripped of all his privileges and immunities so you can have your way with him." The deal was sounding too good to be true for Preston. IST Corp. was the most hated company among the Energy and Transportation companies who were Preston's friends. If he could bring down IST Corp., he would be set for life.

Preston quickly understood why the almighty Col. Brett needed him. Besides the fact if Ralph Honeycutt became president, he could fire Col. Brett and probably would. IST Corp. as well as most of Vasquez Eagle William's clubs, were out of the country. Col. Brett had very little, if no international pull, outside U.S. borders.   He was powerless, whereas the international was where Preston's power began. Preston was the biggest seller of US Military goods, so, even America's enemies liked Preston because he was the man with the guns. America's enemies only had to pay a lot more for the same goods.

It was agreed Preston would travel to Brazil where IST Corp's largest production plant was. Also, he would need to see what The Eagle and friends had going on at Club Shindinkis Hotel and Casino, which was said to be the largest dance club in the world, located in the middle of the Congo jungle in the center of Africa. Meanwhile, Preston got some info for Fiske Braun; Ralph Honeycutt was running for President of the United States—this was really big! One could never tell who strange characters such as Fiske Braun worked for. Preston figured either England or Israel. While leaving Col. Bret's office, Preston passed Lt. Martin. He could not help but to wonder where Lt. Martin would sit, remembering the strain Col. Brett was going through to put the nice and seemingly heavy ostrich skin office chair in his closet.

Chapter 9

PROPAGANDA

June 19, 1994, Dallas, TX:

It was at a small club in Deep Elum, located in the arts and club district of Dallas, Texas in1994 when Steve first had seen Vasquez Williams in action. Vasquez had been trying to hit on Steve's sister Monica when her boyfriend Jason responded by mouthing off about how much money he had, and a spending display to back it up. Jason even dropped his family name. Later that night Vasquez discovered that Monica and Steve were brother and sister. Vasquez proceeded to send his ugly groupies to Steve allowing him to have his first one nightstand thanks to the "Vaz." Exactly one week later, Steve had his sister to get a lease signed for the rundown building that was to become Club Skrew.

Vasquez Williams always had everything his way. He was popular, and he was great with the girls. He had a knack for getting people to do what he wanted them to do. Using his traditional methods of manipulating people to get something from them for nothing, Vasquez talked his friend Steve Lilly into talking his sister Monica into manipulating her boyfriend named Jason McAllister, whose family was into real estate, to lease an old warehouse out to her. Jason agreed to sign a lease, stating it would be three months before payment was due on the warehouse. Payment would be set at $2,000 a month for 18 months. Jason knew his family planned to sell the property to be demolished into a parking lot in a few years if the property value in the area did not increase due to the new shopping center being built about a mile away. To Jason, as well as his father and grandfather, this seemed to be a great deal! They would be getting $2,000 a month, or within two years, $40,000 on property they projected to be a loss due to property taxes and the cost of remodeling or, most likely, demolition. The dilapidated condition of the building was the catalyst for negotiating a three free month clause Vasquez had gotten through Monica. Within one hour of receiving the lease in his hand, Vasquez was on his way to see his new investment.

It was one of those days in Texas that felt like football weather, but it was the month of May with a temperature at about 78°. These days are most memorable because they are probably the last cool day you might feel before every day becomes hot and humid to the point where it becomes unbearable. Vasquez noticed the trees were all in full bloom along the streets as he was riding to his new warehouse located in downtown Dallas the most socially and economically mixed part of the city. Dallas, like most of the smaller big cities, such as Phoenix, Indianapolis, or even Miami seems to have a cleaner inner-city   then places like New York , Los Angeles, or even Houston, which are all only clean where they need to be, but grimy and dirty everywhere else. Vasquez knew he had to get the place up and running within 30 days so he would have a full 60 days of rent-free business. He figured that within 60 days he would at least make $2,000 to pay the first month's rent. He did not have his name on anything, so there was really no consequence to him if this project failed. Yet failure was not an option for this venture; Monica was too fine and he had to have her. She was Spanish and Black mixed with Italian. Steve was also a good friend. Vasquez's parents were of mixed descent, so he had taken all of the best features from all the races. He was a golden-brown color, and was tall, with dark black curly hair, big grayish-blue eyes, and always had a little mustache, beard, or goatee perfectly manicured, and changed his hairstyle to match. He only wore designer clothes and despite not being into sports, he had an athletic body. He always wore shades to hide his eyes, not so much to be cool, but growing up in the ghetto he did not want people to get it twisted if he was 100% nigga or not, and only his eyes suggested otherwise.

Along the way he made many friends and became so popular, he even had groupies. You could always see him with the most popular people or he was enemies of the most popular people. When you have your own following, this was just as good. When Vasquez and Steve first arrived at the warehouse, they could not believe how huge it was. Neither one had ever seen the place. Steve just heard his sister talking about it one day when she was talking about how her new boyfriend's Jason family just gives him stuff and he didn't know what to do with it. Jason was complaining about how his family gave him the rundown warehouse instead of the nice occupied apartment building that he could have collected money on immediately. The three-story, 45,000 sq. ft. building was located in an industrial area in downtown Dallas.

"You know Steve, this is going to work. Within one year, millions can be made. I want you to be one of the managers. You're going to be basically running the place but you know I have to bring in Hawk and Bear," Vasquez said, as he walked over to the lift elevator   that was more for lifting boxes and crates than humans. "I wonder if this thing still works and how much does it cost to get it to work if it doesn't?" Turning his back to Steve he continued, "It's probably going to cost more to fix that lift than the real elevator down the hall over there. Either way, to fix them is probably more than the $2,000 you have to pay for the rent. I bet you the plumbing is all screwed too," Steve added.

"You know Steve, if you want to be my partner; you're going to have to help me pay for these repairs which looks like about $25 Gs."

"Man! I knew it was going to be some bullshit!   I thought you had the money and friends with money to fix the place up." Steve raised his voice.

"I do—Hawk and Bear."

"Hawk and Bear are just like you. They really don't have any money, but they can just ..."

"Make things happen. You know something Steve... money is just a tool. Right now, your name is on the paperwork, yours and Monica. I need for you to sublease the property with all liability being turned over to Hawk. We will give you and Monica $1,000.00 a month each if this works, but we want Hawk in control now." Vasquez was interrupted by a loud rumble of music coming from outside. Steve walked out the door, Vazquez looked out the window, It was Hawk and Bear.

"Boy this place is garbage, how do you expect to make any money here?" Hawk started before he got out the car

"I am going to do like The Mongoose. I am going to apply the Theories of the Great Nothing to my business and let it take me to my destiny.

"Yea, but the old Owl is your greatest rival," Hawk countered quickly.

"We are all friends," Bear interrupted. Steve was totally lost—all he knew was he wanted in.

Vasquez's crew was like no other. It was exclusive as far as Steve could tell. Vasquez, Hawk, and Bear were a sect formed by a voting bloc they had in an elite society they were involved which had some secret knowledge. They never involved Steve as they said, this was not their job, but it was that of the Lion, whatever that meant. For all it was worth, Steve never asked questions as he first managed Club Skrew in downtown Dallas, then The Coolick in Houston, followed by Kisses in Oklahoma City. In all, he ended up with 5 nightclubs he was managing in the South West. Steve had grown very rich and corrupt when in the year 2018 his longtime friend Vasquez Williams fired him. Steve hated everything about his old friend of almost 20 years. When he thought about it, it seemed their whole friendship had been one big party and one big fraud; from the first time he met Vasquez. However, for some reason, he just could not put his hands on; he loved the guy like a brother.

This could be why he jumped at the offer to do some work for the Eagle in January of 2020. It was during the summer of 2019 when Steve started to really feel bitter about his demise from running the five clubs he helped to build. In his eyes, everything was half his, even the new thirty or forty clubs and bars Eagle, Hawk, and Bear later opened. He just knew they had to be doing something illegal. Steve grew up with all of them and Hawk and he was actually roommates in college. Yet, when it came to the meetings, they seem to always be held behind closed doors leaving him out while outsiders who knew nothing about promotion, hospitality, food, beverage, or any entertainment would be listened to. All the people who attended the meetings had code names of some sort— Lion, Snake, Falcon. He even overheard Hawk tell Bear a great elephant was coming to meet one time. Steve contacted the FBI, OSHA, IRS, and every other Federal agency once the reality set in he was never the major player he thought he was. He agreed to work undercover for the Bureau. For several years there was nothing until in 2019 Steve gave a list of names of people who were allowed up to the third floors and into the private meetings of some of the most exclusive nightclubs in the United States. One day, in particular, August 16, 2019, at the riverboat club called Katrina in Shreveport, LA owned by Vasquez "The Eagle" Williams in particular made it into the "Getty File." The day the First Areosport 3000 was sold to none other than Vasquez Williams and he illegally flew it to his club in Louisiana.

Jacob Honeycutt's name topped the list, but the names Bubba Moody Jr. and Clark Johnson seemed to be really out of place beside a Honeycutt on the list. The only other name, which was not an alias, was a Kerry Price whose name Preston was familiar with. The other people allowed up used aliases such as Elephant, Snake, and Owl. After Preston learned about Steve Lilly through his network, somehow Preston pressed for a joint questioning section so he could attend to gather as much info from Steve.

At this meeting with the Homeland Defense Department, Steve was amazed at how many people were attending. Two FBI agents, some State and County from both Texas and Louisiana, probably because that was where the five clubs he managed were located, along with one or two people from the IRS, ABC, ATF, and four or five other agencies. Several photos, maps, and charts covered the walls. They were all seated behind three large rectangular tables. Steve was asked to stand in front of them and tell them everything he knew about the Black Triad as they called them, referring to Eagle, Hawk, and Bear. Big Steve started to sweat like a fat pig in a slaughterhouse as he realized everything done illegally was done by him or upon his order. After a long pause Steve stuttered,

"I... I didn't know there would be so many people."

"Don't worry Steve, relax. No one is going to harm you. Please tell us why all 46 clubs owned by the Black Triad are under different company names," a familiar voice came from the table directly in front of him—it was Officer Bennett who he first spoke to at the FBI. "I don't know. I didn't even know it was exactly 46 clubs", Steve frowned.

"I thought you were half partners with the Triad," a Latino-looking female in plain clothes jabbed at Steve. Steve cleared his throat,

"I ran club Skrew, The Coolick, Kisses..."

"So besides those five clubs, you knew nothing else about the other 41 operations?" A tall very young looking man with a military buzzed haircut standing beside the seated Latino woman said sarcastically.

"Well I guess not," Steve said with a defeated voice. He overheard someone in front of him say he was a small fry and

Propaganda

someone else said he might be useless. Steve became more agitated as he thought about the 41 other locations. He felt he had been screwed 41 times. A hot passion arose in him to somehow destroy the Black Triad; mostly he wanted to hurt Vasquez.

"Well, there is a homicide they caused." The room went silent when Big Steve uttered those words. "His name was Stanley Turds." Steve giggled, which seemed inappropriate when talking about a deceased man.

"Stanley was one of our men," a big Texan said with a heavy drawl, dressed with a cowboy hat, big belt buckle of pure gold, and silver and buffalo skin boots polished to a perfect shine. His badge was showing him as a Ranger.

"Yea, they figured that out, as did Stanley…," Steve replied without the smile. The officers all started to meet with each other. At this time it became obvious to Steve the agents were sitting according to jurisdiction. The local agencies were at one table, the state agencies at another table, with the Federal agencies crowding the final table. They had been conferring for about 12 minutes when Steve stood up and stretched. He walked around the little area they had him isolated in. He looked at the agents scrambling back-and-forth then blurted out,

"Stanley didn't kill himself. I saw on the news where he went to work at the police station and shot his boss, then himself."

"That's exactly what happened according to the official report. Are there any details about this tragic incident you can share with us today?" a more moderately dressed local table agent most likely from Texas asked.

"It's a long story, but we all grew up with Stanley Turds in high school. Your Triad terrorized Stanley just because his last name was Turds. Bear actually put some dog turds in his backpack starting from eighth grade until one year, after graduation at a homecoming, Bear had Stanley's new truck filled with horse and cow crap." Steve was trying so hard to hold back the laughter, tears came to his eyes. He could see how upset the officers were.

"How sick"

"Disgusting!"

"Wish the assholes would have tried that on me." The officers could be heard as some squinched their noses in disgust at the thought of one of their own being treated so harshly in his younger days. Steve continued with a silly grin on his face.

"They must have really dramatized Stanley because all these years later he came after them. I mean Stanley comes to the club all square and gets drunk then starts mouthing off about how he's going to close down Club Skrew in Dallas. I actually deal with Hawk because I can't stand Vasquez. So I mentioned Stanly Turds antics and that he came by all five clubs and said he was with the Homeland Defense Department and decided to shut down every operation we had. A few days later all three, Hawk, Eagle and Bear, were at Club Skrew. I will never forget that night." Steve started to smile as he was reminiscing now; he had everyone's attention in the room. "It seemed like a hometown reunion once the Honeycutt's showed up. All the drinks were on the house.

Hawk told me they were going to do an experiment using Stanley Turds as the test subject. He gave me a script to learn, then told me to be at a particular location at a certain time. I did, and sure enough at 3:30 a.m. here come Stanley Turds on top of the world. He was the happiest man I had ever seen. Then I started reciting the script. I asked him a question as the script required. Stanley was silent for a few seconds then he broke out into tears. He ran out the club and then the next day he went to work and shot his boss, then himself. The next night Vasquez came up to me and told me it could have as well been me instead of Turds. I asked Hawk what Eagle meant by the Comment. Hawk said he voted for me to join the society after

Propaganda

what happened to Stanley Turds, but he lost. He was obviously shaken by Turd's death. He told me Eagle used a subliminal message along with brainwashing visuals. Because he had all of Stanley Turds social networking information, he was able to design a night, especially for Stanley Turds. From the songs played to the food he ate, even the air was manipulated through scents and natural hallucinogens. Several key encounters were orchestrated till the climax when he met his friend from eighth- grade history class, Big Steve Lilly." Steve looked somewhat sad at that moment—probably his true feelings showing.

"That's a hell of a story but there is nothing there to implicate any of the Black Triad", the little Latino woman at the table in front started.

"Well, they are fine-tuning the technique, so they..."

Steve's cell phone started to ring with a strange ring tone. He has the new SuperMax cyberphone with small deep base speakers with up to 100 watts output starts pumping to an exhilarating dance beat with several sounds that were strange. Steve's entire demeanor changed as he starts to bob his head and then stomp his feet.

"Mr. Lilly! Mr. Lilly! We need for you to turn the music down and continue to answer our questions!" one officer was heard. Steve threw up one hand and makes a fist and started pumping it. When another officer interrupted him to turn down the music the fist turned into one finger, the middle one, he pumped it several times then hit the talk button. Steve put the phone to his ear it was Vasquez the Eagle.

"Damn you, Steve. The Elephant was right. You are now Steve the Rat from now on. Wear it with pride." The phone hung up. Steve threw the phone on the ground destroying it saying he had nothing else to say as his eyes danced around in his head and refused to cooperate any further.

From August 2014 until January 29, 2020, several different agencies from every State the Black Triad had clubs in, ran some sort of investigation but never found any evidence of serious criminal activity. Only when a file labeled "Black Triad" landed on Col. Brett's desk was it noticed that several officers who investigated the clubs retired from their respective forces within one year, some even taking security jobs for the mega-clubs that popped up outside some of the micro-cities. Preston also noted, since 2014, The Black Triad focused on international locations.

Preston's old six senses started to flare up soon as he learned of a "Black Triad." He just knew he had found something he could make millions through confiscations while destroying his enemies. He decided to take a day off, go fishing with his grandkids, relax, and get some quality thinking time.

December 31, 2016, New York City:

Hawk was first seen in public with some of the new technologies. However, always to be the trendsetter, Eagle wore the indestructible shades everywhere he went. Once, while giving an interview for a show on Cyber Television,

Channel 134 Music World, the host Guy Smitarini joked,

"It seems it would be kind of hard to get a date if you can never make eye contact."

"Have you ever been to any of my clubs, Mr. Guy?" Eagle shot back.

"Well, of course, you would have to be either a hater or a square not to have…"

"Humph… I can have any female I want any time and place." Some oohs and aahs came from the hip and trendy crowd that included some big-name entertainers. It was well known Guy Smitarini had been dating the hottest Model/Actor in the Western Hemisphere, Zessa Si' for more than a year, and tabloids were suggesting he was ready to marry her. Guy gave his famous down-low chuckle signifying, to those

Propaganda

viewers who were familiar with the show; something was not as it was supposed to be. He also gave his famous three-second stare into the camera, mocking his guest as a wannabe hipster. Eagle, after living abroad for the past decade setting up his club and mega-bar franchise in Africa and Asia, sense of fashion was a little offbeat at times, to say the least. His style was to wear the most expensive name-brand gear regardless if it matched or not. Sometimes he was a hit, but other times he looked as if he was dressed 1980 throwback style as he did in this interview with Guy who, being the fashion guru he was, quickly seized the opportunity. Guy started with his finetuned tenor voice that had a light Portuguese accent,

"I can assure you that neither I nor most of the guys in your club have had much to worry about..." which ushered in more oohs and aahs than before.

"To be honest with you, he probably has to buy his love— that's why he needs so many damn clubs," Guy said this looking into the cameras. "I mean come on, shades in the club or any dark place is just so...um not cool." The Eagle interrupted now flashing his smile, the one that earned him a position in China's Night Life magazine as one of the 100 most beautiful people after he was responsible for the opening of 42 mega-bars and casinos over an eight-year period along the China coast.

"These shades are worth more than you make in a year", Eagle jabbed leaning back on the couch and kicking up his feet. Guy knew he had this weirdo cornered now. Although Mr. Eagle was this eccentric billionaire who coowned hundreds of nightclubs around the world, Guy was no slouch. He was an actor and had a music single on the charts while being the host of this show— one of the most popular shows on mass media's hottest new format. Internet and TV all combined into one totally interactive media where you can watch a show and by its end, whatever commercial you had seen, the product could be at your door. He made over $8 million last year...

"Well, just to entertain any logic in that statement, seriously what makes those million-dollar shades, my rich and strange friend?"

"Well for one, besides protecting my eyes from all the harmful radiation, these shades have ultra-vision technology, so I can see everything clearly even in total darkness. They're also indestructible along with the clothing I am wearing which is made of a material that can repel heat and bullets."

"I bet you would never like to prove it... Come on; is that what you are feeding the ladies upstairs?" Guy used a gesture with his head and eyes, further mocking the Eagle.

This was upsetting to the Eagle because there had been some accusations of young women being fondled and raped in some of his establishments "upstairs".

"Anyway Eagle, Vasquez Williams, or whoever you want to be, you need to remodel your dress code." The Eagle reached under his jacket and pulled out a jewel-handled .357 Desert Eagle. The audience gasped as well as Guy Smitarini. He took it off safety, turned it around, and handed it toward Guy Smitarini who was scared to take the gun.

"Here... Here! Take it you bitch, you!" Guy reached out and took the gun by its jeweled handle. "Okay now you prove me wrong hoe!" Eagle's smile was just as pleasant as when he first took the stage.

"I...I..P.. P.. Please..." Obviously shaken Guy cried and the gun started to slip from his sweaty, loose grip. Eagle caught the gun right as it fell from Guy's hand, spinning it as they used to in the western movies, then placed it back in his shoulder-mounted holster. As the gun was slipping from Guy's hand, Eagle said with a southern drawl,

Propaganda

"Shut up bitch and give a man his gun back 'fore I make you squat and piss like a bitch." He then stood up and walked off the stage with long, slow strides.

January 1, 2017, Paris, France:
Zessa was awakened by a phone call from a gossiping friend telling her to check out a rerun on Channel 134. Although she liked Guy a lot, it had nothing to do with his celebrity or even his looks. It was more about his sensitivity when it came to him turning her on. Having grown up in a Third World country, Zessa was accustomed to men looking at her as if they wanted to ravage her like a savage animal. She hated the stupid comments and foolish gestures they should have known would never get any play.   Her best friend Tonka, who was one of the most sought-after models in the world, was from Fuji and shared a lot in common with Zessa besides modeling, even though their public images' were opposite. Zessa betrayed the wholesome innocent type who was at times unsure about the newfound features of her young 18-year-old body. Zessa was tall and slender like a traditional model, but she had a very large and firm butt and perfect sized breasts. Tonka was short for a traditional model, but her full lips and brown skin made her stand out. Men went crazy over Tonka's perfect little brown body and puffy lips. She looked like a little girl that had matured too soon, too innocent to be touched by a man. Her personality was that of a bad girl who was a heartbreaker. Zessa looked at her girlfriend Tonka with wide eyes,

"Oh my god! Did you just see that?"

"Like yea... Your man just got totally punked in front of the World"

"I bet you I can get those spectacles off of him," Tonka said sheepishly.

"I want to look into his eyes and see his soul," Zessa continued.

Tonka laughed as she flashed a sly smile back at Tonka.

"He probably has a hook eye," Tonka giggled. She always seemed to make a joke of everything.

"Hook-eye? What's a hook eye?" Zessa giggled back with a look of confusion on her face.

"Oh girl, you don't know anything. A hook eye happens when you are fishing and somehow the fishing hook ends up in your eye."

"Oohh... how gross" Zessa skirmished. Tonka started to giggle again, "It's fascinating how many people have hook eyes when you think about it."

"Not everyone is from an Island where people fish every day. I am sure that's why so many of your family and friends had hook eyes." Zessa joked back. Tonka hit Zessa over the head with a pillow as the two guys laying beside them on the double King-size bed started to laugh at Tonka for having hook eye family members.

"If your fish hook eye mom and sisters are as fine as you, they will still get a man," Gustavo Grintroski added with his deep booming voice. He had met Tonka at his friend's Garrett Marquez movie premiere party, slash Oscar award party, the night before. Gustavo was the hottest guard in the IBA and so tough he actually signed a contract to play receiver in the NFL for one year. It was one of the most talked about deals in sports history, and for the first time in NFL history, an expansion team, the Hawaiian Sharks, made a serious run for the Super Bowl in its debut season. They took one of the greatest but oldest quarterbacks and paired him with their record-breaking first-round draft pick rookie receiver. The Sharks then went on to build a formidable defense through free agency and top draft picks. The final piece of the puzzle came together when the Sharks billionaire owner was able to work a deal with the Las Vegas Clippers, the IBA basketball team Gustavo signed to. Gustavo was allowed only 107 reception attempts during the regular season and an additional 20 for the playoffs. This

Propaganda

would minimize the chances of him being injured. The Nevada Clippers made millions off the deal since they practically leased their player to the NFL team. Both teams made millions on the teams' merchandise, as their teams became the most talked about in their respective sports. The Hawaiian Sharks made it deep into the playoffs losing a close heartbreaker by four points in a wild roller coaster of a game in which Gustavo had only two receptions left on his contract. He scored one touchdown and gave his team a critical first down on fourth and long to keep them in the game. It was the most emotional thing in recent sports history as the cameras zoomed in several times on Gustavo crying in the second half because he was not able to get in the game and help his team win. He silenced many critics of his so-called "million-dollar attempt contract" the Hawaiian Sharks gave him when most Americans were losing their homes. It was also gifted players such as Gustavo who were instrumental in helping the IBA (International Basketball Association) become the number one watched and attended professional basketball league in the world, totally eclipsing the former NBA of the United States. Gustavo reached over and picked up Tonka who had only some sexy lingerie on. She had shed everything else before getting into the hot tub earlier. Gustavo straddled Tonka across himself facing him, took her top off, and started to suck her natural, size C breast. Tonka pulled her panties to the side as he pulled out his manhood and inserted it deep inside her and he started to make love to her. Years later in his tell-all book, Garrett Marquez would write the most memorable day of his life was the morning after he had won the five Oscars and awoke to the sounds of Tonka Chung being screwed by Gustavo Grintroski. He said he watched for about 30 minutes, and then he started to make love to Zessa Si beside them.

"*After a few minutes we all switched,*" Garrett would later write. Because he did not clarify who switched with whom after being an alleged homosexual, Gustavo and Garrett would have a huge falling out over the book and never speak again. It would also hurt Zessa's marriage years later as well when the video of that night surfaced.

Preston gathered up all the grandkids he could. He managed to get five of the eight, as his oldest daughter refused to cave in to the pressure of putting her kids on a jet alone to fly all the way from Colorado just to go fishing with Grandpa. She actually prayed in church on Sunday for Jesus to spare her daddy's wrath because she knew how much his grandkids meant to him. Right as his youngest granddaughter with blonde Dixie pigtails, started to scream as the large fishing pole she was holding dragged her into his private lake on his ranch, an idea came to him. Preston first ran and saved his granddaughter from being dragged under by the 60 lb. grain-fed catfish she had hooked. He then recast his line and continued to put his plan together.

Chapter 10

DEMOCRACY

August 16, 2018, Shreveport, Louisiana:

The Great Elephant started to speak after they had finished vaporizing the purple and blue buds with pink hairs.

"The first thing I had to do on my quest for enlightenment was find myself. Once I did, there were several demons beside me on my right hand, and the left-hand side that was controlling my life to suit their purposes." He paused and took a deep breath, then made eye contact with each man in the room as a way to assure each one's attention. Hawk opened a $3,000 dollar bottle of cognac, and then started pouring himself, Eagle, and Bear healthy shots. Snake and Falcon were very tentative, as they would have to relay information to the Lion who was not able to be at this gathering because he was in India opening up a manufacturing factory for a new clothing line. The Elephant continued with a little bit more volume and bass in his voice.

"Once I am sure I met one demon named Greedious Gluttoness after I spent over an hour overeating at a Chinese buffet. I ate until I was sick in the stomach. Later, while walking with a bad stomachache, which I inflicted upon myself, I looked around me and all I saw was the result of Greedious Gluttoness' hand in our society. It causes so much waste in the form of crime and injustice giving society a stomachache. There was another demon I read about name Lilith who lured men and women into deviant sexual acts."

"Um… could you please clarify what you mean by deviant?" The Snake, who was the older brother of the Lion and minority shareholder of the IST Corp., was the second to believe the Theory of the Great Nothing and trusted the Great Elephant. Extremely athletic, the Snake had a chip on his shoulder since his younger brother went to the IBA. This could have been because he was actually faster than the Lion, but the Lion was stronger. The Great Elephant continued,

"Well, at first I thought Lilith was just the demon of homosexuality so I felt I wouldn't have any problem with her." Absolutely forbidden, homosexuality was punishable with death amongst those recognized with the animal signs and wore the medallion. "Now I believe there is only one use for the sexual act of humans, procreation. This means a man and woman has to be physically and spiritually attuned to produce a child so wasted sex episodes, which includes homosexuality, sex with animals, masturbation, and lustful promiscuous fornication are all useless residue of a felled society. In a perfect society, every man would have a woman and every woman a man."

"I can understand some of the technical stuff like metal-infused marijuana, but this is not a church, it's a house of fornication. We will always vote with the sinners, this is where our money comes from," Hawk said as he beckoned Kodak to give him another shot. He then adjusted his oversized Rolex that cost about $85,000 and moved his gold chain to be seen more clearly, especially the medallion with an eye and upside down pyramid surrounded by hundreds of diamonds. He was one of the shortest ones in the crew. He always kept a short haircut called a "bald fade" and had greenish-blue eyes that contrasted with his brown skin. He claimed that if any woman looked into his eyes for more than three seconds, he could have her. As he got older, he would always joke, "it may take a longer stare, but I will always get them."

"Enough with the sermon, Mr. Elephant man. You are the one who made all of this possible," Vasquez Williams said from behind his huge desk. The desk made from a huge mahogany tree stump with shelves carved into it and the top polished with fine crystal molded into the wood. Connected to the desk in the front, was a twin-size bed covered in lavish royal blue sheets and purple bedspread with all the finishing.

Democracy

His desk chair was like a small throne. Adorned with a large gold-plated eagle with stretched out wings holding the planet earth in one talon and the other connected to the right side of the chair over Vasquez's right shoulder. It was a certainty that someone would screw some female on the little bed every night so they called the desk "Sure Stanky."

"But we have a problem with ol' Big Steve the Rat" Vasquez continued with a sly grin on his face.

"Hawk has already made arrangements for a Rat trap but in keeping with tradition, we will take a vote before the rat trap is deployed" Bear spoke out with his deep thoughtful voice. His signature mini-fro glistened in the light from the natural berries and juices he used to make his natural nappy soft. He had on one of his unique tailor-mades, silk suits with ostrich skin boots. A thick chain of gold and platinum weighing a pound draped to his stomach with the same iced down medallion they all had. Bear, at 6'3", 320 lb, coal black color made him look as formidable as he was. He was the third owner in many of the club operations with Hawk and Eagle so he made several hundred thousand dollars a day, the Elephant continued,

"Thou shall not kill is what our legacy must be if we want to be different than those who have positioned themselves as enemies before us. If we do not, we could lose the blessing of the Lord and all your ambitions will fail. So I vote no and, as agreed, my vote carries the Wise Owls fat "no" and the Honorable Gorilla's big "no" for three votes of "NO" to the Rat trap." The Great Elephant started the voting. He was casually dressed, as always, for a party night. He did not have the means of the others. No 300.5 million-euro Areosport 3000, the Areocar model which could travel at speeds in excess of 1000 mph., nor the expensive jewels, although, on his pinky finger was a platinum ring with elephants cast in gold. Also, around his neck was a silver chain link necklace, the same $180,000-dollar medallion the others had. He wore it tucked under his shirt, as it was the most valuable thing he owned. After the Elephant's powerful three votes and speech, it went all the way downhill for Steve the Rat. Eagle, Hawk, and Bear voted for the Rat trap. Lion, Snake, and Falcon voted with Eagle's block, so Operation Rat Trap was set in motion.

February 7, 2020, Washington, DC:

Preston knew Getty was on a lot of people's shit list over at the Energy Department, and now was the time to strike. Preston worked out a brilliant scheme in which he created a plausible scenario in which Ralph Honeycutt, by splitting the minority vote, would cause President Lee the election indirectly. With the Energy Department backing him, he would then get the White House to take out Honeycutt preemptively. President Lee could not afford to go against both the Defense and Energy Departments; she either went after Honeycutt or be seen as a fool. In return for saving the Energy Department's existence, and getting President Lee reelected, Preston decided he would ask only two things of the White House. The termination of Getty and half of Col. Brett's so-called responsibilities turned over to him. This would render a crippling blow to the Homeland cronies while putting a check on Col. Brett's power. It was just a matter of time before he would have to deal with Col. Brett anyway, Preston figured. Either way, he was still in line to succeed President Lee in 8 to 12 years as the "old wise Patriot from the Defense Department." Preston began to make his rounds building his case.

Day one—He had a very warm reception from the Energy Department. people; they indeed wanted blood.

Day two—The White House was even more embracing. There were those amongst the party who wanted to use the recent incidents to open the door for President Lee to become a three and even four terms President.

Democracy

Day three—it was an early Sunday morning before church when Preston opened his US Daily News and read the front-page headline:

"Two Court House Massacre Suspects Apprehended." Preston felt his master plan crumbling around him.

February 8, 2020: Washington, DC:

Getty was excited to inform the committee he had discovered the names of two of the men involved in "The Court House Massacre." At the end of the meeting, Col. Brett congratulated him on a job well done.

"I would like some sort of bonus for the other two." Getty half-joked to Col. Brett.

"Sure $100,000 dollars due—don't worry about bringing in the others. We will use H.I.T. tactics to get the names of the other two bastards" Senator Thompson committed.

"We need for you to focus on the 'Cybervision Network Hijackers' for now." Col. Brett said for the fifth time during the two-hour meeting. He liked the way Getty made his X Department look so good yet took no credit.

One of the accused shooters, named Steve Lilly, was a club manager. He claimed a mysterious man paid him a million dollars to do the job; caught only because he talked too much and led the investigation to himself. The other alleged shooter, named Kerry Price, after Homeland Defense agents surrounded his home, he admitted to masterminding the whole Court House Massacre because the Judge, Sheriff, and District Attorney killed his daughter.

As the days passed it became known that Steven Lilly was also known as "Big Steve" by thousands of party goers, and he was the former half-owner of a club in Dallas called Club Skrew and several clubs in other locations. This brought up Vasquez "Eagle" William's name but because of the threats of his big lawyers kept his name out of the media. Steve claimed he did not know Kerry Price organized the other assailants and the whole operation. They tortured Steve first. His interrogators discovered he had been brainwashed by a systematic method of administering drugs, and pleasure stimulants, that were usually of a sexual nature with music being the delivery method. Later he was directed to carry out the attacks. Besides the million dollars, he had no other incentive or recollection as to what he did, but under hypnosis, Steve would recite his actions as if he had been programmed. He explained how he put on a wig and "had to protect the Clown man" referring to the other gunner. They put Steve away to rot a few years before his trial. They now turned their attention to Kerry Price. His motive was quite different.

Kerry Price was an average looking American White man who was living in Fort Worth, Texas. Born and raised in a small town called Thawada, TX, he stood 5 feet, 10 inches, and had a little beer belly. He graduated high school in 1990, was married once and had only one daughter named Gloria Price. Despite his confession, the FBI and local officials decided to use the Heighten Interrogation Techniques, or simply H.I.T., approved for use on United States Citizens by an executive order signed by President Lee in 2014. H.I.T. allowed methods such as a variation of waterboarding (called bobbing for apples when used on U.S. Citizens), electric shock up to 36,950 volts, sleep deprivation of a maximum 23 hours a day, and starvation in the form of a 650 calories a day diet. Up to five-story butt pyramids, as well as subjection to any experimental interrogation technique deemed necessary by the commanding field officer or civil commander was also allowed. After two weeks of torture, law officers knew no more than the day he was arrested at his home. Finally, it was decided to send in the smart people—the Secret Service and the CIA.

Douglas Willoford, a Triteck Industries top executive, and Preston Ross were both present doing two of Triteck's Information Gathering Device or IGDs demonstrations. The

Democracy

first session was to test a new device. Kerry Price was chosen for his stubbornness and back talk. He seemed to be unbreakable. Willoford's job was to sell the Federal and State Governments a pocket-size Swiss knife-looking device with 31 different gadgets that could be used to torture a person to extract information. Willoford started his presentation in front of some 30 people,

"A person is not ready to tell the truth 'till you have made them shit on themselves." They then demonstrated the effect on two or three prisoners as witnesses looked on.

Dressed in only thin, ragged, white translucent pants, the first one started to shit and piss his paints as a small vice grip-like device slowly crushed his Achilles tendon. The other man's bowels released while an extremely thin needle was pushed 8 inches into the bottom of his foot and up his shinbone —only one very small drop of blood, like a pinprick, was visible after the special needle was removed. Kerry did not shit nor "break," as the officers called it when a prisoner breaks down begging for mercy and willing to provide any information needed. Preston was one of the few men present who was disgusted by the presentation. The second day was worse as Willoford used high-frequency microwave device he had plugged into the wall. It was obviously cooking the insides of Kerry, as burnt meat could be smelled. Kerry screamed and defecated everywhere. This grotesque scene was the actual protocol written and taught as proper procedure for interrogation and the testing of new devices. All the IGDs ended up approved, but without Preston's vote. His no vote almost cost Willoford a sale and started a rift in their friendship.

X- Division's Special Unit was allowed in after a week; Getty was back in charge. After a few days of feeding and allowing Kerry to sleep more than two hours straight, Getty pieced together a report with likely suspects. Seeing the condition of Kerry Price and noting Big Steve total incapacitation due to the shock of the torture, Getty suggested Heighten Interrogation Tactics (H.I.T.) may be not only unconstitutional but also detrimental to the information gathering process. He also noted a company called Triteck Industries, a weapons contractor, manufactured the torture devices.

One day, after Getty had left the maximum-security facility where Kerry was being held, all hell broke loose. Some local officers came in from the Thwada, Texas and they were angry at the crime Kerry was accused of. Considered a Federal prisoner, State officers could not interrogate and torture him—only Federal and Homeland Defense personnel. The two local officers became even angrier. Phone calls were made and tensions were raised. The whole time, Kerry Price could hear the Federal and State agents arguing over the right to come in to beat his ass then torture him. Finally, it was agreed, since the local officers had driven so far, they would be given four hours alone with Kerry to interrogate him with only approved H.I.T. methods—no experimental techniques. When the arguing stopped and went quiet, Kerry made his mind up.

After a few minutes, Kerry could hear the officers deliberately shaking the oversized jail keys that were designed to make an extremely loud sound to induce psychological terror as the sound would eventually become associated with pain. The two men walked into the interrogation room, which had become Kerry's cell. He was the most special of all the residents at this unit due to his alleged crime, so this was one of many atypical amenities made for the alleged ringleader of the Court House Massacre. The interrogation room had mirrors all around and comfortable sofas forming an octagon that went up three levels and sat up to 72 officials comfortably. Small desktops for portable cybervision pads hovered for note taking. 1000 watt HID lights remained on continuously so only silhouettes of the people above him could be seen from the ground floor Kerry was on. Two tall, fat officers came in, one a big Black man who was well over 6'6" and had been making the most noise, and the other, a White man, who was just as big but a few years older, wearing a cowboy hat and boots. Two guards, one Asian-American and the other a Mexican-American, escorted them.

The giant Black man walked in first holding the new small pocketknife-sized I.G.D. with a long sharp probe-like feature telescoped out about 2 feet and featuring a small black fist at the end. A loud high-pitched scream was heard and then the sound of glass shattering. Only three of the fifteen interim students and two of the other observers said they had seen what the camera captured. Soon as the big Black officer entered the room, Kerry stabbed him in both his eyes simultaneously with the ends of a pencil broken in two. Kerry then used the big man's momentum to push him into the

mirror wall sending blood splattering as the broken glass cut deep into the dark flesh. The next guard through the door was the big White cowboy officer. Dressed in a white shirt with a silver and gold badge, he actually had his belt in his hand wrapped around his fist one time as if he was going to beat a child. This really infuriated Kerry to the point he was ready to die. A swift hard kick to the balls dropped the officer in the doorway, blocking it. The video showed Kerry, hollering like a madman step back, grab a piece of the broken mirror, and start slicing the blinded big Black officer jugular vein about seven times on the left and five on the right. The Asian-American officer pushed the big White officer out of the way as the Mexican Officer charged up his shock stick to 50,000 volts. Both entered the room almost at the same time. Kerry grabbed an ashtray, threw the ashes into their eyes, and blinded the Mexican officer who then accidentally shocks the big White officer rendering him unconscious. With the broken glass, Kerry stabbed the Asian Guard in the face with such force he cut his own hand. The Asian guard ran to an unbroken wall screaming while trying to clear his vision from ashes and blood. As the Mexican officer attempted to step over the big White officer passed out on the floor, the big White officer started having a heart attack. Kerry quickly took the belt out the White officer's hand then charged out the door, kneed the Mexican officer in the groin, grabbed him by the head, proceeded to wrap the belt around his neck while biting him in the face, then suffocating him by crushing his windpipe and left jugular vein. After a few seconds, the Asian officer charged back after he regained his sight. He had discovered, after looking in the mirror, that he will be disfigured for life, and he was furious. The Mexican officer had passed out with permanent brain damage and was now dying. Kerry fist fought with the Asian officer for a few seconds, knocked him out, then ran down the hall. Eventually, Kerry was swarmed by 20 guards and was shocked 53 times with 50,000 volts, frying his brain. Kerry died with a slight smile and a tear in his eye. Somehow, he had managed to keep a picture of his daughter Gloria, despite all the strip searches because he had her picture in his hand.

Chapter 11

EQUAL PROTECTION OF LAW

March 2019
West Texas Desert:

David Hill had been the acting Warden at the George Williams Correctional Facility in Texas for three years. It was one of the most violent female penitentiaries. He had started as a correction officer and worked his way up over a 20-year career. It was one of the many units built in the nineties when the State of Texas quadrupled the number of privately held prisons. The K Kircle Group Inc. owned more than 150 facilities in seven States including the George Williams unit. The construction was the same as the rest— two huge 20-foot steel fences with razor wire on top encircling each other separated by a 30-foot trench field with razor wire. The outer perimeter fences were in the shape of an octagon with guard towers at each connecting point for a total of eight. Inside the fences' perimeter were the prison facilities consisting of 23 interconnecting dorm units that were six-story high, hexagon-shaped buildings comprised of 10 two-person cells per side totaling 120 prisoners per level. Each two-man cell was nine feet long by seven feet wide (9'x7') and consisted of two iron bunks and a toilet. There were six levels stacked on top of each other allowing for 720 prisoners per dorm. The 16,560 prisoners per unit count were the estimate, as prisoners were always revolving. There were a few other large buildings connected, including a chapel, an education building, infirmary, and most importantly, the manufacturing facilities.

The George Williams unit manufactures furniture, processed food, soap, as well as a host of agricultural products. The inmates were told the furniture was sold to schools and Universities in the United States, but Warden Hill had orders from all over the world, especially Europe and Asia. With the price of labor being zero, Ellison and Son™ (which was the trademarked brand name of the K Kircle Group products) expensive handcrafted furniture could compete with China's and India's cost. Ellison and Son was a premium brand name and sold at the highest euros since it had the "Made in the USA" stamp. The only thing that mattered to Warden Hill was filling the orders for Ellison and Sons Fine Handcrafted Furniture. Warden Hill knew his salary and his job depended on the production of his "workers" and so did everyone under him. If there were any problems, delays in shipment, or quality control problems, he would have to pay for it, like the time he took a 10% salary decrease although the company reported an 18 % gain. It was because he was late on getting a 47,932-chair order to Iraq. Considering his options to close down the factory for three days to be sure most of the 3,500 "trustee" inmate workers would not be involved in a big ensuing fight or putting rival ethnic gang members who are feuding in a factory full of possible weapons was simple under prison warden rules of old. Now he just did not know what was expected of him. His mighty workforce refused to work which put him in the prickliest situation.

After 18 years of marriage, his first wife divorced him as soon as their older son graduated high school. He begged her to   at least wait until their youngest graduated in four years, but she said it would be useless because she knew he would "just" become a prison guard after high school. After the divorce, Warden Hill was a broken man and became somewhat of a brutal prison warden. His brutal effectiveness soon caught the eye of the K Kircle Corp. who offered him a job at the George Williams unit at twice the salary that the State paid. The first thing Warden Hill did was got himself a girlfriend half his age and she cost him twice as much as his whole family. Costing even more than his young girlfriend was his new Harley- Davidson and brand new fishing boat had which many payments. He could not afford any trouble at work, not right now. He was an independent man with a proud military background. Most of the males in his family had served in the military and were working for the State as correction officers, thus this seemed to be a natural step after military life. The State of Texas, the military and U.S. Government were all the same thing to Warden Hill and his family, but this private Corp. was something else. Patiently, Warden Hill had been waiting for the day to tell the proper-talking asshole with the big title who was supposed to be his boss from Ohio to kiss his ass or, even better yet, kick him in his. However, for now, the money and freedom kept him in check. He enjoyed the unprecedented freedom from inmates having no Constitutional rights nearly as much as he enjoyed his high salary. By working for a private corporation instead of a government agency, the protections in the Bill of Rights, which are protections from the government, did not apply. Warden Hill always kept this in mind. After he ate breakfast, he thought about being on his boat with his pretty little girlfriend and a smile turned into an angry mug as he picked up the phone and called the guard's lounge.

"Attention all C.O. S. We will be having a meeting in 20 minutes unless you are in the lock-up sections. Your attendance is required!" Warden Hill's voice boomed over the loudspeaker. Because of the facility's size, it took Warden Hill about 23 minutes to walk to the officer's lounge where the meetings were held. The officers knew when the Warden said 20 minutes he was upset and you better not be late or you would get written up are maybe sent home without pay.

"Captain Redding, those lines have been down for more than 24 hours. Inmates just refusing to work is not acceptable," Warden Hill started even before all of the officers were present at the emergency meeting that he scheduled at 3 a.m.

"We have done all we can. There is nothing else we can take from them. I contacted corporate in New York, and they refuse to upgrade the food menu as the inmates are requesting. They claim the cost would be unacceptable. They also refuse to do anything about the infirmary or adding education courses," Captain Redding replied apologetically with a southern accent.

"I think we need to separate Gloria Price who seems to have started the whole incursion," Officer Tonya Blaylock, a large African-American female guard shouted out. Warren Hill turned to her and said,

"Who the hell is Gloria Price, Captain Redding ... Lieutenant Caswell… who the hell is this Gloria Price that's screwing around with my money?! Nobody knows anything!" he was spitting as he talked and starting to sweat, as he turned red.

"She's housed in J wing, so she does not work in the factory," Officer Campbell an older White lady with gray eyes who looks as though she should have been an elementary school teacher said, while raising her hand.

"I don't understand how someone who doesn't work in the factory can keep 3,500 employees from going to work. I want her placed in solitary for 30 days, then shipped off my unit. At 1600 hours I expect all factories running or I will replace each and every one of you." Warden Hill slammed his fist two times on the table then left the central guard area to his office down the hall. He sat at his desk and started to sift through the orders he had, every now and then glancing at the monitor of factory 1's main entrance to see if the inmate workers had started trickling into their posts.

The guards knew exactly what they needed to do. They divided into three large groups to show force. Three groups each containing 120 men and 204 women guards each would go to the worker's wing, open the cells one at a time, and "shake them down," confiscating contraband. After losing some of their property, they will be given a choice of going to work at the factory or continue to lose personal items such as commissary, even family pictures, and letters. Meanwhile, 10 officers would go and get Gloria Price, restrain her, and then put her in solitary confinement. Once they separated Gloria, officer Blaylock escorted her to her new home for the next 30 days. An hour later, officer Blaylock returned with Gloria's properties including a cell phone, some purple marijuana, and sleeping pills officer Blaylock just recently added after it was searched. She also included a Pamphlet of Faith from her father who had become a jailhouse preacher since he was unjustly given a life sentence. Tonya spent nine minutes in the cell alone with Gloria where they made love for eight of those minutes. After Tonya left with the letters to the leaders of the work revolt, Gloria sat back and ate the cold Mickey D's burger her lover brought her and dozed off for two days from the tranquilizers.

She awoke with an officer she had never seen before kicking her awake. Before she could swear at him, he hit her with a small bat in the ribs. He did these two more times and then turned and walked out of the cell locking it behind him. Gloria could not take a breath to scream. The mighty leader of the revolt had a very slight stature standing only 5 feet tall, and weighing little more than 100 pounds. Officer Blaylock was not allowed to feed the inmates in solitary confinement for the next week's schedule. It appeared her plan to take care of her baby failed. It was in the Sunday paper she read about the inmate who was beaten to death in a riot at George Williams' named Gloria Price. Her broken ribs had punctured her lungs. She suffocated on her own blood from the broken rib she received from the officer's baton.

July 13, 2019 Cleon City, Brazil Amazon Jungle:
The Snake pressed his ring hard into a piece of paper, imprinting his seal onto the letter addressed to Prometheus Green-Inmate #TX17463755 Judge H.P. Sanchez, Unit Pennyworth, Alabama. United States

August 28, 2019
Pennyworth, Alabama Judge H.P. Sanchez Unit:
The Gorilla opened the letter from the Snake and then started to read aloud to the six men gathered at the table in the dayroom area. One was a Latino guy, stocky build with tattoos covering both arms. One side signified his rank in the Mexican Mafia; the other side showed his loyalties to one of the largest gangs in California. Beside him stood one of those rare six-feet-four Mexicans, also built like a mountain, with tattoos of Aztecs and Inca art. The grey painted area had eight table stations outlining the Day Area where all the inmates gathered to either watch TV or gamble on cards, dominos, or whatever situation could be considered game. A few engaged in ferociously charged chess matches. All the tables and chairs were metal and welded to the floor or each other. If you bumped into any object, it would hurt, giving the feeling of being inside a gladiator cage. The other two guys were Black ones from Compton, the other from Chicago. They were the shot-callers for two of the main rival Black gangs. Two White guys at the table were from the largest White gang throughout the entire system. Just because you were of Aryan blood did not guarantee your right of passage into the Tight White Crew. On the inside, they called themselves The Tight Whites. On the outside, Hollywood, through movies and documentaries, called them the Aryan Blood Prison Gang portraying them as ruthless killers. To join the Tight White Crew, a strict initiation process was required, in which most did not succeed. Their organization was immaculate with small guys following

strict orders of their bosses so, when told to go sit in on a Gorilla sermon, there was not a problem.

The Gorilla had somehow set up a kind of charity commissary on every unit, so everyone was curious as to what he was trying to pull. The Gorilla started reading as he assured the people what he was reading was neither from his mouth nor from the hand of the rich and powerful man who sent the letter, The Snake. It was from a wise man named Mach Brown who had ancient wisdom. Because Sir Gorilla stood tall at 5 feet, 10 inches and was so solid with muscle, he looked very intimidating. He had very dark skin, pointed ears, and when you looked into his eyes he looked fearless. With pride, he read loudly.

"Thank you, Lord, for giving me one more day on Earth to do only your will, I humbly submit myself to you and stand before you as a tree beside a river only accepting your nutrients and the light which feeds me, comes from only you. You have told me to only bear witness and proclaim, thus what comes from my mouth is only your fruit, and this I must do. I have left to the people, in the form of writing, that which you have communicated to me since before I was in the womb, and as long as my spirit has existed. You have told me to tell the people, What is the Law?' and It is not from men! No constitution, writ, code, law, proclamation, ordinance, or excuse to take that which man did not give shall exist. This includes not only life but also liberty. Even a man would bring you the Law of eye for an eye and tooth for a tooth but only an immortal demon could contrive the concept of prison!"

At this point, other inmates began to gather around the table, 20 men listening intently. The entire south wall of the day area was barred opening up to a huge hall four stories high and 54 two-man cells long. Inmates on the first two floors in the front eight cells also gathered at their bars, listening across the hall into the day area. The Gorilla in a heated, passionate voice, repeated the last two lines of the letter again, which, in return, the largest man in the room nicknamed Big Blue because of his dark skin color, turned the volume down a few levels on the old fashion television control he seemed to always guard. This was unusual since Big Blue was more of the old convict type who minded his own business and usually kept the TV blasting so it could be heard far down the run. Maybe he had received some of those blessings the Gorilla talks about in his commissary account. The Gorilla continued reading.

"Lucifer's tool of electricity is modern-day man's magic alter to idols. Where adultery and homosexuality are legal, then pedophilia and bestiality will be just as common with masturbation being the most prevalent, as they are all one in the same—the demon Lust. Moreover, the other demon, Greedious Gluttoness is one of the most powerful here on Earth because the humans have allowed the demon to manifest itself physically, in the form of money; humanity brought seduction on themselves. However, to the defense of humans, a select few amongst them had more knowledge than the masses. They first used magic then electricity to dupe their fellow humans into a system that made them subjected to Lucifer and his Demons. Up until now, humans knew no other way. I will put down the truth providing an option, but since no human has reigned over any other human's conscience, then it is for the person to accept him- or herself. But I can assure you, no one can travel unless they are of the one righteous way."

-The Theory of the Great Nothing
Mach Brown

The Gorilla then gave somewhat of a sermon lasting 33 minutes. Although, filled with profanity with somewhat of a religious undertone, to most hearing him speak it would have sounded more political. Caesar grabbed Ellis and whispered,

"I will die for you brother," in his Mexican accent.

Equal Protection of Law

Ellis reached out with tears in his eyes, looked at the Gorilla square in his eyes and said,

"The brotherhood is with you to the death." Ellis really did not have much of a choice; he had received a letter the day before from his boss telling him to go along with whatever the Gorilla planned. The letter had no return address, only the name Mr. Price in the upper left-hand corner.

Every word the Gorilla said was written down, and a transcript of the speech was mailed out to the Gorilla's associate who printed 167,124 copies. These were mailed out to random prisoners, along with 10 euro (which equaled about $114.00), being placed in their commissary account.

The next month, another random 167,124 inmates received 10 euro. They placed funds in the inmates' accounts regardless of race, sex, or religion. Pamphlets were mailed also. For months, this activity went unnoticed, then, as the crime rate began to decrease inside the prisons, the inmates began to demand education facilities, proper health-care providers, and then finally Law libraries.

The Homeland Defense Department Justice Division wanted to know where the monthly funds were coming from so they launched major investigations. The report passed up the chain of command until finally, it all landed on Col. Brett's desk. Col. Brett discovered the funds were coming from overseas, donated by millions of foreigners from all over the world. At first, they seemed to be spontaneous donations of a sort, but Col. Brett's senses told him it was all connected. The bulk was coming from Africa. It was more his distrust of new people rather than his limited foreign contact list which had initially hampered Col. Brett's investigations as to where the funds were coming from for the prison inmates. He pulled out the nice ostrich-skin office chair from his closet when a few minutes later his secretary informed him Mr. Preston Ross was here to see him. Preston immediately noticed Col. Brett was much nicer than the first meeting. Col. Brett had flight tickets to both Africa and Brazil with Preston's name on them in plain view.

"I got approved for a 450-million-dollar budget program to figure out what's going on inside our prison systems," Col. Brett said in a solemn voice as he handed Preston the official Federal CR5150 authorizing the transfer of government funds into Col. Brett's department's account. "I can do whatever I want with these funds as long as I figure out what's going on and neutralize any threats."

"I see the tickets with my name on them; I suppose you're going to give me half your little ol' CR5150 to take those tickets and leave the country." Preston was being half-sarcastic.

"No, but I will give you $75 million to get me what I want," Col Brett shot back in a booming authoritarian voice. The next day Preston Ross would be on a flight to Brazil. Before he boarded his flight, he contacted Fiske Braun and updated him on his plans. Preston did not mention the $75 million but he offered Fiske to join him and he stated he would cover all costs. Fiske agreed to meet him in Africa; they would gather info together on Shindinkis, the huge resort and casino located in the heart of the Congo jungle the Black Triad owned, which they claimed was sovereign from all governments.

Chapter 12

TWIN TOWERS

Sunday, March 8, 2020
Washington DC 7:00 a.m.:

It started with his daily newspaper's headline: *Ralph Honeycutt to run for President.* Preston was making his way to the airport for Brazil, the TV news media was going wild with the announcement that Ralph Honeycutt was running for President of the United States to challenge President Mary Lee's historic third run. In the taxi on the way to the airport, he heard Ralph Honeycutt's name on the radio station. As he entered the airport, he saw two buses with a huge Ralph Honeycutt smiling face along the sides. Ralph was sporting a big afro with his fist held above his head in a black power salute with the "America First" in big red, white, and blue letters in that dreaded "blinged-out" font as the campaign slogan. The one font with an obscene amount of large diamonds Preston hated most. Ralph spent 20 million euro on advertisement space in one day. Astounding the world as Ralph Honeycutt appeared on every major cyberstation that day. At 10 a.m., Ralph gave an interview to the BEC—the largest cable network in the E.U. He stated something to the fact,

"If the elections were not done fair, he would not congratulate President Lee on a job well done." He also stated, "He could not accept a theory of Electoral College defectors which originally awarded President Lee the election in 2012." Ralph Honeycutt argued since President Lee's victory, the Patriot Party régime has, "caused America to fall to the seventh largest economy" and "appeared to be headed toward war with China and the entire Islamic and Arab world with no allies if President Lee is allowed to stay in office." These statements caused a big scare around the world. Don Abernathy, President Lee's political strategist, confided with his close friends how Ralph Honeycutt's opening assault and scare tactics were brilliant.

The Patriot Party controlled not only the White House but also both Houses and most of the Supreme Court. The accusation hurt like stitches, but because they were so unprepared, the White House would not be able to counter with positive spin until the next day. Nothing to this point had been a real force of opposition against the Patriot Party. One of President Lee's first anti-terrorist laws was directed towards communication entities. It forced cybervision networks to adhere to certain standards of decency by prohibiting negative talk about the Government or its officials without the material first being reviewed by the Federal Communication Censor Bureau (F.C.C.B.). Not adhering to these laws could cause heavy fines and even prison.

It was around 11 a.m. and Preston was halfway to Brazil when the Cyber TV network he was watching interrupted with the top Spanish news commentator Luis Gomez showing Ralph Honeycutt holding what appeared to be an American elementary school textbook. Preston spoke fluid Spanish so he could make out what the broadcast was saying. They were explaining how the schoolbook had written that Latin-Americans were the second largest population in America, which Ralph Honeycutt claimed was false cause in reality; they were the largest racial class. Ralph turned further in the book and saw where it listed the United States as number one in several categories such as economy, military strength, and percentage of college graduates per capita, which was also not accurate. Ralph Honeycutt went on to explain that this type of misrepresentation of facts was how the Patriot Party was manipulating the American people with

Twin Towers

lies and created a dangerous situation for the United States, since its people were not adequately informed about their true circumstances.

It was around 12 noon when the movie Preston was watching was interrupted with news that five top recording artists from three different music genres were to conduct a free concert at the Lincoln Memorial to celebrate the announcement of Ralph Honeycutt's Presidential run and the new big announcement that his Vice President running mate would be Bubba Moody Jr.. Although Preston had met President Lee on a few occasions, he did not know her personally, but he knew Don Abernathy well enough to know he was probably pulling out the rest of his hair right now. At about 1 p.m. the biographies about Ralph Honeycutt started Preston to ponder when President Lee's spokesperson would make some sort of comments in opposition. When the voice speaking in Portuguese with English subtitles begin talking about Ralph's childhood, something caught Preston's attention on the screen. Preston paused the broadcast and rewound it to the subtitles were in big white letters "attended Thwada High School." strolled alone the screen. Preston listened and read about how Ralph De'shawn Honeycutt had graduated from Thawada High School in Texas as a top athlete and was given a scholarship to play both football and basketball at FSU. He went on to an illustrious career in the IBA. After the IBA, Ralph formed the Industry Standard Trading Corporation (IST Corp.) with his brother Jacob Honeycutt and first cousin Tyrone Honeycutt investing their money heavily into the clothing industry where he made a few million euro. IST Corp. manufactured the clothing either at the Amazon jungle facility located somewhere near the Peruvian border or at its Indian manufacturing facility located in Kashmir Kush region. Ralph's smiling face appeared as he explained in English, with the Portuguese narrator translating, "It was Jacob who got Bubba Moody Jr. on board and the rest was history."

After the commercial break, which prompted Preston to order Micky D's for his grandkids because of the toys included, the program continued. Images of Big Bubba Moody Jr. the great hockey star standing 6 foot 9 inches at 300 lbs., appeared. His gold hair and blue eyes defined him as the ultimate Nordic warrior, as he has been called since he knocked out the undefeated best pound-for-pound athlete in the world, Mixed Martial Arts Champion, Marlon Gracie, in a billion-dollar charity match. Big Bubba started his own clothing line called Bubba Wear. Costing as much as $1,000 for jeans and $400 a shirt, Bubba Wear was the most popular brand in the world, selling millions of units a year. Bubba Wear was a status symbol worldwide for everyone who owned the clothes, but inside the American cities and towns, the brand had a deeper meaning. Many rich foreigners had been robbed, even murdered for the coveted two and three thousand-dollar jackets, backpacks, and shoes by White American teens and young adults. Preston visibly frowns and he knows those same $1,000 jeans, IST Corp.

manufactures for $2.00 at most.

"Here's how Ralph Honeycutt spends the money," Preston thinks. Preston remembered Thawada, Texas is where the Courthouse Massacre occurred. Preston changed the cybervision channel only to find the number one Hip Pop artist, Lil Boe Boe, on a makeshift stage in front of the Martin Luther King Memorial performing his hit song "Booty Man." The cameras panned to show there were a few thousand people gathered on the lawn, but in the background, you could see thousands more lined-up as far as the eye could see. The camera panned back onto Lil Boe Boe right as a young lady with a huge butt backed up to Lil Boe Boe then bent over in front of him placing one hand on the ground with the other twirling above her head, prompting Lil Boe Boe to start

performing simulated sex with her from behind. Preston slammed the cybervision monitor closed with a total look of disgust on his face and just stared into thin air for about 10 minutes taking it all in. He asked a flight attendant to bring him a drink, something he rarely did. Later he asked her to bring him a Vicodin muscle relaxer so he could pass out. The nurse returned with a credit card slider prompting Preston to pull out his ID and slide it through the device. A green light blinked with a ching sound, allowing him to receive the prescription medicine while on the fly.

Before Preston was able to doze off, he looked up Bubba Moody on the web. Bubba Moody was well known, as there had been several documentaries and a few movies made about his life; but with the intensity of the past few years in Washington, Preston had no time for television and movies. Bubba Moody Jr. was only 46 years-old but a billionaire at present, earning 2 billion dollars a year. He was the man that made being an Aryan Skinhead cool and sexy. He was CEO of the Corporation that owned several clothing lines and four of the top 10, Platinum-selling artists. He had four Grass Roots, three Heavy Metal, and two Hard Rock groups signed to his record label. He purchased the newest major league baseball team, the Mississippi Rebels. In addition, he was the owner of the number one hockey team, the Anchorage Vikings, who were known for their violence but was also key to his success.

Bubba Moody Jr. inherited a very small percentage of around 3% of the fledgling Alaskan hockey team from his father Bubba Sr. a crab angler who had moved to Alaska from New York on a whim when he was young. While growing up in the freezing waters of Alaska, on the fishing boats, Bubba Jr. became extremely athletic on ice. Bubba would skate alone around dangerous obstacles even in storms on slippery decks he could always keep his footing. When he returned from sea, he would use his athletic abilities on ice to dominate hockey first in high school, and then through college. It was around 2013 when Alaska became the fastest growing state due to first, the exploration of its natural resources by mining companies. Then, in around 2014, foreign manufacturing corporations began to set up manufacturing facilities inside of Alaska itself. Countries were represented as international corporations with names such as OmniTeck Inc., which was from the European Union, Sunrise Industries, Wu Tong Industries and Top Corp (all from China), and Vaistar LLC, a collaboration between Mexico and Venezuela. Bubba's father always told him, "Corporations and countries were the same thing." Bubba was schooled by his father to believe they were both just a group of rich men whose families have been doing what they do as long as the countries and the corporations have existed. Every time something bad happened to his father, such as losing a job or paying taxes, he would hear an ear-full about "the damn government and corporations being the same bastards his great, great grandfather fought during the Civil War and were part of a big conspiracy to screw him."

After Bubba's family moved to Alaska, Bubba's father had nothing but contempt for the new micro-cities because for one, they did not benefit him or his family in any way, shape, or form. Outside the micro-cities, the rest of the United States used the inflated dollar and it was hard on Americans. There was no middle-class, only the rich and the slave-like working-class of Mexicans competing with the prisons free labor workforce. The people inside the micro- cities were the closest thing to a middle-class. but Bubba, Sr. believed up to 90% of the cities' population were immigrants, both legal and illegal, mostly from China, Central America, Africa, and India. All the money they made was sent back to their mother countries after they leached the American resources and left behind only pollution. When the concept of company credit$ moved to the mainland of the U.S.A. there were people who worked passionately against it. These members of the American Patriot Party claimed the new companies brought too many foreigners and adopted many local, State, and Federal laws to accommodate the international corporations. They claimed America was not for its citizens anymore because foreign corporations and rich foreigners had preference inside the United States over its citizens. Bubba Moody Sr. became a devoted Patriot. On July 4, 1993, he joined his first political party, the American Patriot Party. A few months later he started to complain that although the Patriot Party was the majority and always gave speeches about what was wrong with America, nothing ever got fixed yet it seemed all the politicians and their families were getting rich from the international trade.   Once the city of   Anchorage started selling municipal bonds to fund its very own professional hockey team, Bubba's father lived by the philosophy,

"If you believe in something put 100% into it so if you fail it won't be for lack of effort." He began to invest the majority of his earnings into the Anchorage Vikings' Stock. It was not until after his father's death that Bubba realized his father had been buying the Bonds so he could have a say on who plays for the team. Bubba's father thought if he bought enough of the team, no one could ever stop his son from playing Major League Hockey since he would be the majority shareholder and could play whomever he wanted. Unfortunately, Bubba senior fell into freezing waters somewhere off the coast of a small south arctic island while crab fishing never to be seen again. Bubba senior had only managed to get 2.8%, to be exact, of The Vikings. Bubba Jr. was almost broken by his father's death. He felt his father died in vain and never got to see his son reach greatness. Bubba decided he was going to have big money regardless, to honor his father as well as himself.

A good athlete attending a small high school in Alaska had many downfalls; no matter how good he was, it would be difficult to be seen nationally. Bubba attended Alaska State University and nearly won a national championship until he was disqualified for breaking a guy's nose and arm when he was already inside the penalty box. An opposing figure standing 6' 9", and over 300 pounds, he was quick on his feet and said to be able to sprint 40 yards in 4.5 seconds or less. Skating around with the grace of a figure skater he could actually move like Mohammed Ali would in a fight on the ice—an unstoppable scoring force breaking several NCAA scoring records in his first three seasons. After his first season at ASU, representatives from Russia to Canada solicited him to play hockey for them.

Some even wanted him to play football or basketball for their IBA teams. Bubba turned down all scholarships and then went to the Vikings' training camp and asked Coach Ike Schectolf if he could work out with the team for free. After only a few workouts it was soon evident Bubba was the best on the team. Coach Schectolf was so impressed by Bubba, he persuaded the board of owners to offer him a one year contract for the league—a minimal $450,000.Bubba respectfully declined. Instead, he requested to be able to play one game for free then after that one game; he would discuss what he was worth.

The NHL has no mercy. The Vikings' first game was against a team that made it to the playoffs the preceding year and the Vikings were expected to lose by double digits, which in hockey is most disgusting. The sold-out arena in

Edmonton, Canada, with an attendance of 32,000 Canadians and 14,000 Alaskans, received a most delightful treat—an entertaining game, as Bubba Moody Jr. scored five points on his own, gaining the nickname Big Bubba. Although the Vikings lost nine to six, Bubba was in a much better bargaining position. He wanted absolutely no money, He

Twin Towers

asked for 5% worth of the Anchorage Vikings' municipal bonds to play for one year. Along with his father's 2.8 % he inherited, it gave him 7.8% allowing him a say on the Anchorage Vikings' Board of Owners.

Bubba kept getting 5% a year and no salary for 3 years. By the third year, he had 17.8 % shares in the number one ranked hockey team in the world. The NHL MVP asked for his 5% share and 25% of all the team's proceeds along with a performance clause allowing him to gain an additional 10% of the teams' municipal bonds along with several other perks if the Vikings won a Championship. The Vikings went on to win back-to-back championships with Big Bubba Moody Jr. earning $643 million in salary alone. More important to Big Bubba Moody Jr. was the 47.8% ownership in the Anchorage Viking he had earned. The three years before Big Bubba signed the big contract, he had made a few million in the music industry, along with millions of more fans and admirers.

When you play a professional sport, it makes it a lot easier to get your foot through the door in other entertainment venues, especially if you are six-foot-ten, 300 lbs.   blonde hair,   blue-eyed, and considered one of the world's 50 most beautiful people by several gossip magazines. Once age and the party life caught up with him, some felt the billionaire was not worth the 48% of all the net revenue of the team. Therefore, he didn't play anymore, but upon his departure from the Anchorage Vikings as Director of the Board, his last action was to sell all remaining shares to Bubba Inc. for a ridiculously low amount. This gave   Big Bubba Moody Jr. complete ownership of the Anchorage Vikings in exchange for three World Championships and two runs, deep into the playoffs, putting Anchorage on the map.

Moody's reality show really took the world by storm. The media used his show to create a new type of racism that was deemed acceptable. They showed big Bubba's life compared with everyone else's life. They filmed him leaving his office, going to dinner, and then home. By the time the video was edited, it made Bubba look like a White supremacist in his interactions   with people such as; his Asian secretary, who was made to appear to be a spy for China, and the Arab cab driver who wanted to kill him just because he is Muslim. The disgusting Black guys whom the editors go to great lengths to show Big Bubba's physical superiority to and the sneaky Mexicans defined as anyone born south of Texas. Jews were made to look crafty—just another white person with a different religion. Critics never believed Big Bubba years later when he confessed he never watched the reality shows even though they were number one in America and E.U. for two straight years. He said,

"After I watched one episode, I quit…"

Preston pondered how a good kid like Bubba got mixed up with the Honeycutts and bet he regretted it.   Preston awoke with a beautiful olive-colored flight attendant, who had a strange French accent, shaking him awake as the Vicodent had done its job well. Preston considered himself well-traveled. He had visited about 40 different countries, yet for some reason, he had never been to Brazil or the Congo region in Africa. *"Maybe it's just something in my blue blood which makes Third World countries unattractive to me,"* he thought. Once he stepped off the plane he was immediately shocked at the modernization of São Paulo. Literally expecting the smell of sewage and filth, he had to mention to his wife how much better it smelled then New York City or London. Even though it smelt good and looked, good, Preston refused to eat the local foods only eating at familiar American fast food chains. His wife enforced his thinking, telling him she heard they ate snakes and bugs in Brazil and Africa.

Middle-aged and set to retire soon, he just wanted to get as much money as possible. Preston was an old Republican from West Virginia. In their 32 years of marriage, he had cheated once with his high school sweetheart and that was about twenty-eight years ago. Sometimes he sees a beautiful woman he thinks of having sex with her, but then remembers how troubled he felt after the one time he gave in to temptations. He remembers most how he tarnished his perfect record with his wife and has to lie to her for the rest of their lives. Preston almost tears up as he thinks about his wife alone at home without him, especially now that the kids are grown. *"She would have never been so weak,"* he thought as he started to get an erection as he imagined holding Amanda in his arms, her green eyes staring into his blue eyes, as they take a long kiss. He smelled her familiar sweet breath as it accelerated with excitement as it did when she was 19. He pulled off her top exposing perfectly sized C breasts, but they are brown. Preston noticed something different about this vision of his wife. While Amanda's 55- year-old face converges with the way he remembered when she was 19, the perfect size C's and big booty on Amanda belonged to the tall Brazilian mixed-race teenager standing in front of him waiting on a bus. She noticed him staring and turned away. Preston hurried to a cab and asked to be taken to the most lavish hotel in the city. Thinking to himself, as he rode in the taxi to his high-rise hotel, how did Brazil get so developed so fast? In some places, it was ultramodern designs and high- rise where he expected to see slums.

Once at his hotel, he rested a few hours. As soon as he turned on the cybervision, there was breaking news everywhere of Jacob Honeycutt, Ralph Honeycutt's halfbrother and business partner, arrested on a host of charges from drug possession to weapon possession. After listening for a few minutes, Preston discovered after leaving a club, police pulled over Jacob Honeycutt's Party Bus and charged Jacob with everything that was on board. No bail was given nor was any phone calls allowed. He was placed under "intensified custody", one level below "H.I.T." because of commits he made when being arrested. Preston smiled and thought, *"President Lee and Don Abernathy are starting their counterattack. They create negative spin at the cost of poor Jacob Honeycutt."* Preston contemplated if that infamous Honeycutt temper would take Jacob from "intense custody" to being on the Heightened Interrogation List. Preston marveled at how brilliant a move it was to incarcerate Ralph's brother. *"Maybe it would snatch some of the disrespectful tone from his rhetoric by putting him in his place."* Preston thinks. The Incarceration of Jacob Honeycutt set the tone for that day.

Preston fell asleep, waking early, and starting out to the IST facility located 400 miles away in the middle of the Amazon. He arrived late afternoon, so he had to get a room in a small hotel inside the town built around the IST Corp.'s manufacturing facility. Based somewhat on the micro-city philosophy, the town Cleon, Brazil had a population of about 85,000 people, most of whom worked at the manufacturing facilities of IST Corp., except they were paid with Brazilian currency, which was taxed heavily by the Brazilian government instead of company credit$. There were only about three hotels in the town.. Everyone had housing and the hotels were only for tourists. Because of the closeness of the community, it was obvious to everyone Preston Ross was an outsider. He purchased the nicest suite at the largest hotel in town. A rather nice accommodation on the top floor of a nightclub called Tiptoe. Club Tiptoe, owned by the Black Triad brought in some 10 to 20 thousand people mostly international tourist nightly depending on the event and was part of the local economy. Club Tiptoe was said to be similar to Club Shindinki, but Preston did not go to the club, cause he felt he would do all the clubbing he needed to do in Africa at the notorious Hotel and Casino, Club Shindinkis, especially with Fiske. After a warm shower and nice dinner, Preston figured he would watch cybervision to get caught up on happenings in the U.S. while ordering supplies

Twin Towers

for the house and farm. He would then get some sleep before he toured the IST facility in the morning. He ended up staying awake all night.

Chapter 13

MR. AUDACITY
Monday March 9, 2020 Cleon City, Brazil:

Preston took a warm shower because he did not care to soak in the large Jacuzzi bathtub in the main bathroom; he just could not imagine soaking in the Brazilian water, because it somehow reminded him of Mexico's water. After he sprayed his bed several times with disinfectant, he picked up the keyboard remote and turned on the nice 72-inch 3D cybervision, and to his disgust, there was Ralph Honeycutt on stage in a camouflage-colored tuxedo. He was in Washington on a stage with the Martin Luther King, Jr. monument behind him as a backdrop. Preston rewound the telecast to the beginning when it showed Ralph coming to the stage with a procession of what appeared to be over a hundred men, some dressed exactly alike in black military- type outfits with blue glowing pinstripes. The men had on what appeared to be a ski mask but thicker, like helmets with dark goggles with respirators built in. They did not march in formation, they just mobbed along. Preston rewound a little further and it showed the beginning of the news special. The channel was interpreted into English in real-time. The newscaster started out with breaking news of Ralph Honeycutt making a stunning arrival at the concert given on his behalf upon his announcement of his run for President of the United States.   As the cameras zoomed in, Preston changed the channel to an American network as a final act of defiance, but there was Ralph, live on stage on every major channel. Preston thought, *"This A-hole is probably spending more money than I'm making for my little chore for Col. Brett."* Preston had no choice but to listen. Rewinding all the way to the beginning it showed Ralph arriving in a rainbow-colored Areosport 3000 along with nine, what looked like, very large Areocars having long extended van like rears. When they landed, 10 men came from each of

Mr. Audacity

the van- looking Areocars. These were the ones whose black outfits had the blue glowing pinstripes. Once Ralph reached the stage, the music changed. A miraculous sound unlike anything Preston had ever heard before came through the speakers. It was like a trumpet with human voices and had an unnaturally loud deep bass and it seemed to vibrate or rumble into the body. It made your heart start to beat faster. It rumbled for it seemed several minutes, but after only a few seconds Preston heard Ralph start speaking. this gave the effect that Ralph's voice was a continuation of the miraculous sound. The camera zoomed in on his nappy looking Afro, uncombed and glistening in the light. His Afro mane, brown skin, and features, especially the muscular physique from his IBA career, made him look like a lion. There was total silence for a few seconds, only the rumble of the bass voice trumpet sound. Then as the camera got a close up of Ralph, one tear could be seen falling from his eye. He spoke inarticulate and to the point.

"My fellow Americans today is the future—right now is the furthest anyone has seen of the future. Even the next minute cannot be guaranteed, as no one can decisively tell you what will happen next. I first asked the question are you more American than human? You have to ask yourself this question if you sit back and let your allegedly freely elected government kill people? Who has authorized the United States government to send our military traveling around the world and kill people? This is not what we elected them to do. You have not seen Brazil, India, or even China attack countries in the past two decades, but the U.S. has made a sport of invading small countries. The U.S. is covertly or illegally overturning governments and waging an all-out war on every continent. We have been fighting a war on terrorism, which is an inanimate object, for more than 20 years, breaking every international law there has ever been written, as well as our own Federal laws. At best, they just change the laws to accommodate their crimes—sometimes they just don't give a damn what they do."

Preston could not believe what he had just heard; to him it was almost treasonous. He first tried to call his wife, but she did not answer. He thought to himself that she was probably fast asleep. He then called his friend Willoford who said he was watching, but it seemed edited with a delay. Once Willoford turned his cybervision to an international network, he could see and hear what Preston was seeing.

Ralph Honeycutt continues with his loud squeaky voice,

"There's has been absolutely no regard for the 100,000's of innocent bystanders who were killed, maimed, or left homeless and they do all this in your name, the American citizens. Do you know what you are all about in the eyes of the other world's citizens? You are all about murder, rape, and the greedily stealing another nation's wealth. You the American citizens of the United States of America are stupid, arrogant, evil, and racist because of the actions of the United States government. Right now as I speak, the majority of the people of this world are ready to take up arms against this evil nation. They see the United States as the symbol of all that is evil. Think about it—our whole economic system is based on greed and came from slavery. Speaking of slavery, it seems to be an issue that's been swept under the rug. America under the Lee Administration endorsed a prison growth industry which may have led some clowns to illegally, unconstitutionally, and immorally kidnap my brother and hold him hostage under the disguise of legality. You see, I have been classified as an African American—as such, I am treated a certain way in America according to the way I look. Right now for every one African-American you see on TV, more than ten thousand are incarcerated. This includes all sports, film, even reality cybervision." Two huge graviton mega-screens displayed statistics as Ralph spoke. A military cadence softly played in the background. He continued louder as he started to pace the stage,

"There are millions of Black folk warehoused without hope waiting for the mercy of their captors! In 1865, at the end of the civil war, there was said to be 4,000,000 slaves here. It is now the year 2020 and there are 15,832,098 descendants of slaves incarcerated in conditions worse than slavery! I will speak the soul of those so-called African- Americans." Ralph started to walk around the stage. The black glowing pinstriped people formed an open V- shape around Ralph. "First there can be no Black bourgeois class in America! How can a Black person walk around talking about he's bourgeois when your people are still treated worse than second-class citizens are, and it is the year 2020? From 1492 'till today, there has been a straight line of racism and discrimination until right now; when the first African American who is a true descendant of slaves and Native American Indians has decided to run for President to make a real change for all Americans!" The camera panned showing a huge, cheering crowd which had grown to over 150,000 due to all the free food and drinks plus a chance to see some of their favorite rock artists for free. The air was thick with cannabis and synthetic smoke.

"How can someone say they are of a bourgeois class when their brothers, fathers, and sons are being systematically placed in what is nothing more than concentration camps. Moreover, I can assure you when you go to the cities, you see their wives, daughters, and sisters selling themselves or they are incarcerated too. Now how can there be an African-American family? Even if some do survive, there still cannot be an African-American sane community, only ghettos. A bourgeois American Black man is like a Jew riding around, chilling in Europe in a Cadillac in 1940, rolling through ghettoes and concentrations camps thinking, 'Better you than me." There was frantic applause at this point.

"The upper-class niggas, the elite ones, the gifted and talented 10 percent, the African-American leaders, how stupid you look now when faced with the truth." He paused and walked toward a large speaker. "It's the destruction of the Black family is why I can no longer tolerate these racist primitive regimes!" He banged his fist on the speaker close to his microphone magnifying the sound like thunder. "It's the arrogance the Neo-Confederates carry into the courtrooms as they unjustly issue out ridiculously long prison sentences to black and brown-skinned men and boys as sport is why I can no longer tolerate bigots as my leaders!" He banged the speaker again. "It is the murder and rape of smaller countries under the banner of freedom and liberty, when the American justice system's prison cells are filled with hundreds of thousands of people accused of crimes with no victim or damages, proving there is no justice." Again, he banged his fist on the loud speaker. He walked toward the middle of the stage. The glowing pin-striped suited people formed a half circle around him.

"My Latino and Hispanic brothers you and yours are starting to disappear too. First, they classified you as White, remember the 2010 census? They only gave you three choices to choose from: White, Black, or Asian. Of course, you are both neither and all of these; you are Native Americans with your own ancient culture, yet many of you chose White, believing there had to be some benefit for you by being "White" in America. Once you become a White Hispanic, you could no longer complain about discrimination. You can no longer say the prison systems are disproportionately filled with Latino and Hispanic men because they don't exist legally anymore. You are now classified as White, although you do not look like nor share the same cultural backgrounds as most of the White police, judges, and juries that convict you. The Latino and Hispanic men will not be able to complain about unfair wages due to race because their race does not exist anymore. I will tell you why it was so important for the Mexicans and Latinos to become White in 2010. So now, in the year 2020, the 1,800,000 Mexicans killed in the so-called Mexican Drug War and the 9,391,228 "White" classified inmates detained indefinitely who is Hispanic with brown skin look better statistically as white thus hiding the truth. Nine and a half million broken Hispanic families, the backbone of their community, detained indefinitely. Maybe the American Hispanic and Latino bourgeois class who descended from the Native Americans then wanted to be "White" should be treated the same way as the African-American bourgeois who are descended from slaves but now love the White master kids more than they love their own. As for the ignorant, fancy, sell-out, so-called African-Americans, they must go!" Laughter and cheers are heard.

"My platform is to give every man and woman the right to vote, regardless of who or where they are, as long as you are American. American means two grandparents were born in the United States. Yeah! Yea, this big ol' patriotic thing is out of hand when foreigners are gaining privilege over natural-born American citizens because the color of their skin makes them part of the Patriotic Party..."

Preston didn't see what all the hype was about after listening to this guy speak for only two minutes. He felt if Ralph managed not to get arrested, he would be defeated at the polls handily because the people who would vote for him could not vote. Then it hit Preston like a flash of lightning. Col. Brett was going to try to confiscate IST Corporation.

That was what Col. Brett did. The Department of Homeland Defense had many new laws on the books to confiscate land and businesses; all Col. Brett needed was good, third-party confirmation of a violation, then he would move in.

"The bastard gave me a few million so he could get the billions" Preston half mumbled to himself. Ralph Honeycutt's whiny high-pitched voice interrupted Preston's train of thought.

"Finally, someone I could hate more than Getty!" he thought aloud of Ralph. A slight smile flashed across Preston's face. Ralph stomped across the stage shouting,

"Yea, yea, it ain't nice is it? Yeah! Ain't nothing nice I have said so far and it's only going to get worse! You see I will be your first Black President. I am not a mixed breed with split allegiances and compromised agendas. Nor am I a downtrodden brainwashed Uncle Tom. I cannot be bought and I am not scared. To be honest with you, big Bubba Moody Jr. asked me to run for President. It is somewhat surprising, isn't it? You know he is my running mate so I can't be prejudice." The crowd cheered louder than it had previously and for some time. After a few seconds, the crowd calmed enough so Ralph could be heard,

"They never saw the Honeycutt and Moody, Jr. ticket coming. What it represents is trust and understanding. It shows a willingness to make the necessary concessions to achieve advancement in standards of living for everyone, thus advancing civilization as a whole. Our platform is simple. First of all, the African-Americans who were descended from the slaves, with at least one eighth, yea the octoroon, Negro blood will be given one and a half acres of land. This land is going to be in the States which used the slaves in the 1700s, rebelled in the 1800s, discriminated in the 1900s, and has now decided to incarcerate for the 2000s. In addition, all Americans born on U.S. soil and with at least two grandparents born in the United States will be given the one time option to purchase one and a half acres of Federal Land at the low subsidized rate, the equivalent price of half an ounce

Mr. Audacity

of gold. Second, every person born in the U.S. with at least two grandparents born in the United States will have the right to vote. Yes, this includes convicted felons, people incarcerated, and crazy people too, because crazy people are humans too. Third, there will no longer be an Electoral College. Its whole existence suggests that the American democratic system is a hoax. Next, we will require committees of 144 randomly chosen citizens selected quarterly to act as the Grand Jury of Appeals. These State- level,   Grand Jury of Appeals will sit above the highest Courts in every State to review all requested felony cases in which people are imprisoned. If 108 or more of the 144 Grand Jury of Appeals members vote against a State judgment, all court rulings will be reversed. Of course, the U.S. Supreme court will be subordinate to the Supreme Jury of Appeals consisting of 144 randomly chosen lawyers each sitting for 18 months. Finally, I will totally dismantle the Homeland Defense Department because it's only using up federal funds and terrorizing American citizens. This bureaucratic beast has created three classes of citizens: The Elite, consisting of the corporation owners; high-ranking politicians; and media personalities. They are protected by the second-class, consisting of the government working- class, such as police, prison guards, and all other State and Federal workers. These people do very little work under the guise title 'public servant.' They are indeed well paid 'public servants' to their upper-class masters. The third class includes everyone not in the first two classes who are not rich or receiving paychecks and benefits from the government. These Americans are preyed upon by the Elite and   their 'public servants' in the form of taxes, fines, penalties, bails, charges, surcharges, fees, and tickets. If you refuse to pay, then you receive prison or death. The 'public servants' confiscate, incarcerate, and then violate your God-given rights one person at a time. Under my presidency, you will be free from these ridiculous charges. Only a 12% flat tax, with surplus returned to contributors at the end of the year and at the end of their lives, in the form of Social Security. All Americans will be given lifetime, full medical and dental benefits. The 12% pays the doctors and nurses better than they are paid now with more money for research. We will cure cancer and other major diseases to extend human life expectancy by at least double within five years. The 12% pays for unlimited education so everyone can go to college. Under my administration, every member of society will be productive. The greatest endeavors humans can conceive will be possible once we start sending the people convicted of murder and rape to explore, live, and work at the bottom of the oceans and other planets to redeem themselves. Our society will become more civilized when government's employees can no longer legally participate in the hypocrisy of murdering and raping citizens accused of crimes. We will work together with…"

Loud sirens were heard in the distance coming from all directions. The camera shifted from Ralph Honeycutt to show several menacing looking large black buses with armor and visible weapons **Homeland Defense Militia** written in big white letters stood out prominently. They were the Special Assault Buses or (S.A.B. for short) and they appeared to be fully armed with 50 caliber machine guns, high-powered water hoses, and even the new high-frequency sound weapon the military designed to bust eardrums and cause pain to make crowds disperse. Over 50 of these buses, each with over 50 heavily armed special Homeland Defense Militia personnel converge on the crowd. It looked like another 200 or so other local and old Federal agencies officers, some of whom Preston recognized were also interacting with what were probably the Captains of the Homeland Defense Militia. Ralph Honeycutt had stopped speaking when the second wave of sirens was heard. What appeared was almost

Mr. Audacity

twice as many of the huge S.A.B.s, some with H.I.T. Unit written on the side in big red letters. Preston laughed aloud when he saw those S.A.B.s. A loud scream of the microphone and amplifier was heard as Ralph Honeycutt's squeaky voice came back over the speakers and the camera switched back to him. His face was frowned up and he looked very angry.

"Here they come, the oppressors. Don't anyone worry. Our First Amendment's right to freedom of speech protects us. Oh! I forgot. The U.S. government did away with the Constitution in 2012 when they turned this country into a fascist dictatorship with international masters. Today though…" Ralph shook his middle longest finger in the air at what appeared to be the main congregation of government officers and public officials gathered across the lawn. The camera zoomed in to show their reaction. They all appeared pissed—someone even threw their longest middle finger back. It appeared to be Getty.

Preston rewinds the telecast then zooms in and sure enough, there was Getty standing on top of a bench throwing a big middle finger back at Ralph. Preston never thought Getty to be the patriotic type or be a member of the Patriot Party as there was practically the rank-and-file of the Party in charge. For an instant Preston felt proud of Getty for showing Ralph Honeycutt how America really felt about him. Officers started yelling orders at the police and Special force units picked up the pace to get to their positions. Ralph started to speak again.

"You are all protected by IST technology! I will speak the soul of these so-called African-Americans. The United States once had a true African-American president…" some of the crowd started to boo. As Ralph took control of the crowd, he noticed the 100s of officers in blood-red body armor and full shields taking up position as he continued. "Yes, the African-American President's father was from Africa while his mother was a Caucasian American, but he was not a Black -American such as I. He is an African- American or

MexiAmerican but he was not a Black American, a Nigga like me.

If his father had been a White man, would he have been a Caucasian American?   How racist is it to classify a person who is equally half of two as the least desired of the two halves, as if they are somehow contaminated. As far as I am concerned, all the history books should distinguish the fact that the United States of America has only had Caucasian Presidents and one of mixed-race, if race is to be considered. I am not an African- American as neither of my parents was Africans. To call me an African-American is to insult every Black man or person of color who suffered and struggled in this country for not just equality but the most basic right of liberty. I am no more an African-American then the White man born in Virginia is a European-American. Under my Administration, race will not matter but will be dealt with for what it is—ignorance." Loud applause was heard.

The camera zoomed to where some officers are starting to push some of the crowd out of particular areas, causing sections of the crowd to separate. At the other end, you saw local police begin to make arrests and several drug dogs sniffing around. Ralph took off the camouflaged tuxedo jacket replacing it with a black jacket with glowing pinstripes. It appeared the crowd was starting to evaporate then Ralph waved his hand towards the technician booth. The loud bass voice trumpet sound blasted and then rumbled.   With this, people started aggressively pushing back at the Homeland Defense units.   The Mud Stumpers and Jungle Rockers who did not give a damn about politics, but were there only to dance and rock out with their favorite music groups began throwing beer and food at the officers. Ralph yelled at the top of his voice exciting them even more, "What are these fools doing? Why are they here!

Nobody called them. They are working for President Lee!

Mr. Audacity

See how they attempt to take away your freedoms." It appeared someone from above had had enough.

First high-pressure water was sprayed on the crowd from the S.A.B.'s causing a stampede, then the high-frequency weapons opened up causing mass confusion as people were trampled to death. It looked gruesome, but Preston knew Don Abernathy was dancing with joy; he would have the news stations spin it all as Ralph Honeycutt's fault. This was the big league of politics—play hard or go home—and it appeared Ralph was going home as the cameras showed him put on one of the ski mask-looking helmets and started to run toward the end of the stage. One of the black-suited, glowing pinstripe people grabbed Ralph. He pointed to Ralph's legs and then they turned and ran toward the Aerosport 3000 and large Aerocar vans or Areotruck CVEG as they were later named. The race was on—once they made it to those highly maneuverable crafts, nothing in the U. S. arsenal could touch them, as the Eagle had painfully demonstrated. Preston was at the edge of his seat to see if he would get to see the big mouth arrested on international cybervision like a common crook. One officer was making his way to cut off Ralph. To Preston's delight, it was Lt. Martin; he had the angle on

Ralph but Ralph made a football jump, complete with the Heisman Trophy stance at the end, making it to his Aerosport 3000. Then, to Preston's amazement, he heard gunfire as several of the S.A.B.'s opened up with their 50 calibers on Ralph's Aerosport 3000. All the Areotruck CVEGs took off, accelerated to 500 mph, and faded away. Preston thought they were all cowards. The cameras showed other S.A.B.'s menacing silhouettes moving across the park lawns with absolutely no regard for the thousands of scrambling hysterical people below them in order to take aim at Ralph's Aerosport 3000. It's obvious they wanted to totally destroy it. After a full minute of what seemed like an eternity, the gunfire stopped. Tens of thousands of rounds had been pumped into Ralph's craft. After a brief silence, the Aerosport 3000 slowly rose to about 500 feet then the passenger door opens upward. One of the men was wearing the black outfit with blue glowing pinstripes stepped out and then fell to the ground, landing hard on both feet and one hand then sprang some 200 feet to the nearest S.A.B. He then grabbed the .50 caliber gun and ripped it from its mount, smashing it against the side of a vehicle then spins one-half rotation hurling the torn gun barrel at the next S.A.B. piercing a small section of its armored side. Assault units opened fire on the blue pinstripes suited person, the blue strips glow brighter and sparks could be seen. It appeared he too was impregnable to the bullet fire. After ripping the high-pressure hose and high-frequency sound weapon off the S.A.B., the lighted man jumped to another S.A.B. then started to dismantle it in a like fashion. Preston calls his wife, but she does not answer, he thought it was somewhat odd. He called back a second time then after a few minutes she called him back. He told her to turn on the cybervision to see the action in Washington. After a few minutes, she said she could not find the channel he was watching only news bits of a commotion, but not as he described. Preston then noticed what appeared to be a newscaster, but with a Bubba wear shirt, sagging jeans, and then to his astonishment the camera operator passes him a blunt. Preston slowly turned up the volume. The newscaster was a White guy but had a ghetto accent.

"Yea, yea—the revolution is being cybervisionized right before your eyes. You see how our new government will defend its citizens in the face of radical assaults on the human race." The camera panned and showed the blue glowing pin stripped guy demolishing a S.A.B. like some comic book character. Then the camera panned the opposite direction showing mobs pulling special assault officers' battered bodies from some of the busted S.A.B.s. Others were fighting with police officers who had run out of ammo after shooting at the glowing guy. Preston shut off the cybervision. Immediately his phone rings. He just knows it is Col. Brett but to his surprise, it is Fiske Braun. He speaks cool and calm, though Preston can hear explosions in the background.

"This changes things quite a bit. We need to meet in Africa at Club Shindinki within 48 hours. Also, I think you should consider moving all your family to Europe for a while. I will meet you at the bar in the Cydonia Lounge. Until then, you want be able to contact me." The phone went dead. The next call was from Col. Brett. He sounded out of breath. Along with the explosions, you could now hear rock music in the background,

"Those damn niggers and ignorant poor White trash bastards have gone crazy! Damn it! Damn it! Over 100 billion in US Defense money scattered across the Capitol lawns like garbage. Now you understand don't you? You know weapons. We need you to find out what manner of technology these baboons are using. Look...get me what I want and Getty's yours unless he gets me what I want first, then maybe you, or his..." Col. Brett hung up. Preston laid back to take it all in. He made all the necessary plans to leave for Africa the next day. After only about 2 ½ hours sleep, his alarm went off. He was off to the IST Corp. South American Manufacturing Facility.

Chapter 14

WHITE BOY KINGDOM

Preston started off doing fine; he signed up for the basic tour of Industry Standard Trading Corp. Brazilian Division facilities. The two square-miles of grounds were decorated with lots of rare tropical plants so it was very easy to not be seen. There were few areas guarded, and he noticed the guards were sitting down smoking and drinking. Preston hopped off the electric tour train and headed toward the door marked "HIGH SECURITY AREA - PROPER AUTHORIZATION REQUIRED" in big red letters. He quickly picked the lock and stepped into a hall that stretched at least a quarter mile. There were several doors on either side, and the ceiling was about five stories high. Each door had a name above it, but the name appeared to be in code. One room had "HOT WATER" labeled on its door while another had "CHUG GUN," and yet another had "40th GENERATION." Finally, he came to a door with "C.V.E.G." —he was so excited; he could hardly wait to get on the other side. He hoped that he could get an incomplete unit to sell to Tritek. Once he busted the lock open, he laughed to himself how primitive their security was. He turned a corner when he heard footsteps. He hurried to some stairs until a guard yelled,

"Hey! What are you doing?" The guard stopped and questioned him. Preston noticed he had an accent—local boy he thought to himself. Using an Australian accent, Preston convinced the high guard that he was a major customer who had simply lost his way.   Preston was soon on his way. Again, Preston chuckles thinking to himself, *"How stupid niggers were regardless of where they are from."* He observed an assembly line with about 400 workers building Areocars unlike any Preston had seen before. They had thick sides like armor and what appeared to be some kind of weapon being mounted on the front and rear. He had seen enough. He headed out and stopped at the door labeled "CHUG GUN." He had to see what was behind that door. Once he busted up the lock with a small hammer device, he then made his way to the top of some stairs. There were only about 100 people working on a shotgun-looking device. Preston could see several other people working in a separate area. He made his way to the other side when he heard a voice from behind,

"Hey fool, what the hell you think this is?" It was Tyrone Honeycutt, Ralph and Jacob's first cousin—the boss of this South American Manufacturing Facility and the pride of the Honeycutt family. Tyrone was the shortest of all the Honeycutt dark-skinned and with a little-man mentality. Of course, Preston did not know who he was. To him, Tyrone looked like a young little Black dude who had a blunt too many. Preston did notice his necklace —a huge piece designed of gold, falcon trimmed in platinum, and loaded with diamonds, holding an elephant in one talon and a lion in the other. Preston smiled and then put on his best English accent (he always heard Black people like English White people better than American Whites).

"Yes, I am quite sorry for trespassing. I do think I am lost."

"Yea you are lost. You are now a kidnapped fool."

"What? What are you talking about? I am so fascinated by the Areocar; I just had to see every aspect, every corner of this magnificent facility… this greatest accomplishment of man."

"Ooh, yeah."

"Yes, yes indeed."

"Okay, since you are so fascinated with our accomplishments, I will take you on a tour of our facilities, but remember, you are officially kidnapped and you will do what I say, else you get it."

"Sure. I would be more than delighted to get the inside tour!" Tyrone kicked Preston in his ass.

"Naw, I said yo ass is kidnapped! Like your ancestors did my ancestors. You have to do whatever I say else I am going to beat yo ass and my people here working like they don't see us ain't going to let me lose the fight." Preston looked around and notices everybody working appears to be muscular. They shoot angry glances at   him but continue what they are doing.

"Okay., Chap, I will go alone. Violence is not necessary."

"How about you drop the corny accent cause I know who you are." Tyrone pulled out a purple cigarette, it was some Grand Daddy Purple rolled in   transparent   rolling paper.

"Ever since you made the transfer 200 miles away, we have known everything about you." Tyrone fired up his exotic cigarette and blew the smoke in Preston's face. The skunk and grape smell was not exactly unpleasant to Preston but the manner it arrived was. After another long drag and a few coughs Tyrone continued,

"Once you checked into our hotel it was just a matter of time before you would be here kidnapped… Anyway, this is where we make our Chug Guns. I guess you don't know what the chug gun is, huh? It holds 30,000 rounds and fires a molten alloy slug. I will not tell you the exact ingredients we are using in the 'single ought' .01-gram slug since the formula can be changed for different effects. Observe." Tyrone walked over and picked up a chug gun. It looked kind of like a square-shaped shotgun with a drum on the bottom.

"Here, feel this."

Preston took the gun—it was light as hell. Tyrone never took his hands off it and immediately snatched it back.

"It's made from a lightweight composite material which is basically recycled wood and plastic from garbage. A chug is a special alloy pellet about the size of a dust particle weighing .01 of a gram—so small, one canister clip holds 30,000 rounds. Every time you pull the trigger, a chug is accelerated along the barrel reaching at least 987,000 feet per second. Along the way, several chemical reactions occur causing the chug to combust into a molten piece of matter reaching more than 500,000° F. Right after it leaves the barrel, the chug begins to enter a semi-plasma state. It will go through any body armor. It will go through walls and it rips through titanium like a hot knife through butter. Only your tanks made of depleted uranium could stand up to it, but we got that Hot Water for them, hea, ha, ha, ha." Some workers start to giggle as well when Tyrone said, "That Hot Water." Preston wonders what in the world it could be, but by now, he was hesitant to ask too many questions—his host seemed quite hostile.

Tyrone pushed Preston in the back to usher him out. They walked out into a long hall and then walked to the door with 40th GENERATION written on it. Tyrone took out a set of keys and unlocked the door. As soon as he opened the door, strong smells like diesel fuel, pine trees, lemons, and a nasty fart hit Preston. He recognizes it but not ever as pungent.

"Here put these on." Tyrone handed Preston some shades. "You're lucky. In a couple of hours the lights would have been off."

They walked around the corner—Preston's nose was right—the room was filled wall-to-wall with marijuana plants. The plants were also along the walls in rows, five stories high, or about 60 feet up.

"Here is my favorite project. You see, these plants are all clones from one special plant which was fed heavy metals and other chemicals made its hemp fibers 5x stronger than normal. Out of nearly 1,000 plants, only one survived the toxic chemicals. We naturally called it, "The One." We cloned it, then took the clones, along with another 2,300 plants, and put them thru the same heavy metal feeding regiment, yet only the clones of "The One" survived; their fibers twice as strong as their mother—"The One." That was generation two. We continued to clone and enhance each preceding generation, producing the, ha, ha, ha, ha… Well, you saw what happened at Cuz's coming-out party… We repeated the process and refined a plant with the perfect properties. This is why your bullets are useless."

"There is no way I am going to believe a damn weed plant is stopping 50 caliber bullets." Preston responded.

"We also line the suits with 94-sided synthetic diamonds in a pinstripe fashion. An intense electrical current is pulsated through the uniform creating a strong electromagnetic field which repels metal and various waves along the electromagnetic spectrum, such as heat, gamma, infra, ultra, and a few others the Wise Owl thought might hurt our men. Also, this electromagnetic energy along with some nano-hydraulics allows us to toss your vehicles around and bend your metal like rubber. You see, ha ha ha… while you White boys were busy placing sanctions on alleged dictators in far-off lands, that starved millions of poor children in their country, but affected the rich of the country in no way, we were busy studying the muscle fibers of ants and we now have our nano-hydraulics… ha, ha, ha! Tyrone started laughing harder when a sick expression drew across Preston's face as he realized what he had witnessed the night before in Washington was a reality as was this hostage situation.

"What's wrong White boy, you sick? All of a sudden, the world is not as you planned it to be? Let's go to my office, I just got a bright idea. Maybe they will trade you for Cuz."

They walked all the way down the long hallway. There were 14 doors with strange names. Preston wondered if behind each door, there really were such advanced technologies. After a long silence, two big dudes joined them. This was when Preston began to feel like a prisoner. Preston figured it was time to start thinking about self- preservation.

"So my friend, what are your plans for me?"

"Beat yo ass."

White Boy Kingdom

"Oh… I mean, I have not harmed you in any way. I was just…"

"Spying on our operations for your racist country or a private company—one of the two, it's all the same. We should kill you but we are not barbarians like you."

"What if something happens to Jacob?" one of the big dudes walking with them asks.

"If something happens to Cuz, then we going to do the same thing to the fool right here," Tyrone countered. It was silent for a while as they exited outdoors and walked to a tall building about 10 stories high. It stood out with the jungle in the background. Preston was starting to worry about his family now. With the incident in Washington, Jacob Honeycutt would be a target of the Lee Administration along with the rest of the Patriot Party. *"They may use Heightened Interrogation Tactics which means they will be sticking gerbils up my ass, to say the least,"* he was thinking as he started his short elevator ride up to the top floor to Tyrone's office.

His office was like the evil twin office of Col. Brett. In place of German field marshals were Marcus Garvey, pictures of the slave with his back scarred by his Master's whip, Frederick Douglas, Malcolm X, and a group picture of the original members of the Black Panthers laced the walls.

Tyrone sat down. His large, Col. Brett-like desk, with its dark mahogany and cherry woods and marble finish, seemed twice as huge because of Tyrone's small stature. "You see those two pictures over there?" Tyrone pointed to the pictures of Harriet Tubman and John Brown.

"Do you know who they are?"

"The pictures seem to be quite old—I can't quite make them out."

"Preston Ross, like all White boys, you only see what you want. You think you own this world, huh?" Preston fought to hold back a grin 'cause of his current situation. Even if he were to get out of the office, he would have to travel some 200 miles to be out of reach of Tyrone's workers. He felt it was best to keep the best company until opportunity presented itself. Then Tyrone yelled,

"If the Declaration of Independence is to be taken literally, they are the mother and father of this country! That woman is the bravest American woman who has lived thus far. She risked her life on numerous occasions to travel into a hell created by your ancestors to bring freedom to a country, created as a free country but was not free. Could you have been as brave as Harriet Tubman?" Preston remembers reading something of Harriet Tubman in middle school—maybe one paragraph, then again on a trivia game show.

"Oh, I know of her exploits indeed; a Black Moses so to speak."

"Moses was already Black, so you can call her the female Moses. You would have tried to stop her the same way you are trying to stop us." Preston started feeling more uncomfortable.

"That man there is one of the bravest White men in American History. John Brown died fighting for freedom, justice, and liberty for a people the Supreme Court of the United States said was not human. Was he simply fighting against what would today be equivalent to animal cruelty or do you really think he considered the Negro to be his equal?"

Again, Preston found it hard not to crack a smile at his situation. He knew he had to get out of this one so he would have one for the boys back at the country club. Tyrone noticed the little snicker and then all hell broke loose. He threw a big, heavy stapler at Preston and split his forehead with a ¼inch gash. Blood started to stream down Preston's face. Now, Preston was keeping his cool. Here he is, a 55 year-old esteemed, highly respected U.S. citizen. To have some young savage disrespecting him was almost more than he could handle. He was keeping his cool now for the grandkids, although they would be well taken care of if something should happen to him; he had reached his limits with the physical assaults.

"Hey! I am no sissy coward! I am U.S. Airforce Lt. First Class! I'll die right here before I let you insult my dignity."

"Dignity?" Tyrone looked at Preston astonished. His face was frowned up as if he smelled a nasty smell. "What gives you more dignity then my kinfolk Jacob your people have caged like an animal?"

"Your kinfolk broke the law and therefore he was arrested. It has nothing to do with me."

"Slavery was your law also. It only affected certain people of Color. This tells me you are capable of having discriminatory laws. If slavery is not proof enough, let us try Black Codes, then Jim Crow. Repeatedly, you show me you can and will make discriminatory laws in an allegedly equal justice system. If I am not in the rooms when you make your laws, then don't apply them to me. Jacob broke no law. It was just one of your customs to restrain Black men against their liberty. It's a sport to you. Like cattle rustling or breaking a horse; reminds you of having us in shackles."

"I am not a racist. I... I just don't socialize with Black people. I only interact at work, and I am most fair in my dealings."

"The only people you are dealing with are so-called Latinos in your garden and as maids. Our plight was much different in the United States—we don't have our own country. It was bad enough you didn't give us an inch of land or a drop of freedom after you freed us, but you started to persecute us with your concentration camps disguised as prison systems while moving toward a final solution. You see, we know you plan to exterminate all the useless eaters in North America and then turn America into one big Las Vegas where the rich of the world can come and do as they please with the Latinos as the slave labor workforce." Preston was shocked. He had heard talks of all these plans but always in fraternal or secret society meetings.

"Do you think Black people should be given land?" Tyrone put the opposite fingertips of each hand together and looked Preston in the eye.

"No, slavery was over a long time ago and you have had plenty of time to recuperate. Look at yourself —you are wealthier than I am. You are the American Dream." Preston musters a smile.

"I had to work much harder than you and sacrificed more. I suffered when I was young until we came up. I had to break your laws that were nothing but artificial barriers to hold me down since when breaking your laws neither victim nor damages could be realized -except for the "State." I had to watch most of my family and friends suffer as they realized the American Dream was a lie and they were still slaves waiting for your prison growth industry to catch up with them. I watch the ones who could not evade the traps of your racist justice system spend 20, 30, 40 years in prison for less than misdemeanors. I know my history. I know you White boys came over here and took millions of acres of land for free and then bought millions more for minuscule amounts which only amounted to token jesters. You then divided it up like booty, passing it down thru generations, while Blacks were to be slaves for centuries to come. Now you say all is equal and fair as if your capitalist society was not built on slavery. It's like running a 1,000-mile race— some have jets planes while others have both their legs chopped off and are then asked to crawl to the finish line." Tyrone stopped his rant. He climbed onto the desk then pushed a purple cigarette in Preston's face. Preston could see green, purple, and orange buds with pink hairs and so many crystals —it looked like it was sugarcoated through the transparent cigarette paper. It smelled like blueberries, chocolate, grapes, and a sweaty gas station attendant. Tyrone sat on the desk cross-legged and lit the rainbow-colored cigarette with a gold trimmed falcon shaped lighter with rubies for eyes. He took a long, deep drag and blew the smoke in Preston's face.

"It's some of that Blueberry Armpit fool. Only one man in the whole world has this strain. The asshole sells only old school, three finger bags for $10,000 U.S. dollars. He is in the Guinness Book of World Records and everything, for the most expensive plant—calls himself Ghost…asshole. Oh well, I got it. This is my American Dream." He took another long, deep drag and again blew the smoke in Preston's face. Preston looked around at the stocky dude sitting in a chair by the door smoking a huge, fancy water pipe with some stinky smelling bud. Another guy was by the window, also a little more than a 55 year-old dude would care to handle. He was smoking a blunt.

"I refuse to talk to an idiot. I am going to start your punishment now. Hit this here fool—else we going to beat yo ass." Tyrone was motioned Preston to take a puff with the look of "or else" on his face. Preston took a long drag, inhaled, and then blew the smoke in Tyrone's face. What the hell, he had smoked plenty of reefer back in college. The taste was quite delightful and fruity with a charcoal finish. Immediately his mind went to a plateau it had never been before—everything was more vivid. His heart was beating faster; his breathing slowed and became deeper. He started to cough violently with saliva running down his chin. He could hear laughter all around him. He closed his eyes the first thing he saw through the tears was Tyrone Honeycutt coughing violently with smoke coming out his nose, tears out his eyes. Then when some saliva slipped out uncontrollably (with a little snot prompting Tyrone to turn away reaching for some napkins to clean up), obviously, ashamed of not being able to hold his smoke. Preston uncontrollably started laughing. It was the most awkward situation—Preston wanted to hit the Blueberry

Armpit again. Tyrone knew this and never let him hit it again. He keeps passing it to the two guards. While torturing Preston by not letting him hit the Blueberry Armpit again, Tyrone got a phone call. He then looked at Preston and said,

"I have a big meeting to attend, so you have to come with me since you are my hostage."

"Can I ask where you are taking me?"

"You'll see when we get there. Sammy, call Nate. He is going to be in charge while I am gone." Tyrone got up and staggered toward the door, "Come on asshole, we have to meet Hawk, so move out... give me your hands!" Tyrone put a plastic zip strap around Preston's wrists tightly.

"Oh! I will lose circulation," Preston yelped. "I bet ja Cuz's handcuffs was a lot tighter than these when yo people got him," Tyrone mumbled. Tyrone and one of the workers pushed Preston out the office and into the hall. When they reached the elevator, to Preston's surprise, two nice, clean-cut White kids exited the elevator.

"What's up Big T," the tallest of the two White dudes starts as they both give Tyrone and his worker the high-five handshake and dap.

"Yo, Nate dog! I need you to hold down the place for a few days. Bear should be coming soon, but you can handle it," Tyrone said as he passed Nathan Walker the half-finished Blueberry Armpit spliff.

"Oooh, is this that special?" Nate took a big puff of the cigarette then passed it to the other guy with him, as he started to cough. "I will keep everything steady," Nate said, as he caught his breath. His partner was now exhaling smoke and coughing violently.

Tyrone then led Preston to the roof. There was an Areosport 3000 sitting there waiting. It looked metallic black; the outer skin was dark-colored, micro-solar cells that glittered in the sunlight. Preston had never been this close to one of these crafts, as only the super-rich bought them or

White Boy Kingdom

governments tried to duplicate them as soon as they were built. He could not help but notice the ominous "Chug Gun"-looking apparatus at the front and back of the craft. He was sure he had not seen it on any of the photos of the craft.

The door opened upward out hopped Hawk. He was dressed extravagantly and beckoned them to hurry. His grayish, green eyes looked at Preston like a dagger. Preston was always amazed at the many contrasts of Black people. Hawk was brown skinned with grey-green eyes and reddish hair, but 100% nigga. Loud music boomed from the craft and smoke poured out.

"Get in fool," Tyrone said as he pushed Preston into the backseat. A beautiful petite young woman was asleep in the back seat with her bucket seat leaned all the way back and looked quite comfortable.   A small Asian-looking young woman was sitting beside the sleeping girl busy working the cybervision hologram screen.

"Man, I think you should drive. I don't trust the automatic pilot or the anti-crash feature," Hawk said as he yawned.

"It's cool if you are at least 30,000 feet when   you engage it—an alarm goes off at 20,000 ft., then at 10,000 the music automatically shuts off," Tyrone said as he took the driver's seat.

Hawk walked around to the passenger side, put on his double-breasted seatbelt, and leaned his seat back until it was most comfortable for him and uncomfortable to Preston, smashing his knees. Hawk closed his eyes and then yelled out,

"Tonka, watch this mothafucka behind me!"

"K," replied the little Asian woman.

After a few seconds, Hawk opened his eyes then walked around and tied Preston's hands to a bar under the seat. He cast a skeptical look at the little Asian woman then hopped in the front seat and closed his eyes again. The Asian woman never once took her eyes off the cybervision screen. Tyrone went to the trunk and got a small box and a six-pack out of a cooler. He handed Preston and the Asian woman a beer. He then sat in the driver's seat and started to roll up three, huge Blueberry Armpit spliffs. Upon finishing his task, he pressed a button and it seemed as if the insides became pressurized.

All of a sudden, Preston felt himself being lifted off the ground then accelerated forward. Looking out the window and at the odometer, the odometer said they had accelerated from zero to 400 miles per hour within two or three seconds, yet he felt only a slow, gradual pressure of maybe one G. It seemed like his seat was slowly sliding backwards as if the whole cabin of the vehicle was a gyroscope. He watched the odometer peak at 958 miles per hour as they continued to climb to 70,000 feet. He was awestruck by the contrast of the sun rising over the horizon to the east and the moon to the west with nothing but clouds below them, like an ocean. Then, to his astonishment, the odometer continued to rise until it steadied at 1,853 mph, nearly twice the speed the craft was supposed to be capable of. He noticed that the little young Asian woman had turned away from the cybervision to marvel at the beauty of this reality few humans would ever get to experience. The sleeping woman awoke, looked at him, and then began to marvel at the sights for a few minutes until she dozed back off. Preston thought she was one of the most beautiful women he had seen in his life. Her blue eyes and dark complexion gave her a very exquisite look. Her body appeared to be in perfect proportion. He knew he had seen them both on the cybervision a few times. He figured they were dumb models. He felt angered by these beautiful women journeying with low-lives such as these clowns. Tonka made eye contact with him; his heart skipped a beat. Something about her made him want to protect her. Her smell was sweet and inviting. The thick, musty smell of the Blueberry Armpit Tyrone started to smoke overpowered the sweet smell of the two women. He passed it to the Asian woman who took several big puffs, coughed each time, and then passed it to

White Boy Kingdom

Preston. He took the biggest puffs he could and then, out of nowhere, Tyrone turned around and started slapping at him reaching for the spliff screaming, "Give me that! Hostages are not allowed to smoke this good stuff." After a few minutes Tyrone began to work on Preston again; this time, with an audience, he seemed to go all out.

"Hey asshole, you think the Asian girl wants you because you are a rich White man that conquered the world. Your Indo-European white supremacist lie was all-good until the Nazis decided the Jews and Slavs were not White people. Tonka, do you know how the so-called White race came to seem to dominate the world over the Asians and Black people?"

"Asians rule the world now; cause China and the Koreans…"

"Shut up! You think you know everything. I am talking in the past, before 2012. Just shut up and listen." Tyrone passed his spliff to Tonka after scolding her. After she took a few puffs, she seemed confused about whether to pass it to Preston or not. She smiled at Preston and then gives it back to Tyrone. Tyrone took a couple of puffs and then passed it to Hawk, whose eyes were closed, but had his hand out to receive the spliff. Tyrone continued,

"White boy, you hear me out because I know your biggest secret. Some so-called White men got together and came up with the Indo-European lie creating a greater Caucasian race stretching from the mythical Atlantis to all of Europe, half of Asia, half of India, half of Africa, and all of the Middle East. What is so evident and so messed up about the whole scheme is everywhere there appeared to be a great civilization, they had to be White—such as in Africa's Egypt, Asia's Babylon, and all of India itself. Now you want to claim the Aztecs, Incas, and even the Black Foot Sioux? "

Tyrone pulled his leather boot off and his sock. He showed Preston his foot and looked at him with an angry mug that Preston understood was the line he dare not cross. "You White boys would teach our kids this false truth attempting to make it a reality for their future. This is why you have to love Hitler and the Nazis because they proved just how big and fat of a lie the whole Indo-European, great "White" Caucasian race scam really was. As he stressed the word "White," his angry, sinister looking mug turned into a big fake smile as he also threw his hands up in a universally friendly gesture." He then switched back to a very angry, menacing scowl. Continuing his sermon,

"The Nazis said the Jews were not White folk excluding them from the elite White boy club. They even had the genetic proof. Ooh, the Jews hated to hear they had been cast to the realm of mixed, impure, and unknown racial genetics that placed this old ancient race of people in a category along with Mexicans, Arabs, and Aborigines." Tyrone switched to his sad face.

"The Slavs, Russians, and every person born anywhere in Asia were next. They were right there with the Jews. They could not be considered White folk; just several generations removed Asian mulattos. As such, both the Jews and "inferior Slavic" Eastern European, Russian, and other Caucasian Asian type were slaughtered by "real" White Boys just like the Ethiopians were. Now, Preston, you White boys think you are slick given those same people— Jews, Slavs, Russians, Persians, Arabs, and once again, the man from India, who's darker than an African, the same coveted White status? Even the Latino was classified as a "White" yet treated Black sometimes" Again, as he stressed the word "White," his angry, sinister-looking mug turned into a big fake smile as he threw his hands up in a friendly gesture. Then he looked directly at Preston with absolutely no expression and rasps,

"They were all preferred over me and my brothers as their reward for participating in the White man's world order. With

White Boy Kingdom

the fake banks, fake money, and prejudiced credit system, all built to make the White boy dream a reality at the cost of the nigga who was to always be his slave along with the China man. What is the inside joke? The nigger has always been only a few votes away from being a slave from the day he was born. This is why America, the dirty ol' White boy kingdom must be…"

"You talk too much when you smoke, Mr. Falcon," Hawk said as he turned on some loud music.

Preston felt a hand on his leg. He looked to the side and Tonka hollered in his ear, above the music, that she was horny. She then took Preston's free hand, stuck it down her shorts, and then gave it back to Preston. He was so high, he smelled it, and then licked it in what seemed like a gesture without thought. He was immediately aroused and was not afraid for his life as much. She then yelled into his ear so only he could hear that she would help him get free when they got to Africa. *"Finally, someone who has come to their senses as the amount of trouble they are going to be in when someone figures out what happened to me,"* Preston thought. He would personally make sure Tonka and her sleeping friend got off lightly. At the end of the day, Preston felt his privilege would spare him. The music turns down then Tyrone's mouth starts running again. Preston's euphoric high was destroyed.

"Everything about America was to be for the benefit of only one race of people, the European White man. America has always been a leading eugenics enthusiast, sterilizing the Black man while holding them inside your prisons. So you think you are the master of my procreation just like during slavery when you forced every immoral act known to man upon my ancestors?"

Preston had had enough; he was going to speak up for himself,

"I voted for the first African-American President of the United States because I liked his character and approved of his policies. I think I am far from a racist!"

"That man had nothing to do with us or our cause. He was a White man with African ancestors. He positioned himself as the descendant of the wise African kings who sold the slaves to the Europeans, not a descendant of the slaves who were thrown off ships into the ocean for fish food and beaten until their spines showed through their ripped flesh. He was not of the ones who hung from trees or was dragged behind pickup trucks. His agenda was that of the European White man as he fought against the red, the black, and the green. When he did not ask for any retribution to the slavery, which is to this very day keeping our people in slavery, offered not even one penny of the fake money or one square inch of land, which was just as much ours as theirs. He did not even offer to make the racist slave-creating credit system fair. All this, after not offering the formal apology from the entities that perpetuated the atrocities upon us... fuck him. He was no better than the others." Preston was speechless.

Chapter 15

ESCALATION

Washington DC Monday March 9, 2020:

The oldest and wisest of the rank-and-file of the government officials evacuated as soon as they saw the first multi-million-dollar S.A.B. vehicle demolished. Some headed for their underground bunkers, others for the airport. Ironically it was later rumored the Retired Judge was seen leaving in his own signature color, blue and gray Areocar with his young intern.

Getty noticed that everyone retreating was yelling orders to their subordinates. Col. Brett made his way toward his office after sending his bird-dog Lt. Martin after Ralph Honeycutt. Getty figured Col. Brett was more worried about protecting his office than the rest of the Capitol. After a while, Getty saw the Jets flying over the capitol and then heard two simultaneous large explosions. Large debris started to fall so Getty took shelter in the subway. He already knew exactly what his next assignment would be—to find out what IST Corp. had going on—and he knew that, because it had to do with weapons systems, he would eventually have to get some information from his nemesis Preston Ross. IST Corporation was stationed overseas in South America and India, neither of which Getty had ever stepped foot on.

After the two explosions, it seemed the police and Special Homeland Defense Units were getting control of the crowd. Most of the people had dispersed. The smaller their numbers the easier it was to subdue them. Soon as Getty reached street level he saw police and Homeland Defense Units beating and hog-tying anyone they could get their hands on. Behind them were the parking meter officers and security cadets rounding up the detained citizens and throwing them into large cargo containers hauled by 18-wheelers. Getty then saw something he had never seen before. One of the Big Black S.A.B. units with the big red H.I.T. written under the big white HOMELAND DEFENSE Insignia started spraying yellowish orange foam onto a crowd of people. The foam started to harden and stopped the fleeing people in their tracks locked inside a foam-looking blob that was hard as concrete. The hardened form of the substance still looked like a foam, as it had air bubbles. Later, officers would come and spray chemicals that dissolved the hardened foam and chipped away the remaining material to free the now prisoners. Everyone was arrested; even women pushing their babies were arrested with the children being taken into custody by Child Protective Services.

It all started with one woman yelling, "You killed my baby!" as soon as her mouth was free of the Secure Foam™, which Getty later learned the substance was called. Apparently, the Secure Foam was designed for the bubbles in the soft foam form of the substance to become air pockets when it hardened so the captured person could breathe until he or she was apprehended. Unfortunately, sometimes the Secure Foam would get into the nostrils and mouths where it would harden, suffocating its victim. Maybe it was a bad batch because most of the people captured did not find the air pockets that day. There was one woman whose face Getty would never forget. She looked as though she could have been a young model no more than 18 or 19 years old. A total look of terror was on her face as she strained to take a breath only to realize the one before was her last. Her eyes budged out her head giving the only sign of a death mask. Getty then witnessed something that sickened him. One of the parking ticket officers, a clean-cut, African-American male who was following the S.A.B. spraying the Secure Foam, after applying the dissolvent, snatched a thick gold necklace from around the lifeless young girl's neck. Getty walked over and tapped the parking ticket officer on the shoulder very

Escalation

hard. The officer turned and immediately pushed Getty back as tensions were high. Getty said,

"You are going to turn over the necklace you took off that poor girl's neck!"

"Who the hell are you? What the hell are you talking about?" the parking meter officer yelled as he reached under his jacket pulled out a sting rod with 50,000 volts of electricity sparking. Getty carried no weapons except a small knife. He knew if he started a confrontation with the officer, his partners would swarm him. Identifying himself would do no good as the city's Department of Vehicles and Streets employees would not even know Getty's Federal Department even existed. Getty stepped out of reach of the sting rod. Then he yelled at the nearest parking ticket officer who was feverishly applying dissolvent to Secure Foam around an old White man and his dog who appeared to be alive.

"Oh Please! Please! Officer you have to save my little sister! She can't breathe! Hold on lil' sis, I'm here!" He then moved toward the body. The parking ticket officer who had been helping the old man and dog rushed to Getty's side applying dissolvent and pulling the girls slumping body off to the side before realizing his efforts were futile. He then screamed,

"My God not another one, she's gone man! Your sister is dead!" Getty moved up close to the girl as the other parking ticket officer who had stolen the girl's necklace started to move to the next citizen who was suspended in the Secure Foam. He starting to apply dissolvent; Getty figured his greed was calling him as many more victims were left. Getty acted as though he was heartbroken by the young woman's death. He put his hands to his head as if to hold back tears. The young Latino ticket officer who had tried to help Getty save the girl looked as though he was trying not to break down into tears, as he turned and hurried to the next person whose motionless silhouette you could see trapped inside a Secure Foam mound. Getty then made his move.

"The rotten bastard! That lowdown scum stole her necklace!" Getty yelled as he cast a ferocious look at the thief parking ticket officer. Again, as soon as Getty steps toward him, he pulled out the sting rod. Getty made sure the other parking ticket officers could hear him as he yelled,

"Give me back the necklace you stole or you will have to kill me right here!" The thief officer swung the sting rod at Getty who weaved and punched the crook in the face once, then threw a knee to his stomach. The thief officer fell to the ground as Getty jumped back from several parking ticket officers with their sting sticks out. The officer who had tried to help Getty yelled,

"What the hell is wrong with you?"

"He stole my sister's necklace! It's in his shirt pocket...gold!" Soon as Getty said this, he had to dodge a sting rod from one the parking ticket officers. As more officers surrounded Getty, the one who had tried to help initially went over to help his fallen comrade who had the breath knocked out of him by Getty's knee. He stuck his hand in the thief officer's shirt pocket and pulled out a large broken gold chain with a charm of the girl's name written in gold letters.

"Let him make it! I got him!" the officer yelled as he held out the necklace wrapped around his fist. He walked toward Getty and handed it to him. Getty put the necklace in his pocket as he vowed to himself that he would make sure it got to the girl's family. He then rolled up his sleeves and started to help where he could with the cleanup. After a half hour   or so, he reached into his pocket to retrieve the necklace and charm so he could put it in a bag with the girl's ID, having retrieved it also from her body. For the first time he got a good look at it. The chain was very thick and worth a few thousand euros. The letters on the charm were filled with diamond studs spelling out her name "Summer."

Escalation

There were still more than 100 vehicles roaming the area, all using their weapons on the crowd. The one Last Areosport 3000, the rainbow colored one Ralph Honeycutt arrived in, swoops down beside the blue glowing man who had wreaked havoc on about 30 S.A.B. The door opened up, two people jumped out and pulled the glowing person in. The Areosport 3000 takes off straight up into the air until it was invisible to the naked eye—about 60,000 feet.

"You just can't leave those people! Bubba Jr. shouts as he pulled the helmet off the glowing suit.

"We can't just reveal our tech for petty reasons. We are in the world's eye and everything must be done by a committee with consideration for the whole... anyway, why in the hell is Big Bubba in angelskin?" Ralph yelled sounding as if he was still giving a speech.

"You're through with the one-man debate, Lion. I let Bubba use it to get some revenge for his fans and father... you saw them—they didn't give a damn, they were killing," Bear said as he started inserting a key-looking device into the collar area of the angelskin suit—the glowing outfit Big Bubba was wearing. A loud explosion was heard as the Areosport 3000 started to shake. The slug guns at the rear and front of the craft started firing automatically. Ralph and Bubba grab what looks like video game controllers from compartments hidden behind a wood grain finish. "Oh shit!" Bear yelled as he grabs the leather with wood grain finish steering wheel pulling up and smashing the acceleration button. The Areosport 3000 rocketed nearly vertically to about 80,000 feet in just a few seconds. Then Bear banks it right and started to dive. It was a clear day so the four fighter jets that had fired the missiles triggering the Areosport 3000 new auto-defense system could clearly be seen. Ralph and Bubba each grabbed what looked like a video game controller. The cybervision screens showed the moving jets as red triangles. Bubba and Ralph guided a green X over the jets and pressed a button. The chug guns fired softball size white-hot matter, which was in a plasma state. Two of the jets explode into fireballs. Ralph and Bear look at each other as if they were surprised by the effectiveness of the weapon system. They placed the green X over the other remaining fighter jets but do not fire right away; the jets break off their engagement. They decided to fly to Africa and drop Bear off at Shindinki's then call it a day when Ralph and Bear simultaneously received a video text from the Owl.

About a minute later, Ralph received a text message from the Great Elephant asking him to have his camera crew start filming the deceased victims on the ground in Washington. Ralph made a cybercall then switched the monitor from defense radar back to cybervision. After a few minutes of viewing several victims, the camera zoomed in on the young woman whose gold necklace Getty retrieved from the thief parking ticket officer. After a few seconds, the camera moves on showing several other bodies until the footage abruptly ended as the camera-wielding man was beaten, then arrested. After a few minutes, Ralph and Bear simultaneously received a text from the Great Elephant. After they read it, they looked at each other strangely, then, Ralph took a deep breath.

"We are going to get Jacob, and then we are going to free the Gorilla", Bear said so Big Bubba would know what was up. You know we have only two Angelskin suits he adds. Bubba quickly replies,

"I guess I will be staying in the craft. What about Kerry? I have not heard a word from him. No bond has been set or any mentions of a trial… are we going to get him… oh, we don't know where the hell he is!"

"If that's the case we might as well go get big Steve— we can let him run something overseas… just not in Africa," Bear

Escalation

said as he shuffled through music songs to play; the trip to where they were holding Jacob would take a little more than 45 min. at top speed. A call came in on the cybervision monitor; it was Vasquez "Eagle" Williams. After years of not trusting anything electronic for communicating, they had gotten into a habit of calling each other by their "animal manifestation" as the Elephant called it, when they communicated with each other; especially since 1992 after Harold the "Mongoose" was killed after the filming of ancient ruins on Mars incident. Eagle was hysterical, yelling,

"You can't do it! The Elephant is crazy... we have..." He reached for another cell phone moving so fast he dropped it then scrambled to pick it back up. He yelled, "We have at least two votes against what the Elephant suggested me and Hawk." As if right on cue, the cybervision screen split in two with Hawk looking cool on one side and Tyrone

Honeycutt piloting another Areosport 3000 coasting at 70,000 feet at about 1400 mph. on the other side

"Forget Elephant's plan—it's ludicrous! He will mess up our money, all money. I vote no. Bear what's your vote?" "No," Bear's deep voice was heard.

"Look, Snake will be free within the next few days. His incarceration is nothing more than a publicity stunt for President Lee.   Don't let the Elephant have his wish of messing it up for everyone...ten million dollars from Hawk and I have to sway ISTs hand." Eagle pleaded.

Tyrone looked over so his face covered Hawk's side of the screen.

"Falcon votes y'all go and take Snake back, two votes for Elephant", he said then leaned back. Right as Ralph got ready to speak. Eagle looked up from his phone with a sly grin,

"Birds of a feather flock together. No need to vote Lion, the Wise Owl has decided it... four votes against Elephant." Vasquez cut off his cyberphone; His image on the monitor went black. Ralph checked his phone and sure enough, the Wise Owl had voted with Eagle, Hawk, and Bear, to let justice run its course with Brother Snake.

"Don't worry Lion, we got a hostage worth more to them than Snake… I'll see you at Shindinkis in 6 hours or so." Falcons said as Hawk and his screen then goes black.

Ralph turned and headed toward Africa, specifically, Club Shindinkis. Ralph thought how appealing the suggestion Mr. Elephant made was. He was quite all the way to Africa.

The Gorilla and Snake received the message at the same time a day later. A coded text message sent to a guard at the county jail and prison holding them. Both were furious their family and friends who had the means were not coming to get them as the Elephant had suggested. Usually they went alone with him on even the most radical ideas. They have made it this far, why turn back? Jacob Honeycutt, for his part, did not vote. What was asked of him to give approval to would take things to a completely new level and he did not want to be responsible for anyone else's life. He, like the Owl, had the gift of ingenuity. They could fix anything; they were natural handyman. Although Ralph was the face of IST Corp., Jacob was the one with the master's degree in engineering. He took the Theories of The Great Nothing and applied them. Jacob hired the top 152 scientists and engineers from Third World countries. He paid them a fraction of what their under-performing Western and Chinese colleagues were paid but got much more out of them.. He had the dream to be totally self-sufficient with energy and demanded the perpetual aspect be applied even though in the long run IST Corp. would lose fortunes by not limiting the Areocars capabilities. He was by far the most rational of the three, as Tyrone and Ralph tended to have anger problems. He was also the only Honeycutt male who had been married to one woman for more than 28 years with kids and

Escalation

grandkids from just that one woman. He had never been in jail before but he kept the Gorilla in mind and stayed strong. Jacob Honeycutt was confident his million-dollar attorney would have him released on some form of bail on his next court date if the charges were not dismissed. The Snake sent the message back,

"If on my next hearing in two weeks they don't release me then pop goes the Snake."

The Gorilla decided to make the move after being incarcerated since the summer of 1988 when he was 16 years old. Charged with serious crimes for a teenager, aggravated assault with bodily injury and attempted murder he had learned his lesson for sure after the second year. For the other 30 years, he was just a slave of the State. For 20 years, he worked in their factories and in their fields to keep his sanity and pass time. Then, one day after he read how the United States military dropped bombs killing 15 innocent people (mostly women and children) trying to kill one bad man. On the same day, the same government gave $300 billion dollars to private companies allowing them to pay their executives millions of dollars in bonuses while simultaneously keeping them from going broke even as that same company was evicting families out of their homes. On that day, he refused to work anymore as a slave for free. He yelled every day for a month for hours; he wanted to see his mother because he had not seen her in 14 years. He was then placed in solitary confinement for three years.

The Great Elephant reached out to him and let him know he had an ally on the outside who knew the evil of those who had imprisoned him and was not afraid of them. The Great Elephant gave him some predictions as a sign, every last one of which came to be. He wrote and told him in 1994 when the Lion, Falcon, and Snake were not even speaking to each other cause of a family dispute. The Elephant wrote, *"They would have a kingdom to the south, in another world, along a river of many tall beautiful women if they cooperated. They would race above the clouds faster than sound and even have the ear of the world as a dignitary if they pooled their money."*

The Gorilla also believed it was The Elephant's suggestion to Hawk and Vasquez that they should use brainwashing techniques similar to those used by military and religious groups on their partying patrons, which made them have legions of consumers worldwide. Hawk just followed the blueprint, although no one can underscore the charisma of Eagle for adding to their success. The Gorilla reminisced about the fine life all his rich pen pals must have been enjoying all those years. He then took out a picture of his high school sweetheart, Cynthia Honeycutt, and started to masturbate looking at the picture. He cleaned up, and then took out an obituary of his goddaughter Gloria Price. A tear rolled down his cheek. He was crying for the first time in 30 years. He was crying first soft, and then it turned loud. Other inmates came to their cell front. They had heard many cries but not like this one before. It was not a cowardly punk whimper. It was more like the one you would hear from a wounded soldier saving a fallen comrade, a battle cry. It was the cry of a man who was ready to die. Then it went silent.

Chapter 16

JUST FOLLOWING ORDERS

March 10, 2020:

Prison guard Robert Hawkins was an average kid from small-town U.S.A. who like most White non-Hispanic young adults with no criminal background, ended up working at a prison. Working for more than 6 years, 70 miles from any city with more than 50,000 people in Pennyworth, Alabama; he just recently was hooked up with Prometheus Green, the big shot convict who was running the yard. Robert thought Prometheus was such a sad case. They shipped him from the Texas State penal system 8 years ago as a chronic troublemaker. He had been locked up since he was about 15 or 16 years old for a fight at school 30 years ago when he tried to kill some White kids. He said before he came to prison he had been jumped and beat up several times by older Black kids in the projects where he grew up, yet no one ever went to jail. He had one big fight in which he fought how he was taught and he got a 60-year sentence. He insisted he was a great football player although he did not even play past his junior year in high school and he said he was good with the ladies, yet again, his last girlfriend was in high school 30 years ago. After getting to know Prometheus, Robert knew for sure, he had his back.

After 8 years on the yard, Prometheus saved his life at least on two occasions. Once when there was going to be a big riot, Prometheus informed him not to come to work that day. One officer was killed and another was seriously injured; in situations like prison riots, the situation is totally out of control so even if you are a good guard toward the inmates tragedy can happen. A few years later, Prometheus warned him about a crackdown by the State and Feds on prison guards providing drugs and cell phones. Robert scaled back his operations to consist of only food and condoms and sure enough, his superior officer and two subordinate trainees were busted, and given strict probation, as prison is the worst nightmare for prison guards. Now it seemed it was time for payback.

Prometheus wanted to be free by any means necessary. He offered CSO, Robert Hawkins, $250,000 to gather some more people to collect a $5,000,000 reward to free him. Once free, he would just go to Africa or Brazil and live out his life. Robert accepted it, and from that day on, he called himself Bobby Hawkins. CSO Bobby Hawkins had a 48-hour deadline to meet or Prometheus said he would get someone else. He gave Bobby a debit card and pin number attached to a bank account with $50,000 as down payment and start-up funds. Prometheus's plan centered on paying off anyone who would attempt to stop him from leaving. Designed where there was to be no bloodshed, "the plan" started with a routine riot which Prometheus thought was smart, but then it got sloppy. Somehow, within 48 hours, CSO Bobby Hawkins had managed to bring in nearly a dozen or so dumb conspirators including (in order of entrance into the caper): his fat lazy coworker—CSO Renaldo Gomez, a Catholic priest, two deputy sheriffs, a strip club owner, three strippers, the leader of a gay prison gang, and finally assistant warden Ned Cantor. Bobby actually owed $150,000 more then he would receive if successful.

Prometheus made it outside the gate parameter without a shot fired. His police escort was there waiting. The two deputy sheriffs were each paid 50,000 to take him to a hotel and $50,000 apiece not to tell his partner, although they were sitting beside each other the whole time. Several Homeland Defense Units stopped them with four S.A.B.s filled with nearly 200 heavily armed troops. Prometheus noticed helicopters, then two fighter jets flew overhead. He then told the officers to stop the car then hopped out and attempted to run into the woods. Bobby then heard several shots fired. A Lt. Haraesio Martin was credited with the kill.

March 13, 2020:

The Prometheus Green incident was the final straw that broke the camel's back. President Lee's actual statement was,

"This will prevent criminals like Prometheus Green from terrorizing our communities." as she signed a secret executive order that had been setting on her desk for years. It gave States the ability to dispose of inmates considered as terrorists or incorrigible. A combination of events, particularly the destruction of 21 S.A.B.s, two top-secret experimental fighter jets being shot down, and several American lives lost at the Honeycutt / Moody, Jr. rally played a role in the signing of the executive orders. The incident in Washington at Ralph Honeycutt's Presidential run announcement was portrayed by the media and United States government as an anarchist and terrorist attack. The Cybervision Hijacking was also another reason cited for the new laws. To qualify for immediate extermination, an inmate needed to meet three of the following criteria:

Have a life sentence or combined sentence of more than 40 years. Been previously labeled a terrorist, conspirator, or collaborator by the United States Department of Defense, or been convicted of the following crimes by a Federal or State court: treason, sabotage, arson, murder, sexual assault, aggravated robbery, kidnapping, assault with use of weapon, a drug offense with possession of a weapon, and any crime against a public servant. Had not received a visitation within last 12 years.

The only system approved for use was Tritek Industries Mass Sanitary Disposal Carriages (M.S.D.C.'s). These large building units were hauled in sections on 18-wheelers. Each one was roughly larger than the average container about 70'X 15'. Some of the larger facilities required convoys of ten or more 18- wheeler big rigs when they installed the "PortaShowers" as they were called. Once assembled, they worked as efficient showers requiring less than 18 hours to assemble to underground plumbing and electrical transformers. Inside, was a huge fully functional shower facility that could be easily cleaned.

The inmates always marveled at how clean it always was in the showers. It was made of some space-age material that always stayed the same temperature and was stain resistant. Depending on how many sections assembled, a minimal 100 inmates could shower as each section had 50 showers with 25 heads on each side of a translucent wall. The little glass translucent wall gave some sense of privacy between the two sides, which was unheard of in the penal system. Privacy indeed was not the intent for the little glass wall. The materials of the divider wall, as well as the other walls, were filled with small fiberglass-like tubes that release non-ionizing microwave radiation when the "little red button" was pushed. In addition, the Warden had a key, which needed to be placed into the machine and turned 180 degrees inside a hidden compartment.

On March 14, 2020, inmates on 33 Maximum-Security and Aggravated Surrogate facilities were sanitized. Attached to their units two years prior the inmates were lead into the (M.S.D.C.'s) Porta-Shower units. The guards who were running the shower were not the usual guards.

They were special State and Tritek Industries Securities' private penitentiary subcontractors. They would place 100 to 500 convicts inside the M.S.D.C.s where they would shower as usual for one minute to get the entire body wet. An electrical current of 250,000 volts was sent into all surfaces for 2 seconds rendering all of the convicts unconscious then microwaves at 2.45 gigahertz was discharged for three minutes and 52 seconds. The space-age designed material inside the M.S.D.C. muffled sound to only a few decimals.

Just Following Orders

Also, the microwaves worked inside out immediately liquefying internal organs within the first 5 seconds so there was no audible sound after a few seconds. After 3 minutes and 52 seconds, only black hard mounds of carbon, phosphorus, calcium, and several other trace minerals weighing on average 45 pounds in the form of charred miniature humans remained. The remains of the inmates were later called "meat mounds." If stored, "meat mounds" were supposed to go 180 days with no odor according to Tritek Industries Securities' advertisements, but this proved to not be true. The meat mounds had to be ground up and fed to livestock on the food manufacturing penitentiary facilities within 48 hours of production because of smell.

On the first day, March 14, 2020, 33 facilities disposed of 5,840 convicts. The next day 48 facilities disposed of twice as many. March 17, 2020, an amendment was added to the secret executive order allowing States to exterminate inmates to include a fourth criterion of "subject being an imminent danger." On March 19, 2020, 62 facilities located in 18 States with the "Porta-Shower" attached disposed of 21,480 inmates. On March 20, 2020, 74 maximum-security, segregated prison facilities in 21 states, disposed of 38,309 inmates including Jacob Honeycutt. Operations were scaled back the next day as most major offenders had been sanitized. On March 23, 2020, the United States Supreme Court secretly put a halt to some of President Lee's secret executive orders.

March 22, 2020, Washington DC 4:00 a.m.:

Hundreds of buses were on the streets of the inner city offering $5,000 to families who would relocate within the next 48 hours. The reason was simple; a catastrophic event was soon to occur within 72 hours. Within 48 hours, 98% of all poor and homeless people had relocated at least 300 miles outside of Washington D.C., others such as college kids and several other teens in accordance with their favorite pop icons, used March 25, 2020, as an excuse to escape the city.

Patriot Party members flew into DC from all parts of the country to celebrate what was seen as a victory for them since all the poor people and rebellious youth were leaving the city that day so the Party members decided to hold a rally. Videos from several miles away showed a bright whitish-blue fireball, about four miles across, and then a mushroom cloud reaching 60 miles into the sky. Washington DC was totally destroyed with what appeared to be a suitcase nuclear bomb. Later several facts lead to alternative scenarios. One such fact was the tremendous yield estimated of 1.4 megaton blast left a very small creator. The blast imploded causing total destruction inside a 9-mile radius but practically spared everything outside the 9-mile radius. There was also practically no radiation fallout. No known entity possessed any thermonuclear suitcase-size devices of more than 200 kilotons and they were huge car trunk size. The slight majority of the United States government had been away from DC but 38 percent of the House, 47 percent of the Senate was there along with 24 state governors, and 5 Supreme Court judges. Also gathered were other prominent business leaders in the form of lobbyists, effectively paralyzing the United States government and the entire world economy for a few days.

Several hundred thousand casualties were reported. Neither President Lee nor anyone from her administration was heard from for several days then, the Speaker of the House, Lawrence Cobb, announced he was President of a new United States Government located in Pennsylvania.

Ralph Honeycutt suggested on his cybervision station, that a poll be taken, and broadcast via cypervision. This poll would allow all Americans to vote for whom they felt could best lead as President, and every other position in Congress, the Senate, and the Supreme Court. Lawrence Cobb and his crew wanted to run the United States the same way, bringing

Just Following Orders

back all the remaining politicians and "…use every resource this great country possesses to hunt down the individuals and the rogue States responsible for the worst act of terror in history." Ralph wanted to take America in an entirely different direction that did not involve war. He asked for a vote to be taken via 21 cybervision networks. Forms were sent out requiring signatures and other identifying data to eliminate fraud. Ralph posted his platforms and what he would do if he was head of a "Dream" Government.

On April 22, 2020, six large media outlets, which had been associated with the Black Triad, began to broadcast the inauguration of Ralph Honeycutt as the first President of the Free United States of America (F.U.S.A.). He received twice as many votes as Lawrence Cobb. Positive information about a new alternative United States government and a new era declared "The Age of Reason" was broadcast. To set the tone, for his first five days as President of the Free United States of America, Ralph worked instead of partied. There was no inauguration ball, no celebration. They took out a big hat, wrote the name of each State on a piece of paper, and then randomly drew from it 50 times. The order in which each State was pulled would be the order the new Federal Government would have to reside in that State for one year before moving to next—South Dakota was the first. Some of the smaller States liked this ideal because it would bring in substantial revenue when the entire Federal Government was staying in town.

On April 23, 2020, a month after Washington was destroyed, President Honeycutt and the "Dream Congress" met in South Dakota. An all-star cast of who's who included some familiar faces in different positions. Hollywood A-List actors, professional athletes, and pop icons received the most votes from their fellow Americans to make political decisions as a Congress. Authors, activists, neighborhood doctors from small communities, and college professors got many votes as

Senators from their respected States. A few intelligent bums, Union leaders, and a small number of traditional politicians got the nod as well from the people. Governing was to be done via cybervision, so they had already decided there was no need for a permanent Capitol City. They offered every American the opportunity to participate in every decision affecting them with the reality of cyber-voting. Records were to be kept of every vote, so fraud was eliminated. There was no more Electoral College. President Honeycutt also signed a World Constitution into law, freeing the poor and minority citizens of the F.U.S.A. from government oppression.

After the media blitz, with some star power, the American people were willing to give cyber-voting and the Dream Government a shot. On day two, the Honeycutt Administration issued out one million square acres of Federal lands to the descendants of the slaves. Some White people complained President Honeycutt was racist. The next day, Honeycutt's administration offered one million square acres of land for sale at $2,750 per acre to only citizens born on United States soil who had at least two grandparents who were born in the United States. If the person was on welfare, a Federal grant was issued allowing them to purchase the land over 10 years. It created a lot of wealth overnight as whole towns and cities were planned around the settlements of 50,000 land shares grouped together in the middle of nowhere.

Many Black people sold their land to rich White people and Asians at cheap prices, so the reparation worked out well for everyone in the end. On day four, President Honeycutt gave a speech announcing his American Universal Health and Education Reform Bill. The Bill passed nearly unanimously with the new Dream Congress and over 83% of the public's cybervision votes. Some of the highlights of the bill stated by President Honeycutt was,

"Universal health care for all American citizens born on F.U.S.A. soil with at least two grandparents who were born in

Just Following Orders

the former United States... Special cards with three identifiers to eliminate fraud including retina, fingerprint and face recognition will have to be used in order to receive benefits... All Health employees will be under Government oversight to ensure excellence and the highest quality healthcare this world has ever seen. To ensure the brightest and most talented individuals strive to be health care providers, large government incentives will be paid to the Doctors, nurses, and technicians who save lives instead of the military contractors who indiscriminately kill people... Massive funds are to go to science and technology industries for the development of cures and treatments instead of weapons development..."

"The Bill also restructures the education system placing it under Federal control. The amount of waste eliminated from State corruption by the misappropriation of funds due to fraud and incompetence was tremendous. Much higher standards will be set including year-round school and 10 hour days. The new education system requires youth at age 13 to start nominal paying apprenticeships (half of the minimum wage) working in various fields of their choice. This system is designed to give the F.U.S.A. a competitive edge since our doctors, scientists, and engineers will have been working on their crafts since the age of 13. It also gives the Free United States of America a massive 40 million-body physical labor task force full of youth and energy. We will provide two meals a day. They will primarily be healthy with minimal unhealthy snack options. This youth task force is literally going to be made of kids who are better with their hands than there head, but "smart kids" will also partake in physical education. The Youth Task Force is going to assist in the construction of large public works projects such as underground cities, Aero Vehicles Guidance Grids, and Massive underground C.V.E.G. generator plants to power cities. Another feature of the Bill is the unprecedented opportunity it provides for millions of poor, underprivileged, and juvenile delinquent type youths by offering them job training and equal opportunity to become anything they choose if they qualify intellectually regardless of their social status..."

"The Health and Education Bill calls for a 75% cut in the former US defense budget and combining all the funds from the Department of Education, Welfare, and a few other obsolete Departments."

When asked how he would defend the F.U.S.A. with only 25% of the defense budget President Honeycutt explained,

"Although it appears we are cutting our defense budget by 75%, in reality, we have more than doubled the amount of money the former U.S. nuclear arsenal received to make sure we have big accurate bombs to issue out unrecoverable damage on any likely enemy. We are starting a program, which will make our troops nearly impregnable to bullets and other modern battlefield hazards making for a hardier and more menacing fighting force. Finally, I will officially induct 1.5 million inmates and convicts into military boot camps with the best drill sergeants and officers focusing on turning them into soldiers regardless of the crime. These will be our shock troops, as we will unleash them in mass on any enemies that threaten the F.U.S.A.; with the threat once released, we cannot control them, so rape and pillaging might occur. These inmates and convicts will be our first on the ground in any future altercations. This will save the Free United States billions of dollars since convict soldiers will be paid a nominal salary of $195 a month. Because the convict soldiers are being paid, they will also have to help work on the most dangerous construction projects and emergency rescue. I think the F.U.S.A. citizens will be getting the most out of their tax money."

On day six the images of President Mary Lee flooded the cybervision channels broadcasting live from somewhere in Europe demanding that all State and local officials take back total control of all counties and precincts in the United States.

Just Following Orders

Several State and local officials began to fly out of the country to organize in England and France to plan the re-subjugation of the American people.

The first resistance violence took place when a group of sheriffs and police tried to stop some formerly homeless people from building makeshift shelters on land designated as their own according to the broadcast via cybervision by President Honeycutt's administration and confirmed by a Congress of their idols. The sheriff and police claimed Ralph Honeycutt was not President of their State and fired upon the unarmed citizens, killing 12. This continued throughout the day with 846 mostly Black Americans killed. The next day 1,372 citizens were killed, including 127 White men and women who were exchanging fire with officers protecting their new land gained through purchases and trade of some 900 acres. Thirty-four sheriff and police were killed. The violence continued out of hand until April 29, after some radical group posted several thousands of Homeland Defense Militia officers home addresses on cybervision. This led to images of an 18-year police veteran being shown holding his three dead kids, who were shot and hung by home invaders.

On May 1, 2020, as the F.U.S.A. citizens lost their stomach for violence, hundreds of tanks and helicopters were moved into all the cities by the remnants of the former U.S. Federal and State Governments. President Ralph Honeycutt released a million men army with "That Hot Water" encased in balloons. The 'That Hot Water" was an extremely corrosive clear liquid that a human could stick his hand into and it would feel like hot water yet slightly uncomfortable to touch. When this same substance touched metal, it totally destroyed it.

F.U.S.A. civilians would just throw what appeared to be water balloons at the tanks and then wait 30 minutes or so. There were so many fumes and sparks, the tank crew usually evacuated before large holes appeared burned all the way through making the tanks look like Swiss cheese. Stories of people destroying M1s and later Challengers with only three That Hot Water balloons, baseball bats, and rocks became common. After destroying 70% of the tanks and a few helicopters with Chug Guns, the attacks stopped. Ralph Honeycutt was accepted as the legitimate President of the Free United States as well as his seated Dream Congress and new Supreme Court. The F.U.S.A. citizens had the right to impeach them all via cybervision vote of a 70% disapproval rating or more at any time. President Honeycutt's speech *"Why is a Tank in My Yard?"* defined the concept of an "Age of Reasoning" where violence initiated by governments against citizens would no longer be used as a means of negotiation. President Honeycutt's most powerful ally may be cybervision, as he has stayed above a 78% approval rating, giving the 22% who wanted to impeach him a long way to go.

Chapter 17

BIG FAT COINCIDENCE

Congo Jungle Africa March 12, 2020:

Preston had passed out from smoking the Blueberry Armpit. When he awoke, he was in a well-lit wonderland of Areocars and Areosports—some models of which he had never seen before. Workers seemed to be doing maintenance on the craft when Preston got closer and noticed they were installing the chug guns. At first, he felt good about his situation 'till he heard Tyrone's familiar voice say,

"Cover this asshole's eyes." They all looked around. It seemed no one had anything handy, and then Tonka giggled as she pulled off her panties.

"Here try this," she said. The other tall, beautiful girl beside her, Zessi Si, looked at her in disgust as Tyrone snatched the panties, and then nonchalantly arranged Tonka's skimpy G-string panties in such a way as to cover both of Preston's eyes. Everything went black for Preston— only an invigorating scent he would never forget. After about a 20 minute walk outside in the hot and humid African sun, the sounds of what seemed like a city of animals heard going about their daily busy lives could be heard. Preston heard sounds he had never heard—"Was it a monkey, lizard, or bird? He was thinking. They stop and he hears them shuffling through clothes as if they were placing on jackets and then he heard laughter. He heard a door open as ice- cold gust of air hit him like a typhoon after the humidity of the Congo jungle made him wet—he yelped and shivered as his captors laughed at his discomfort. Preston thinks to himself, *"These assholes put on coats before they went in."* A 10-minute walk inside a nice air-conditioned building followed when Preston heard the familiar sounds of overcrowded people excited as if they were on vacation. He felt it quite odd no one thought it strange for a man to have panties on his head but because he could not see, he felt it best to bid his time a little longer. After a couple of large doors slammed, it was all quiet. They walked up two flights of stairs and then Preston took what was the longest elevator ride he had ever experienced, straight down for about 10 minutes. They walk through some doors and then took an escalator up. They walked down a hall; Preston heard the familiar sound of a hotel key being inserted into a door and a green light giving the Okay. He was shoved into the room. When the panties were removed   from his eyes and he turned around his heart skipped a beat; he was face to face with Serwin Getty.

The room was like a very nice hotel suite with a 62- inch cybervision screen overlooking two king-size beds. A few stairs lead down to a living room area with a black leather sofa and love seat divided by a glass coffee table. Before Preston could say a word, the Cybervision turned on showing   the now   familiar   images   to   Preston   of   the Washington DC concert/presidential nominee announcement ceremony gone amuck. After a few minutes of the images of mayhem and savagery, Ralph Honeycutt appeared behind a finely polished cherry wood podium dressed in a dark blue suit with a red tie. In the background, there were two American flags. Getty, without saying a word, went and sat on the sofa, leaned back in a comfortable position and crossed his legs. Preston slaps his face with his hand and squeezes as if to control an explosion as Ralph's squeaky whiny voice begins.

"My fellow Americans and people everywhere who can freely receive this signal greetings. Our estimates are more than three billion people all around the world will have an opportunity to experience this moment. My words are being translated in real time with only a few seconds delay. My images are being shown across cybervision monitors from China   to   Liechtenstein,   Argentina   to   Singapore,   and everywhere in between. Less than 24 hours ago as I was

Big Fat Coincidence

announcing my candidacy for President of the United States in Washington DC, myself, as well as several other people were attacked by an organized syndicate of people calling themselves the U.S. Government, and Police, Sheriff, and official names of which we have never heard. Despite what is being perpetrated by the United States and other Nations' media, thousands of innocent people have been murdered by the use of strange and exotic weapons as well as excessive force…"

Preston could not believe it. This guy was right back at it again. Ralph Honeycutt was officially running a guerrilla Presidential campaign from outside the United States. He was going to use cybervision to get his message out. "First things first." Preston thought, as he slowly turned around to face Getty blocking out the cybervision broadcast from his mind. Getty being mixed race at this moment, for some reason, he seemed extremely African-American like, almost Black like Tyrone Honeycutt.

"How was your trip?" Getty started sarcastically.

"You are in cahoots with these IST Corp. bastards aren't you? You have gone too far this time buddy. I am going to make sure you are prosecuted for kidnapping, aggravated assault, and attempted murder to say the least! You will never see freedom again, I promise you!"

"Shut up asshole. I am in the same situation as you. I am a hostage for now… they caught me snooping around. Col. Brett authorized me to come after what happened in Washington yesterday. Lt. Martin is still above ground in the club and hotel area he…"

"Where in the hell are we?"

"At least 2,500 feet underground... It appears these guys took some abandoned uranium mines, reinforced them, turning them into a several million square foot underground labyrinth of bars, hotels, and brothels for the super-rich. They try to provide any experience for the right price. It's totally fascinating… look at this." Getty stood and walked toward the wall. He pointed at what appeared to be a huge abstract painting covering the entire wall. "It's a rare mold which emits a large amount of oxygen. There is also another mold under the carpet that doesn't need light also producing oxygen. The other colors in the artwork are microorganisms that produce nitrogen making this room self-sustaining as long as an animal exhaling carbon dioxide is present. Also, the water system is most fascinating." Getty walks over to a fountain-looking machine with two glass bulb tubes on top leading to a silver faucet. "You see the two glass jars here? One captures excess oxygen from the atmosphere while this other one here captures the hydrogen. It's all mixed here and wa la la…" Getty pulled the faucet handle releasing ice-cold sparkling water. He takes a drink. "It is so fresh and pure."

"How long have you been here admiring the beauty of this place? I could have sworn I've seen you in Washington with Lil Boe Boe and friends doing the booty dance," Preston said sarcastically. He trusted Getty as far as he could throw him with one finger.

"IST Corp. is not the only entity that has fast-moving vehicles. This is my job I suppose to be here. The question is what in hell are you doing here? Of all people I would have expected to see." At that moment, Preston understood that indeed greed was a mighty force. He thought aloud,

"Col. Brett knew these guys were up to something and he wanted to muscle in on their racket, probably take everything in the name of national defense. His fat ass was too much of a coward or too lazy to build his own case so he…"

"Cut you in on the deal to get him what he needed?"

"Yea something like that. How are we going to get out of here?"

Getty started to smile then a belly laugh came out. "Let's listen to this clown first then we will figure out something."

Big Fat Coincidence

Getty giggled pointing to the cybervision with Ralph preaching.

"I don't want to listen to that fool! I would rather listen to the song of death itself than have to listen to that idiot." Getty just looked at Preston with a very serious look on his face for a few seconds as he ranted, competing with the cybervision broadcast volume.

"Listen my friend, we need to know what these guys are thinking so we will know who we are dealing with," Getty interrupted.

"They are your friends! You have dealt with them before haven't you? You gave them this Areocar technology didn't you? What the hell is going on? I can see why Col. Brett doesn't trust you, he should just…"

"Just what? Kill me? Or worse, turn me over to the H.I.T. team? We are not in America my friend and even if we were, it still isn't anything our kids and grandkids are told it is. It's just one big Monopoly board game over there where you and your other 1% friends, all 287,739 of them, have been given immunity and allowed to make as much money as possible with as many human casualties as necessary. I am a human first my friend. I am neither one of you nor your flunky so screw you." Getty rolled his eyes, went back to the sofa, and took a comfortable position looking at the cybervision tentatively. Preston had no choice but to listen to Ralph as he walked around the large suite. He walked to the rather modest bathroom with a huge inviting clear bathtub appearing too thin and fragile to work. There was no need for a shower curtain as all the excess water evaporated and then recycled. Ralph Honeycutt's voice was heard over the cybervision.

"Sometimes we get caught up in the rat race of living our day to day lives and began to feel like struggling, pain, and suffering is the only way to live. We began to stop dreaming and only want to get drunk or high, maybe just have sex and go to sleep. We are fat, lazy, and wanting to die. No more do

Americans look at the stars and say I want to fly around up there. I want to walk around not just on Mars but also on Saturn, Jupiter, or just go to the wildest party city with a population of 20 million and growing floating out past Pluto's orbit. I recently visited a little resort hotel and casino called Shindinkis in Africa. When I went to take a shower, the bathtub was made of a clear material; I later discovered it was called Hydroite™. It has a chemical property to resist water molecules thus permanently and indefinitely creating a quarter inch or more of an invisible barrier of water resistance on a molecular level. This brings infinite possibility to sea exploration. I would like to exploit this technology to its fullest potential establishing the first permanent colony under the ocean within my first four years as President of the United States with a million square foot Hydroite dome in the middle of the Gulf of Mexico. The project will employ millions. Why not? We have the money. We now have the technology. It is time for us to have an agenda as a country besides war and the detriment of other humans.

I also have knowledge of a new propulsion system based on "Rail Gun" technology that will make it easier and cheaper to transport several tons of material via orbit than to ship overseas. With this most promising technology, teams of top scientists have constructed plans for a space city that could constantly be added to—like children's building blocks. A thousand years from now 7 billion people could be living in that space city alone, but we have to start it today. Some might say it is crazy for a Presidential candidate to think like me, but there are some who would run this country who   consider mass   executions   as   a   way   of   population control.

As President of the United States, I will make it my priority to ensure every American has a roof over his head, healthy   food,   proper   free   health   care,   education and   a cybervision in every home to further ensure proper education.   There no more police but instead "resolution officers" with masters and doctorate degrees in sociology and psychology who, along with, scientists and teachers, will benefit with double the salaries our current law enforcement officers and teachers at the State level receive. Their education will be paid for with federal funds, as would the housing program in which every American family will be provided a home. Federal land will be distributed by first a restitution process in which every American who is a descendant of a slave is given one and one-half acres of land.

Next, all poor Americans with at least two grandparents born in the United States will be given the one-time opportunity to purchase one and one-half acres of Federal land at the price of one ounce of gold. Subsidized housing will be provided to anyone who cannot afford to build a home. To make it simple, I will use an example... The White fifty-year mentally ill military veteran and strange-looking, scary Black man who has spent the majority of his life in prison for petty crimes. Both are living under a bridge, stinking and eating out of the garbage. They will now have a home to live in dignity as citizens of the United States. This should create a situation never before seen in American history where every citizen of the nation will have a home.

After Americans have homes, I will make a fully accessible national health-care system in which doctors are compensated just as they are now, as well as their nurses, that will transform our nation into a preventative care system where people are healthier and will live twice as long. The federal government will pay for this complete high standard medical system. Health and education will be connected with an advanced technology social network from all disciplines to encourage and reward innovation and ingenuity. Citizens will share ideas to reach common goals. This new education system paid for by the States will start from preschool continuing through to State Universities and postgraduate studies. I will double teacher salaries as well as the number of supplies needed for a top-grade education. Continued education will be available at home through interactive cybervision channels. Our goal is to make dumb people smart and smart people reach their full potential. In return, all students past the age of 13 years will be allowed up to five hours a day of nominal paying government-sponsored work programs for the construction of mammoth public works projects including an interstate Areocar guidance network and huge solar power grids, covering thousands of square miles to help power the nation. Even outer space and oceanic exploration will be on the table. All paid for by cutting the U.S. defense budget by 75%. The remaining 25 % of the defense budget will be used to sew up U.S. borders by hiring 100,000 veterans only to help keep them employed. Advanced weapons technologies and maintaining our current military arsenal at maximum working condition will consume the remaining funds. America will exist as a nation on absolute stand-down in which no U.S. soldier is involved in a conflict. It is amazing how much you can do if you are not trying to kill people. I will form a special waste committee of only nine people whose job will be to cut waste at all levels of government, shaving 10% off the cost of running the entire government. At the end of the day, instead of entertainers, athletes, and gangsters, American kids will strive to be civil and criminal resolution officers, teachers, doctors, and scientists—all these professions will be lucrative as well as productive…"

"Enough—even, you are killing me. I am looking for a way out of here." Preston interrupted as he started to look around.

"Why is it that you hate me?" Getty said as he turned down the volume on the cybervision. Preston ignored Getty as he walked into the bathroom and then proceeded to piss on the floor. "Hey fool, I ask you a simple question man to man." There was an unfriendly intensity in Getty's voice.

Big Fat Coincidence

"How about for one, you represent everything I do not stand for," Preston sarcastically yelled so Getty could hear him from the bathroom.

"Not that I care, but you don't know me well enough to know what I stand for—you are just a racist", Getty shouted as he turned the volume back up. Preston comes out of the bathroom.

"Okay... I will tell you why you are so deplorable if you turn that crap off." Preston pleaded.

"O.K.…. There." Getty turned off the cybervision.

"Well, I started hating you when you disrespected my son by flirting with his girlfriend, especially in front of my wife. Second, you act so like a stereotypical, mixed race person. It is so arrogant it is disgusting. Third…"

"You know White boy, you are the worst of the worst kind of racist! You feel because of my mixed blood that I am cursed, as are all my seeds.   I don't   need   your White world…" Getty was obviously upset.

"Hey, hey buddy, hold up—looks like I hit a little

sweet spot. Why am I always the racist when I mention your heritage? I mean, I never take offense when you try to alpha male me because you think you have some sort of physical prowess over me, because of your … blackness… I mean…" Preston was obviously getting to Getty. Getty jabbed back,

"I get the picture. You really do hate me. Wow, over a bitch. Now that's disgusting."

"What! You dare call my wife a bitch right in front of me?" Preston was fighting mad. He grabbed Getty by the collar—Getty threw his hands up.

"Hold up buddy. I was talking about the little freak intern your son was dating. She isn't worth the animosity. All you need is a nice body, some booze, and a little game and she's fresh meat. Hell, I think Lt. Martin even hit her. She was such low hanging fruit."

"She's my son's wife now... I cannot believe the way you talk about women. She is still someone's daughter. You are a disgusting man. All hell seems to be breaking loose, I don't know where the hell I am, and I can't afford injury now...That's the only reason I don't take you on right now." Preston was red. His heart was racing. Getty seemed to symbolize everything pissing him off right now. Getty backed up out of Preston's reach, smiled, and then started,

"Ah! My friend I have finally figured you out. Ha, ha, ha... You are weak behind women. You have spent your whole life trying to satisfy one woman ha, ha, ha..."Getty's laughter reminded Preston of Tyrone Honeycutt's laugh. He had had enough. Before he knew it, he had grabbed Getty.

"Now you listen here! I have had enough of your little games. I will kill you if you ever disrespect any of my family again. You hear me!" Preston was ready to fight to the death at this moment. Nothing else mattered.

"Woa, whoa, hold up. We have to work together or we both could end up dead," Getty yelled as he reached up to protect his throat from Preston's hands not yet at his throat but violently pulling his collar. Preston was ready to commit to the battle when out of the corner of his eye, a shiny platinum and gold ring on Getty's pinky caught his eye cause of some strange familiarity. His heart skipped a beat. He grabbed Getty's one hand with both his hands and saw two huge eyes of highly detailed gold owls cast on the same type of ring Tyrone and the fellow calling himself Hawk had on. He pushed Getty off him and just looked Getty in the eyes. Barely audible, he muttered, "When I saw you giving the finger to Ralph Honeycutt, for an instant... I thought you were a patriot—now I don't know what you are."

Getty was wide-eyed and totally taken off guard by Preston's attack, although, he had provoked it. After adjusting his clothes and gaining his composure, he stepped away from Preston a few steps—the smile was no longer on his face. Getty did not look angry or afraid, just surprised. He looked as though he was searching for something to say. He took a deep breath and spoke.

"I gave Ralph the finger so he would know they were going to try and take him out. You see, that finger was the way all of Law enforcement felt about him. I am not going to continue to toy with you Preston Ross. The only reason you are still alive is because of me. I actually like you. Please, do not use any more violence because it will only beget violence. I am going to show you something and then I will leave you to your own destiny." Getty walked over and picked up the cybervision controller.   He sat down and started typing in coded commands.   The huge 6 2 -inch monitor started flickering in a pattern. He started talking to Preston in an entirely different tone than he had ever used while he was entering the data.

"You know, Preston, in the X Department we can access any civilian cyber network and see through their monitors. We have come a long way since spying through computers and cell phone cameras and speakers. Why we can even bounce the signal off mirrors and use mirrors to see everything. I guess the lesson to learn here is to stay away from cybervision monitors, cyber-phones, and mirrors when you are doing dirt. Once you really pissed me off, so since all is fair in love and war, I looked into your home. What I saw was more then I wanted to. I am sure you will understand why I recorded it." Preston's head was spinning. He looked up at the cybervision projection and there was his living room appearing as a stage before him. It was dark. Getty began to enter some more data when the projection changed to Preston's bedroom. Preston felt his stomach in his throat when he saw his wife having vigorous sex with Willoford who was known for being well endowed. Getty threw the controller in Preston's direction. Preston grabbed it, rewound it and then broke down into tears. He zoomed in on Amanda's face in ecstasy from the pleasure she was receiving from Willoford. Getty, sensing the danger, pointed at the door saying, without looking back at Preston, "I am going to leave now. The door is open. You have been locked inside a room with open doors." Serwin Getty turned and walked out the door. Preston stayed in the room for two days. While locked in the open room, he found a manuscript, written by a Mach Brown called the *Theory of the Great Nothing*. He read it several times. There was also a bowl full of Blueberry Armpit. He smoked it all.

Chapter 18

BEHOLD A BLACK HORSE

July 1988:

On this hot humid summer day in July, the temperature was about 108°. They were in the South-Eastern part of Texas in the bayou where the deciduous trees mixed with pine trees. You could hear several species of birds communicating through songs competing with crickets and frogs. At one point, they all seemed to be in unison and then a locust would overpower them with its screams. Mach Brown was working for the Summer Job Training Services (S.J.T.S.), a program for poor youth in the State of Texas. He was working with Tyrone Honeycutt, Bear, Kerry Price, and his half-brother, Bubba Moody Jr. who was staying with Kerry for the summer to save money before Bubba moved to Alaska with his father. They were all a year under Mach except Bear, who was Mach's classmate. Tyrone planned on being the starting running back for Robert E. Lee High School. He was built like a tank at 5'6" and, although he was going to be sophomore, he was one of the strongest kids in the school and could bench press 305 lbs. Tyrone was very arrogant, but he was a proven record breaker, running the ball like Walter Payton with the same body type. His cousins Ralph and Jacob Honeycutt were a junior and a senior—both were bigger and stronger but not as quick.

They were all starters for the Silver Knights of Robert E. Lee High School football team, as were many Honeycutt before. They were working together; their job was landscaping Tawada Independent School District properties from the elementary all the way to the high school—a total of five campuses and two stadiums. They were paid for their hard labor at $3.25 an hour. Years later, Mach would write how the work program only prepared poor kids for a life of hard work for minimal pay because even by the year 2020, the minimum wage was still $3.25 an hour.

The boys would mostly hide in the shade and figure out ways to get out of work. All of a sudden, everyone started to work feverishly. Coach Hank Timmons was driving up. He was the head football coach and athletic director for the Thawada Independent School district. He looked like the typical blood and guts football coach and redneck. He was about 6'3", barrel chest with a hard keg of a stomach, looking exactly like a bulldog in the face. He had been the coach for 30- something odd years. You could always see him at all the big town events. He was treated like top royalty.

He walked up and just stared at his eager audience.

" Do y'all know what the word for the Silver

Knights state run this year is?" Hank Timmons hollered. "It's Intensity!" Hank continued, "You boys need to put intensity into everything you do—the way you work out here today is the way that you're going to work on the field Friday night."

"Augh, coach Timmons, what time is the physical this year?" Mach asked.

"Son, I had the Secretary send out letters last week, and I don't remember your name on any of them," Timmons said with a grave, sad face. Since Coach Timmons was there, the other workers had started to gather including the girls who worked inside the school. Everyone heard coach Timmons tell Mach he was not going to get to play football.

From that day, Mach was in servitude to Coach Timmons so he would actually do what his supervisors asked of him. He worked harder than the other boys. His newfound sense of goodness brought animosity from the other working crew that consisted of all Black seniors with the ringleader being Prometheus Green, next year's starting quarterback. Mach and his crew felt Prometheus and his crew was jealous of their athletic abilities and looked at them as a threat for some of next year's starting positions on the Silver Knights football and basketball teams. Prometheus claimed Mach was a sellout now for working hard and trying to make his crew look bad. Mach was always, "Yes Sir" and "No Mam" to adults even when Coach Timmons was not around—worst of all he was really friends with poor White trash Kerry Price and his half-brother, Big Bubba Jr.. They hung out after school and played video games at each other's apartments in the projects.

One day, Coach Timmons personally came out to lead both crews in the cleaning of the Knights' football Stadium. It was kind of a cool day for the summer, so it felt like football weather. More than once the Coach stopped all the mowing and weed eating to line the boys up and show them some new plays he had in mind for the season. Coach Timmons had a way of turning every task into a competition to pit the boys against each other as he could see where they had divided themselves by class; underclassmen vs. seniors. It was Coach Timmons' tendency to have big Bubba Moody Jr. run the quarterback position while the other for sure starters, such as Tyrone at tailback and big Stanly Turds at the right pulling guard position, that first upset Prometheus. When Prometheus was seen playing safety position trying to defend passes from Bubba Moody Jr., the rumors started around town that "Thwada's Silver Knights had a big White boy standing in the pocket slanging bombs!" Prometheus overheard more than once,

"The only way the Silver Knights can win State is if they move Prometheus to Defense." Comments from Coach Timmons appeared in the papers and interviews stating,

"A quarterback needs to remember his plays," "I always liked a tall quarterback," and finally the worst, "I might need to change my running offense to throw more with a strongarmed, accurate QB." made Prometheus feel funny sometimes. Prometheus, although considered a stud, was not the starting quarterback Coach Timmons was describing.

He stood a solid 5'10" and 170 lbs. in comparison to 15year-old Bubba Moody Jr. standing about 6'4" and 235 lbs. Prometheus was extremely muscular, dark-skinned, and came from a very poor family living in the projects. He had a rough life and he had the scars to prove it. This may have given him a kind of inferiority complex. He always tried to dress in designer clothes even if it was borrowed from one his friends. Football and track were all that mattered to Prometheus. If he got a scholarship, his greatest obstacle would be passing the exams. He was well aware of his future depended on him playing professional football so he could not afford to get into too much trouble. He always used a fall guy who was usually Stanley Turds, the starting nose tackle and offensive guard, and one of the strongest kids in the school. Bear called big Stanley Turds the "Water Buffalo" and "Da Big Ox." Mach called Prometheus the "Hyena."

Prometheus was forever the prankster always trying to get the other crew in trouble, even fired. With Bubba and Kerry, he was overly aggressive with pseudo-violent attacks such as setting dangerous booby-traps and sending big Stanley Turds, who weight 294lbs. to bully Kerry Price who weighed in at 145 lbs. and seemed to be afraid of Stanley. The rules of the "cold war" Kerry and Bubba found them self-drawn into were simple, only body punches could be thrown when you caught the enemy and no weapons. This led to Kerry, Big Bubba Jr., and even the mighty Bear receiving severe beatings from Prometheus's crew, which also included big Steve Lilly and Jacob Honeycutt. Every time Prometheus's crew scored a victory, his horrid laughter was heard for hours. Mach joked after they got Big Bubba Jr. good one day, "I heard Prometheus laughing three miles away!" It was only blood ties between Tyrone and Jacob Honeycutt, which kept it only a pseudo-gang war. It was the craziest situation since Mach was

Behold a Black Horse

trying to protect Kerry and Bubba to look like a good student for Coach Timmons while Prometheus was trying to kill them, but Coach Timmons thought it was the other way around. A basketball game decided the whole matter.

It happened in a flash; again, both crews were working together around an outside basketball court. With Coach Timmons looking on, the girls' varsity and junior varsity volleyball teams started to practice next to them. So, as could be expected, the game got really intense with Bubba Moody Jr. Stealing the show as he proved unstoppable, dominating Prometheus who was trying to cover him. Big Bubba Jr. blocked three of Prometheus's shots and even slammed on him. To add injury to insult, Kerry Price hit several jump shots and got some steals on Big Steve who was actually good at basketball. To win the game, in a come from behind victory, Kerry winked at Cynthia Honeycutt, who was a freshman volleyball player and the apple of Prometheus's eye, prompting Prometheus to D-him-up very tight on game point. Kerry Price faked the three, which he had hit a few times in the game then drove in for the lay-up letting out a wicked aggressive battle cry that got everyone's attention as he went up strong with both hands. The ball started to bounce around the rim as Kerry blows a kiss to Cynthia who, despite being dark brown, obviously blushed, or at least started smiling back. Then the ball dropped in the hole causing Cynthia to start clapping and cheering for Kerry. At that exact moment, loud laughter was heard as the basketball went through the hoop landing on top of Prometheus's head causing him to explode. He was all over Kerry and not throwing body blows. Kerry took a few punches to the face, fell back a little, puts up his guard, and then charged back with a bloody nose. He was a whirlwind of punches catching Prometheus in the eye with a right overhand, then with a left hook that split Prometheus's lip. He also managed to slip two of Prometheus's punches only to catch one hard hook to the jaw knocking him back.

Prometheus backed back and ripped off his shirt. He had a Bruce Lee build with sweat and muscles rippled everywhere.

"You think you bad, White Trash ass White Boy?" Prometheus's growled as he started to bob and weave with both his arms up high like a praying mantis.

"Yea, ol' bitch ass coward, you's a ho to me!" Kerry growled back as he got in what appeared to be a Philly Shell style with one arm high and the other below his chin tucked to his chest also bobbing and weaving. It appeared he knew how to fight as well. By this time, Stanley Turds and Steve Lilly started to try restraining Prometheus as Mach and Bubba Jr. got in front of Kerry. Coach Timmons saw what was going on and started shouting,

"Hey! Hey! Hey! Y'all break that up!" Kerry pulled his shirt off showing a few muscles, wiped the blood and sweat off his face prompting a whistle from a few of the girls beside them on the next court including Cynthia Honeycutt Jacobs and Ralph's little sister. Prometheus went crazy running around Stanley Turds and again tried to sucker punch Kerry who managed to block most of the powerful haymakers. In return, Kerry threw two punches, one a jab setting up a nice hook. A loud sound like a mule kick was heard as Prometheus head snapped back and he fell to one knee. "Ooohs!" and "Ahhhs!" are heard as Big Bubba Jr. started shouting, "Let em go! Let em go!" It's about this time Coach Timmons saw they are at it again and started yelling,

"Hey! Hey! Hey! Y'all break that up!" Prometheus lunged forward, grabbed Kerry around the waist, and he then started to pick Kerry up while running forward, catching Kerry off-balance. The entire time Kerry was swinging punches, hitting Prometheus in the temple and ear causing some swelling around his eye. As they fell to the ground, a loud cracking sound was heard. Kerry's head hit the asphalt causing blood to cover Kerry's hair and stream down his back. Kerry covered himself for a second then started punching up at

Behold a Black Horse

Prometheus who was on top of him punching down. The girls started to scream at the sight of the blood then Bubby Moody Jr. ran over and kicked Prometheus off Kerry. Kerry started to kick at Prometheus as he flew off him landing the heel of his shoe right between Prometheus' eyes giving him two black eyes. Coach Timmons, Steve Lilly, and Bear ran over to see if Kerry was o.k. and to separate the two of them while Prometheus staggered away. Kerry was holding his shirt to his head telling Coach Timmons he was all right when another loud cracking sound was heard. Prometheus had picked up a brick and hit Bubba Moody Jr. in the back of the head. Blood went everywhere as Prometheus swung again and again, hitting Bubba Jr. in the back and shoulder. Big Bubba Jr. caught the brick on the third blow, kneed Prometheus in his stomach, and then proceeded to wrestle with Prometheus for control of the brick. Tyrone Honeycutt ran and pushed Prometheus causing him to drop the brick. Prometheus stumbled back and then punched Tyrone in the face. They started to fight with probably even more ferocity than the Prometheus Green vs. Kerry Price altercation. Bear and Stanley Turds immediately start "squabbling" as if on cue like two grizzly bears throwing blows, only they could survive. "Squabbing" meaning an intense and skilled mutual combat often found in the ghetto. Big Steve Lilly started to stomp on Bubba Moody Jr. who had passed out by now from loss of blood.

Mach Brown had the most delightful smile on his face as if he had orchestrated it all from as far back as a few weeks ago. The only problem was getting Jacob and Tyron Honeycutt to go along with first "cold war" and then the "pseudo-war"—it was most Machiavellian, to say the least. *"I didn't even have to get my hands dirty or break any allegiance,"* Mach Brown thought as he worked his way through the chaos towards Coach Timmons to "save" him. He did just that, first, pushing him out the way of being punched in the face by Bear. Then he kept him from being knocked down by the whirlwind of fist and feet—Tyrone Honeycutt vs. Prometheus Green fight. Mach started to laugh out loud when he looked back and saw Kerry Price jump on big Steve Lilly's back and then proceeded to choke him 'till he passed out, landing on top of the passed out Bubba Moody Jr. whom he had been stumping a few seconds earlier.

In the end, it did not work out as Mach had foreseen. Bubba Moody Jr.'s father went crazy. He was from the East Coast and straight-up prejudice so he pressed charges on Prometheus Green who ended up being charged as an adult and then sentenced to 60 years in the Texas Department of Justice by a Judge Murphy after a jury found him guilty.

Because it was a violent crime with the use of a weapon, Prometheus would have to do nearly 85% of his time before he would be eligible for parole. Kerry Price wrote Prometheus apologizing, explaining his dead redneck father would have never made his mother do anything like that— maybe shot at Prometheus or busted his head with a bat— but never would he have pressed charges on a kid as an adult. Kerry sent him many pictures of girls even some of Cynthia Honeycutt. A couple years later, he even sent Prometheus a picture of his first goddaughter, Gloria Price, whose mother was Cynthia Honeycutt. Big Bubba Jr. moved to Alaska, never coming back to Thwada. Mach was the only other person who received punishment—expulsion from school, even though school had not started yet. He was not allowed to continue to work for the work program and Coach Timmons, who was probably upset for losing his tall White boy with the strong arm, systematically turned all of the other kids against Mach.

At least eight of his starters were working for this (S.J.T.S.) summer program and team building was important. Coach Timmons first made the two crews into just one big workforce making it clear Mach Brown was the enemy and would not be in a Silver Knight uniform opening the door for the other boy's constant harassment of him. They said Mach worked like a slave and kissed ass so they made extra efforts to give him the blues as if they were a pack of hyena, especially when Coach Timmons was around. All these guys were world-class athletes and thus would have had a vicious bite in a fight. Like hyena, they ran in a pack looking for scraps and taking from the weaker kids on the work program who were not on the football team. Mach was too big of game and too dangerous for the hyena to bring down, thus they just harassed him while keeping out of reach and giggling the whole time.

About a week later, the crew was working at the varsity football stadium that set high on top a hill. Coach Timmons drove up.

"If y'all run up this hill 40 times, five days a week, you'll be in about 90% Silver Knight readiness next week when two-a-days start. I won't Y'all there at 5:23 a.m. sharp," Timmons hollered like a drill sergeant.

"Coach, I haven't received a letter yet," Mach said. Coach Timmons just stared at him like, "Why did you even talk to me?—after a few seconds the other boys started to laugh. In their eyes, they all have favor with coach Timmons. Finally, Coach Timmons said,

"You're not a Silver Knight! You do not have what it takes. If you want to play, you have to go through initiation."

"And what's that Coach?"

"You have to run 40 miles in two weeks in order to be a Silver Knight."

The varsity and junior varsity football teams started to practice one week before the freshman team. Mach had to run his 5 miles a day before the other freshman started to practice, so, when two-a-days started for the freshman, Mach was the only freshman to practice run three miles in the morning and then run two more miles in the evening at the second practice. The Silver Knights' practices were big in a small town, so there were many townsfolk that came out to watch, sometimes as many as a hundred. Some would glance to see some strange kid running around the track after practice. They wondered what he had done so bad to have to be punished so greatly. Everyone knew that Coach Hank Timmons was the most merciful Coach and a devout Christian. This kid had to be extremely bad, probably even evil to be on Coach Timmons bad side, most onlookers conceived.

Finally, the day had come when Mach had completed running all of his miles. This day the practice was tougher than usual; all the players had to run 20 extra 50-yard wind sprints,

"Cause Brown finished his Knights run!" one of the racist assistant coaches yelled. Another coach said he saw Mach cheating while running his Knights' miles, so he would have to rerun 3 miles after practice plus the two miles to finish. Yet another coach said Mach left some gym shorts on the floor so he had to run 20 Knight Hills in which a player had to run up a large hill and back down 20 times. Between the practice and 110° heat, Mach was feeling a little dizzy. Everyone seemed to be in a hurried and excited frenzy. He heard the other students talking about picking up their class schedules in the cafeteria. It seemed strange to him that even the education part of Thawada High was not liking him too much either, as he did not receive a letter informing him when and where to pick up his schedule. After a hurried shower, he rushed to the cafeteria. The school was newly built, and it was on three different levels. Everywhere were the school colors, blue and grey.

Mach staggered into the cafeteria. There were three lines formed according to the last name. Built like an opera house or concert hall, teen excitement filled the cafeteria. There was an upper deck, which the cool kids and the seniors along with all of the athletes and the prettiest of the students sat. The lower deck area was where the regular students sat. They had to look up at the cool ones.   At the other end of the cafeteria was another raised section. This was for the teachers only. There were also seats along the outskirts of the cafeteria. These tables were neutral and were actually the best seats in the house since they were against the large, tinted window. Here, mostly couples sat or people trying to get away from their regular crowd. No matter where you sat, everyone could see you since it was all inside one large room. All the students were gathered. Some had not seen each other since the end of school last year. Mach staggered in just in time to get his schedule.

"My name is Mach Brown, and I would like to pick up my schedule," Mach said to the woman at the long table in the A-G section.

"Unfortunately, Mr. Brown, we cannot give you your schedule today because you have not taken your DPT booster shot in the last 10 years," The plump   freckled woman said with a southern twang.

"I have all my shots and I am not an animal. I do not have any diseases. Let me have my schedule please," Mach said with a little bass in his voice.

"It's pronounced an animal… and you will not be registering today." was her response as she placed his schedule to the side and proceeded to call the next students name. The other kids were having a great time comparing schedules to see who was in whose class—an important thing to know when you are a new student, especially a freshman. From the heat and the exertion of practice, Mach was very lightheaded. Everything seemed surreal—people were talking in slow motion. He actually did not even recognize people who he knew.

"Just give me the damn schedule!" Mach demanded.

"You can just go to the office then!" the Lady replied.

This brought laughter from all of the athletes.

"I guess she told you."

"Ha ha ha!"

"He he he!" Peers laughed in the background.

"You are not going to get to go and play football or go to school," a familiar voice joked in more of a sigh of relief as now he would get to be the "star."

"I will just go to the office and talk to the principal myself!"

Because of all the confusion before school had even started, Mach felt they were picking on him. He was used to this. He walked into the principal's office, and he thought,

"They will have to give me my schedule..." First, he demanded to speak to the principal.

"The principal is not in. You need to speak to the vice principal, Mr. Taylor," an older, motherly looking, White woman that no one could be mean to, said calmly. Mach took a deep breath and did not say thank you to be rude to Miss Watson.

"Send Mr. Brown in!" a voice behind a door with the letters Vice Principal on it boomed, making everything seem even more surreal because the vice principal acted as if he knew Mach was coming. Mach never skipped school or did drugs; he had been expelled several times but in junior high. This was high school and different. Mr. Taylor escorted

Mach to his office before Mach said a word Mr. Taylor said,

"I've seen you raise your voice at my teacher. I know who you are, and we are not going to put up with your antics at this school!" Mach stood up and said,

"I don't have to take this shit! I'll go to school somewhere else!" With that, he started to walk out of the office. Mr. Taylor stood up and grabbed Mach by the shoulder to turn him around saying,

"I'm talking to..." Then BOOM! With a loud explosion, Mach pushed Mr. Taylor in the chest with such force that Mr. Taylor flew about 10 feet over his desk and onto the floor with his chair on top of him. Mach continued to walk out in a total rage, not only at the fact that they would not give him his schedule, but they had pushed a 15year-old kid nearly to the point of having a near heatstroke.

Mr. Taylor staggered out of his office.

"Call the police! Call the police!" Mach just stood in front of the school cursing it and telling his classmates what had just happened.

"You're crazier than hell!" said Ralph, who had known Mach since second grade. Ralph was like Mach but he was quicker, but not as powerful. He had the heart of a lion and would later play in the IBA.

"You should run!" was heard by a few friends. "You just messed up your whole career," said Hammonton Wilson who was the biggest and strongest of all, but he was not as agile. He was big and very dark skinned, nicknamed Bear. He hated his birth name and took offense if called it by the wrong person the wrong way. Ralph, Tyrone, and Bear were some of the best athletes in the state—with Mach at their side, they would've certainly won the State Championship in football as well as other sports, but now this had all changed. Sirens were heard in the background getting louder as they got closer. Mach looked at them and said,

"They planned this, don't you forget it." The police came and took Mach away.

It was not 'till several years later, Mach was seen again. With Mach gone, Ralph took a natural lead of the classmates consisting of Hawk, Bear, Vasquez "Eagle" Williams, Harold, and Serwin.

Chapter 19

THEORY OF THE GREAT NOTHING

May 2005
Los Angeles:

Mach Brown sat on his couch watching television. He had the same feeling he had the morning of September 9, 2001, when an earthquake struck downtown Los Angeles and then again on the morning of September 11, 2001. Mach needed only one more piece to put together the device he felt would save the world. Adrian Marshall was giving his last newscast after more than 35 years with the CBC network. The broadcast was showing images of him reporting from the 1960s to the present. Adrian seemed to Mach to be one of the best newscasters, but he had said something about President Lee that someone did not agree with so he was forced to retire. His integrity of reporting was even brought into question. Mach felt most of the reporting on TV newscast was hearsay; only partially true or   at least had some sort of distorted view based on the person in charge's philosophies or agendas. He did not feel Adrian Marshall had done anything particularly wrong. He and President Lee were from the same State so maybe there was something beneath the surface common folk could not understand.

Adrian stared into the camera as images of the stories Americans would always remember from the last 35 years ran across the screen. Then Adrian mentioned the story of the Firefighters   Company, Ladder 6. They were the firefighters who went into the tower after the plane hit. They were saving an old woman who grew tired and had to stop to rest.   A few minutes later, the entire building collapsed killing and destroying everything around them. There was no damage where the firefighters and the old woman were standing so they were spared, not even a scratch.

Theory of the Great Nothing

Mach was touched by the story as he had a strong belief in God, although he would not consider himself a religious man with regard to attending church or being part of a denomination. He had read the Holy Bible several times from beginning to end and had read the Holy Quran to cross-reference his religious knowledge. Before he would open a holy book, he would always pray for God to guide him in his search for knowledge. He was extremely sincere in his preliminary reading rituals, starting with prayer and then a trance-like state lasting several hours. He would later explain the importance of the meditative state in his *Theory of the Great Nothing*. He would explain how humans and all living things have wave frequencies along the same concept as radio, micro, and light but much more complex. He termed these waves soulwaves. He believed these soulwaves are the captured thoughts experienced by humans and other life forms containing everything experienced during the waking hours of a person's life. Every sight, sound, feeling, good act and bad act, are being transmitted trillions upon trillions of light years away to another galaxy or even dimension, in an instant, mostly during sleep. This is possible because thought particles, which the soulwave are made of, make up quarks and antimatter subatomic particles. Soulwaves can travel faster than the speed of light and even through black holes or to other dimensions. He later wrote, *"These soulwaves are uploaded when humans sleep by God's angels, who number in the zillions and needed something to do with their eternal time."*

Mach's Quran opened by the hand of God, to Surah 4 verse 75 -78; he read to himself the English texts beside the Arabic.

"75. And what is the matter with you that you fight not in the cause of Allah and for the oppressed among men, women, and children who say, "Our Lord, take us out of the city of oppressive people and appoint for us from yourself a protector and appoint for us from yourself, a helper."

76. Those who believe fight in the cause of Allah and those who disbelieve fight in the cause of Taghut, so fight against the allies of Satan. Indeed, the plot of Satan has ever been weak." Mach looked in the footnotes to see what the meaning of Taghut was. The footnotes said Taghut meant "false objects of worship or those transgressors who usurp the divine right of government." Mach had seen people steal and cheat to win elections in the United States in both small, local elections to big, national Presidential races. He went on to read verse number 77.

"77. Have you not seen those who were told, "Restrain your hands from fighting and establish prayer." But then, when fighting was ordained for them, at once a party of them feared men as they fear Allah or with even greater fear. They said, 'Our Lord, why have you decreed upon us fighting? If only you had postponed it for us for a short time.' Say, 'the enjoyment of this world is little, and the hereafter is better for he who fears Allah. And injustice will not be done to you, even as much as a thread inside a date seed.' Mach re-read the line aloud. 'And injustice will not be done to you, even as much as a thread inside a date seed." Mach went on to read verse 78.

78. "Wherever you may be, death will overtake you, even if you should be within towers of lofty construction.

But if good comes to them, they say, 'this is from Allah'; and if evil befalls them, they say, 'this is from you.'" Say, 'all things are from Allah.' So what is the matter with those people that they can hardly understand any statement?"

Mach now knew, without a doubt, God destroyed the Towers. God had spoken. He picked up the phone and called his mother. Mach started to spit venom after a few formal greeting to his mom.

"I had foreseen so much evil with the one who stole the election, it tested my faith. I foresaw all the death and destruction overseas, the endless wars. I foresaw the fall of the American economy. If most could have seen what was about to happen, they would of …."

"Don't be talking like that. It upsets me when you get all angry and start talking crazy," Mach's mother interrupted with a soothing voice. She was also old enough to know that you have to be careful what you say over the telephone.

Mach continued,

"By not killing any of them, I figured it would punish the world and teach people a lesson. If I had done it, 911 would have never happened… Not only would 911 not have happened but also all the US troops would not have died nor all the tens of thousands of Iranian and Pakistani women and children. The stock market would not have crashed and there would have never been an African-American President", Mach exploded into his rants to his mother. Of all things Mach had said, his mother agreed with him only about the African American President part as a problem. She had an inherent hatred of Black men somewhat similar to the inherent prejudice acknowledged by White male Judges and prosecutors in the United States' justice system in both State and Federal courts towards Black males.

"Jesus, Jesus. Then they would have had to kill you", Mach's mom mumbled into the phone.

"No! Even though I foresaw this in 1998, the whole 2000 voter scam thing, the wars, and the collapsed economy; it is because thou shall not kill! and no man is above the law. It was impossible for me to kill a human because God's work would not have been done. Now, I am a Word of God. Anyway, the Towers were such a bad place, so bad they still haven't built anything there, because it was toxic. This was a place of injustice. The Towers were where the value of poor countries' money was kept at very low exchange rates reducing those countries to slave labor for the modern, rich countries. The Towers created the third world and was a sanctuary of evil..." Mach continued with his rants as his mother, unknowing to him thousands of miles away, placed the receiver of the phone on her shoulder as not to hear of the blasphemy coming from the mouth of her poor, crazed son. Mach went on for about 10 minutes on all kinds of different subject matters.

Mach survived off his intelligence. By profession, he was a salesman—he could sell anything, even an igloo in Hell. Once Ralph Honeycutt questioned him on this mumbling,

"Selling an igloo in Hell wouldn't be too hard to do considering it is hot as hell in Hell—haa ha he he hee!"

"Yes indeed. Hell is surly hot, but it is to the Devil whom you have to sell the igloo and here is where only a master can succeed," Mach countered. Ralph found wisdom in this and appreciated it, but still continued to attempt to make a mockery out of all of Mach's ideals, yet offered him a well-paying position at   IST Corp. to make Mach's life easier as well his brother Jacob and cousin Tyrone. Mach cordially, but sometimes angrily refused saying,

"My path is from God and not from any men or their money." Tyrone cordially gave Mach a,

"Fuck you then," and decided to go along with his cousins on any decisions, thus making IST Corp. completely sovereign, as Tyrone would put it, casting three votes on everything.

Jacob Honeycutt openly acknowledged Mach Brown convinced him to break down and accept the smallest share of only 20 % as a sacrifice to get Industrial Standard Trading Corp. started when after many years he was on absolutely no speaking terms with his brother Ralph. Tyrone and he were just two broke niggas living in Chicago, while Ralph was a retired IBA player who had swindled away about half of his professional salary with an upside down mortgage living in New York. All they had was some rings Mach gave them with

Theory of the Great Nothing

a Lion, a Snake, and a Falcon molded in gold. The Snake would always point out Mach Brown brought up the idea of getting big Bubba Moody Jr. to get his own clothing line brand going as far as drawing the infamous Bubba Wear logo.

It was sometime around April 2005, after studying all modern scientific theories, Mach had a feeling there was something missing. Flying home from a company meeting he had to attend in Chicago, he realized this nothingness, which scientists called the atmosphere and outer space, was a lot greater than anything man could have ever imagined. If it could lift thousands of tons into the air, then what appeared to be "thin air" was indeed, something! With this, Mach came up with the "Theory of the Great Nothing.", He wrote:

"I am a light walker, The Prince of Dawn. I have all the knowledge of the universe, but because it is so complex, I do not understand everything. I discovered today that time is a circle. I realized about three years ago I should do what I could for the good of other humans or be guilty of aiding the bad guys by failing to act. In the 34 years of my life on Earth, I have come to hate humans. Most people on the planet Earth are foul with a filthy soul and thus cannot travel.

My first memory was when I was lying in a bed beside my mother; we were at my grandmother's house in a small town. I remember tall, black shadows dancing across the walls. The shadows were long and skinny with very large heads and long arms stretching from the ceiling to the floor. I cannot recall how many there were, because they were dancing in a circle around the room. I say they were shadows, because I could not see any facial features and I noticed no clothing. At first, I figured they might be shadows of tree branches from the large oak tree outside the window caused by passing car lights. I do remember there not being car lights at times, and the shadows would still be there dancing. I specifically remember thinking to myself 'it's not the car lights.' I remember this so vividly because this was my first time experiencing the emotion of fear. I remember during this time of my greatest fear, small flashes of illuminated objects shaped like everything in the world, but very small, filled the room. I reached up, grabbed the objects of light, and closed my hand upon some of it. When I opened my hand, something like a light blue force field surrounded first my hand and then my arm and then my entire body. It seems like I could see all the veins, muscles, and bones through my skin because they were lit up, but I could not make out any definite organ. Once I touched The Spirit, as I came to call the phenomenon, it would change from those small random specks of light of everything to larger illuminated objects that formed patterns. The Spirit did not have any feeling or sensation when touched. It was neither hot nor cold and there was no smell, but there were sounds. My mother said she moved away from her mother's house when I was 14- months-old. Therefore, I first experienced the Spirit at 14 months, and I remember. This was my first known memory to me on Earth.

My second memory was me running towards some monkey bars in Brakenwoods Projects when I stopped and thought to myself, "I have come into reality," because from that day forward, I remember everything I have ever done, but most importantly from that moment forward, I have had total control of myself and absolute perception of my material environment. I was about 2 ½-years-old and was at a birthday party for someone else whose name I cannot be exact, but I am sure they were turning four-years-old. The feeling I most remember from that day was jealousy because it was someone else's birthday party and he was being treated like a king. I had never had a birthday party and never have 'till this day and, at that time, I knew I would never have a birthday party. It was also upsetting to me that he was considered older than I was for some reason. It was not until

Theory of the Great Nothing

my recent years, starting around 1993, that I first started to gain perception of my environment that was not so material.

Later in life, I often wondered if other people were also as conscious as I was or were they like animals with no souls. Although I came to accept the fact all human beings have a soul, most human beings cannot accept this fact, causing much of the strife in the world today. It was the belief that animals and other living creatures did not have souls. This made it easier for me to have the belief there could be humans who were not worthy of having a soul. In order for the universe to exist, it had to be based on some form of order and justice. For there to be total order in the universe, then every living thing, including animals as well as plants, would have to have souls. It has to be obvious to any man who has ever stood by a giant tree that it has as much if not more life force then he does. The tree was there before him and will be here after him, living.

This theory can change the world forever. First of all, I have discovered the Great Nothing, which is all the space that contains what appears to be nothing and called "air" "thin air" and "space" and exist throughout the entire universe, not just on Earth, as an atmosphere. Thus, I claim "outer space" is not a vacuum devoid of all matter and antimatter. Its density ranges from the denser elements, like uranium, but invisible to the naked eye and not yet discovered by Earth's humans, to those a lot less lighter than hydrogen also not yet discovered. I feel discoveries in science of our physical universe as of 2005, are only a small fraction of the reality of what the universe really is. Most of the knowledge is based on misinformation inspired by politics and greed; therefore, everything evolving from these sciences is inefficient, and most of the time only one of many different methods in which innovation could have been achieved. An example would be the inefficient, highly pollutant automobile. Surely, no logical person could consider it the best invention for transportation.

The Great Nothing is filled with atoms and particles. These particles assert charges that can be used to benefit humans in very powerful ways. Inside this Great Nothing, are entire universes which some call dimensions. They are not in a different dimension, as to say, but so small or large, they have different concepts of space, and time. They have different concepts of reality, differentiating what is alive or inanimate. The significance of The Human civilization on Earth is equivalent to the importance of a bacterium inside one human on a desolate island. This bacterium in the one human could have occurred any time in the past 10,000 years. That one person's bacterial infection would be considered quite small in the whole scheme of the world, as we know it. Earth could just be a small ball inside a laboratory being studied. It is a fact if only one ounce of matter could undergo 100% particle nuclear fusion it could power the entire United States for one year. With this amount of power stored inside the atom, very large and spectacular civilizations are capable of thriving in the universe.

Separate from my first Theory of the Great Nothing, there is a second theory;—'The Theory of Manipulation of the Great Nothing.' I will discuss the second theory after the first theory is explained more intricately. Let us explore this Great Nothing more deeply.

One must be amazed when a big military aircraft take off from the ground loaded with tons of equipment, tanks, and heavy artillery pieces on board. Better yet, what is even more fascinating is when a bumblebee, whose wings are scientifically too small to support his body in-flight, floats through the air at 30 to 40 mph. To explain this, one must look inside the atom and the magnetic charge. The bumblebee secretes chemicals which cause his body to glide through the air using manipulation of the magnetic force, and the particles contained inside the air, or "The Great Nothing," the bumblebee's wings are only used as routers to guide it through

Theory of the Great Nothing

the air using various magnetic propulsion techniques against the resistance of the air. This is a much more complex manipulation of the Great Nothing than what humans do with their airplanes, which simply has a rounded wing with a straight bottom so the air moves faster under the bottom of the wing than the top, causing the plane to ride on top of the air if thrust is applied. As stated earlier, this Great Nothing is not the same density or makeup throughout the entire universe, so there would need to be different principles of manipulation required to perform the same functions in different parts of the universe. A good example would be if one tried to fly an airplane on a planet that had no atmosphere such as the Earth does, much less dense. Principles that we use now for flight would not work since there would not be enough of this Great Nothing volume to create lift. However, other ways of manipulating the Great Nothing where flight would be achievable exist; such as a method similar to the bumblebee or various other methods made possible by exploiting every benefit of high science. With this, I need to say it would be easier for man to travel at the speed of light than to create an environment totally void of The Great Nothing since man does not know all the ways of manipulating the Great Nothing. This is why a particle accelerator requires more and more energy to accelerate a particle. Matter in the man-made vacuum not yet known to humans slows down, reflects, distorts, and even changes the particles being accelerated."

Mach goes on for several pages with some deep scientific details and accusations capable of changing those who read it concept of reality. I the Mighty Ant was so compelled by the enlightenment; I promised myself I will put the truths down in writing for the rest of the world to know.

Nov. 2010
Los Angeles, California:
Mach Brown sat in front of his computer and wrote:

"I have been using the principles from Theory of The Great Nothing, of which I have explained, to communicate with other entities, beings, and myself whose physical location exists millions of years in the future and millions of years in the past. You would have to travel trillions of light years in distance to reach the locations I have traveled. Therefore, with this simple principle manifested, I declare that all human beings are free from the slavery and oppression of the entities, which you call Governments and corporations. We have decided they are the ultimate oppression of all beings of Earth, including humans. At first, I must admit we had decided not to interfere with the workings of Earth since we have observed that the worst punishments inflicted upon humans were brought upon themselves. Now exists a time we have come to believe that there are humans whose will is to be free of the oppression and the slavery of the five demons, but they are being forced into servitude. Therefore, we will act.

If we were just chemicals and molecules, then it would be possible to duplicate everything that has ever been done, exactly. As an example, you can take any incident in the history of the world; let's say your birth. With the empty void of space as your canvas, you could reconstruct the exact molecular structure of everything that existed down to the exact atom everywhere it matters, which may be a town, if the person influence is to be small, or the entire planet, if one's presence is to be felt internationally. So now you can take one exact instance in any time, say 75 years of your lifetime, and then with the aid of a device that could put all the molecules in the exact order to watch everything that happened in one's life at will. The show would be three- dimensional, with sound and smell with whoever is watching being in the fourth dimension. They could watch one's life like a movie, being able to rewind and fast forward, pause, and zoom in and out. It would be possible to un-fry an egg by simply duplicating the molecular structure exactly as it was before it was fried. Soulwaves would be the medium the data is stored.

Every human being transmits Soulwaves at night when you sleep. This is how the one referred to as God, knows everything a human does in his or her lifetime. Information is also transmitted back explaining why it is necessary for humans to sleep. Without sleep, a humans programming gets messed up.

Manipulation of the Great Nothing - Mach Brown, Nov.28, 2010

Dec 21, 2012
Nevada Desert:
Mach had the old feeling he had to be somewhere. It was supposed to be the day the world ended. The stock markets had crashed. Several countries including the United States Presidential elections were in controversy. There was a rise in suicides in every country. UFO and paranormal activity reports were at an all-time high. Most people hunkered down with their families waiting to see what would happen. The funniest movies were released at this time in most countries. Mach stayed in Las Vegas the night before, where he had won several thousand dollars. He hit nearly every time on roulette and then continued to call the right numbers, side-betting in craps at often 5-to-1 or more odds. He left the casino and then drove 40 miles outside Vegas and traveled down a street named Zxxyz St. At 12.02 a.m., he pulled over and stepped out of his vehicle to marvel at the night sky. He walked off the curve a little into the desert. His heart started to race and then he had the same gut feeling that something was about to happen. He pulled out a little flashlight and starts shining it to make sure there were no snakes. He noticed some nice, volcanic-looking rocks on the ground. He took some and then spelled out his initials. He looked up at the sky— 15 lights covered the entire sky from horizon to horizon in the form of

a "V" shape. It was as if the stars had been swept out of the sky because even behind the humongous lights the normal night sky full of stars did not look the same. It looked like the sky was transparent and something huge was behind it. These same lights were seen over many cities with the most impressive sightings in Egypt and Mexico City. Mach was awe-struck now and afraid, when he thought in his heart, *"Courage is to be afraid but continue."* He yelled out,

"I am the Prince of Dawn, bringer of the light manifested from the word of God! I fear you not!" Mach felt as though the entities behind the lights felt his presence. Maybe he was just at the right place at the right time. After a few minutes, the lights zoomed away. He noticed he was covered in sweat and it was 4:20 a.m. He must have fallen asleep. He then noticed he was in his car. The 15 big lights in the sky all seemed like a dream. Because of the time, he rolled up some Armpit Kush his friend The Owl had gotten from some guy called Ghost. It was strong but a bit harsh. The next generation was going to be crossed with a Blackberry Indica x Blueberry Sativa hybrid to get a better flavor. It was to be called Blueberry Armpit. After a few puffs, everything came back to his mind vividly. Before he had seen the lights, he noticed some nice volcanic-looking rocks on the ground after shining a bright light on them to make sure there were no snakes. He stepped out of the car, walked a few feet, and sure enough, there was his initial. The rocks were there, just as he remembered, with his initials spelled out. Therefore, he concluded he had not been dreaming.

This incident very much inspired Mach to trust his thoughts now. What is important to understand is that it is here the sophisticated technologies began. The first project was the 40th Generation heavy metal hemp plants. Mach sold it to IST Corp. with the promise of supplying them with ounces of Blueberry Armpit. The 40th Generation heavy metal hemp

Theory of the Great Nothing

plant project or "Operation Kitchen Sink," as Mach called it soon turned into the Angelskin Suit. Honeycutt C.V.E.G. Motor™ was another technology he claimed derived directly from the Theory of the Great Nothing's principles.

The first experiment actually took place when the Mongoose and Owl were experimenting with the rail gun technology, sending a football-size probe to Mars in the summer of 1992. After the Mongoose was murdered, Mach took it hard, blaming himself. He effectively dropped out of society and changed his name to The Great Elephant, initialed T.G.E. The Great Elephant then gave his friends "titles" based on the animal characteristics in which he said existed in every human. When bestowing their titles, he gave them a platinum ring with their animal manifestation cast on it. This occurred long before The Black Triad or IST Corp. existed, making the rings so special. Mach Brown was just as broke as everyone else was, yet he had so much faith in the future he had seen, he would spend all of his money on those platinum and gold rings than be totally broke. In 1994, Hawk, Bear, and Eagle started a nightclub called Club Skrew. It was struggling, but they were satisfied with it. The Great Elephant came along with his "experiments into the Great Nothing" sparking first Hawk then Eagle's interest in applying high science to the party industry to increase profits. They initiated the brainwashing experiments. After a few attempts trying various methods, and the unfortunate Stanley Turds detail, they started opening clubs and venues at a rate of nearly one club every three months, even going international. By 2015, they had millions of dollars, euros, yen, and several other currencies in private underground vaults. They had a silent partner though, Mach Brown.

Mach had 99% of the millions in funds received from the Black Triad going into IST Corp. to fund its Honeycutt C.V.E.G. Motor and Angelskin suit. His own, personal Angelskin suit did not have blue glowing pinstripes, but instead an ugly costume-looking one with a mirror fishbowl looking helmet. It was used in the Network Hijacking video. When attacked, only a big white ball of light was seen with the naked eye when Mach tested it. This angel skin suit was designed to survive any environment, including deep space, such as the center of stars, black holes, and quasars.

Another project Mach worked on with IST Corp. was the Chug Gun. From this project came the Element Bomb which he felt could be used as a propulsion method. I will not be specific at all concerning the operations or designs to this particular endeavor, but the Great Elephant was able to put an alloy compound into the slug gun, that would then cause a fusion reaction of 1.4 megatons. The Owl later explained the cold fusion technique used was like taking a giant Olympic-size swimming pool full of water and then instantly forcing it to compress to fit into a coffee cup. Nuclear Fusion occurred releasing tremendous amounts of energy in several forms of heat, microwaves, sound waves, alpha, gamma, and several other waveforms. All of which were repelled by his Angelskin "costume." A suitcase nuke did not destroy Washington, DC as the media portrays. The Great Elephant strapped an Element bomb to his ass, ran down Jefferson Dr. SW towards the Washington Monument. At15th. Street, he leaped 574 feet into the air using his angelskin suit's nano- hydraulics, designed after ant muscle fibers, and then detonated the Element bomb using only soulwaves. Mach said his conscience was clear; the "meat mounds" assured him he was doing the right thing. He labeled it as an experiment of his Manipulation of the Great Nothing Theory. He would tie a chug gun to his back, making it detonate an Element Bomb propelling him to Mars within a few minutes. He could then check out Cydonia personally. To be sure, it was God's hand involved; he made the fuse detonate with only his thought, or soulwaves, similar to a person with ESP bending a spoon. He

Theory of the Great Nothing

said he would say a prayer, if   nothing happened it was God's will, and if it detonated, then this too was also God's will.

I spoke to The Great Elephant personally on March 23, 2020, one day before the Theory of the Great Nothing became scientifically recognized as a fact in Washington, D.C. The Great Elephant asked me to manifest myself as the Mighty Ant because I was a builder of Civilizations. He told me to write all I had seen and stayed true to God and myself; then the rest will fall into place. I will attempt to fill in as many blanks as possible now.

Chapter 20

SCENT OF A WOMAN

March 14, 2020
Congo Jungle, Africa
Club Shindinki Hotel and Casino:

It had been two days of deep thought for Preston. The first day he cried like a baby and felt sorry for himself. He did not eat or sleep. No water touched him so every orifice stunk. It was late on the second day when he decided to start smoking the Blueberry Armpit. There was some paper spray, which you sprayed on the bud and then rolled it up, but this was to new-school for Preston. He wanted to take it back to the 80s, but there were only a few transparent papers from Brazil, so he used it. He disrespected the Blueberry Armpit and rolled up a fatty, the size of his pinky. Halfway through, he passed out. The next day he was refreshed. The first thing that crossed his mind was not Amanda's but Tonka's panties covering his eyes and the sweet fragrance of some strange and exotic perfume she must have been wearing. He wondered where she was and who fucked that sweet pussy last night. The next thought, that crossed his mind, was Willoford's fat, Nordic sausage ramming Tonka. It was Tonka's small body with his wife's face he saw. Amanda was making the same expressions and sounds as she was with Willoford. Preston walked to the restroom. His urine where he had pissed on the floor had evaporated leaving only a yellow stain and powdery residue. The 10 mm. thick Dehydroite™ bathtub looked inviting. It had a memory foam ring around the top so you could rest your head. Preston ran the hot water and soaked. He smoked the other half of the spliff he had rolled the night before. He was oblivious to time and had lost all sense of not only it but also his purpose in life. Nothing seemed to matter. His few billion euros, his four big homes, the powerful job, and then an evil thought started to fill his mind, like the grandkids were not his. That was it! It all comes flashing back to Preston. He started flipping through the past months day-by-day the best he could in his head. *"Did that whore Amanda fuck Getty? Maybe the Retired Judge paid her some millions to blow him. Surely, Lt. Martin had her... that's why Getty brought his name up... he looked into Lt Martin's house and Amanda was there... No, that whore fucked that nigger in my house."* He then pictured Amanda fucking a big Black man and enjoying it just as much as with Willoford entered his head. He had had enough. He was getting out of there so he could confront Amanda face-to-face. No cybercall; he wanted to see the expression when she lied face to face.

There were some complimentary workout sweats hanging in the closet. Preston put them on and then headed to the door. The other side looked like any other luxury hotel hallway except a foot wide strip of water was running sideways along the wall defying gravity as decoration. He felt this effect was neat and actually let out a small, sinister grin. His whole outlook on the world had changed. Just a few days ago, he could not have appreciated anything these damn niggers could have put together, but now they seemed even more civilized than his circle of friends. He found an elevator and noticed it went 80 stories vertically and 350 stories horizontally. Preston pressed the button marked "Lobby." He entered into a dark hall with several glass windows. There were several other people in the hall. Loud dance music was playing, and some people were making out with girls on fuzzy sofa- looking objects. The walls appeared to be original earth rock. When he walked past the first glass window, he looked out and to his amazement saw several blocks of building structures, at least 300 feet beneath him, stretching a few miles into pitch-blackness. He felt as though he was in a skyscraper looking down at a city, although he was underground. Thousands of lights glittered as far as the eye could see. The difference was the lights were not all ugly advertisements but artistically designed specifically to entertain the tourists. Some were obviously synchronized with music; others performed 3-D holographic shows. For an instant, he felt excited with butterflies in his stomach—a feeling he had not had in decades. Like a child set to explore an amusement park, here was something on the planet he had not yet experienced. Just when he was starting to feel good, the thought of his exploring partner, Amanda, would never get to see this place, at least not with him, crushed his brief happiness. He felt sorry for her for being so stupid.

After a minute's observation, Preston realized the sophisticated light shows were to attract well-paying patrons to particular clubs, bars, brothels, and every possible hybrid combination. A person could sit in the window for many hours observing the beautiful spectacle of lights, just as several couples were doing as they passionately kissed, but he had to escape. He felt as if he was still a hostage until questions were answered and those who had wronged him had paid their price. He moved on down the hall toward the lobby sign. The next glass windows offered a different view where he could see glass windows all along the rim of the massive cavern. He now understood the horizontal elevator.

Once he made it into the lobby, a busy casino greeted him. It all seemed like total madness to him that so much could be built 1,000s of feet below the surface. He wondered who these people were, but deep down inside he felt he knew— most likely the world's rich and privileged and their overgrown kids. From his recent experiences, he knew he was being watched. He decided to find the Cydonia Lounge and hopefully, Fisk Braun who was supposed to meet him there. As Preston walked through the casino, he noticed the thick smell of marijuana and the unforgettable smells of opium and hashish. "*Now this is gambling with a twist,*" he thought. He found an exit and was amazed how crowded the streets were.

Scent of a Woman

He figured there had to be at least 100,000 people, probably more. Most were drinking. Some were in costumes, while others were half-naked. A mob of huge men and two 6-foot women with big white SECURITY glowing across their chests stared at him menacingly. One started talking on some type of communication device and then they all started laughing at Preston. He decided to move with the flow of the crowd down the street. He noticed there was always someone with a glowing SECURITY written across his or her chest in sight and they were always giants. Huge open-air nightclubs' music competed and the excitement was overwhelming. Human circles formed around street performers who were performing circus-like acts with modern day twists, slowed the flow of traffic to a crawl. Above him was an elevated ski lift-type multi-passenger train silently sped by under total blackness above it. A guy pushing a cart selling beers and mixed drinks caught Preston's eye. He decided to drink one beer to take the edge off. He stopped the man but then remembered he had no money. The beer vendor smiled as if he empathized with Preston's predicament and then handed him his favorite beer. Halfway through the beer, he decided to ask a few questions to get some sense of direction. A store called Cloud 9 caught his attention, so he walked inside.

All around him, girls were dancing to 80's music on top of counters, while their boyfriends snorted different colored powder beneath them. It was overcrowded and most people were dressed retro. Preston read a lit menu board serving six types of cocaine: Metro, Scorpion, Fish Scale, Pineapple, Peruvian Flake, and Strawberry. The percentages of the cocaine's purity were listed beside them as well as the origin and a brief history of the product. The same information was found on drink cards placed on each table. Preston thought the drinks looked cool, as fruit floated on blue and pink ice swirls. A beautiful dark-skin, Persian-looking young lady, maybe 20-

years-old, placed her hand around the back of Preston's neck and leaned into his ear and yelled over the banging music,

"Will you get me something to get me started?"

"I… I can't. I don't have my wallet," Preston replied. He was genuinely upset he did not have any money. The young woman made a sad, pouting face. Then she started to wiggle to the beat as she sipped her rainbow-colored drink. She had a very nice athletic body and was dressed in a short leather skirt with a designer "Bubba Wear" shirt, probably the $1,000 type. Preston leaned back over and asked,

"How do you get to the Cydonia Lounge?"

"I have been here for three days and I only know this place and my Hotel… oh, and Club Heaven about three blocks from here. You should really check it out—here try this." She pushed her colorful drink toward Preston's lips— the sad look in her eye found compassion in his heart, so he took a sip. The traditional taste of the Mai Thai drink made with 151 proof rum and 30 proof fruit liquors mixed with sweet fruit juice to smooth the potency, washed down his dry throat. She smiled and then started to dance a little more. About this time, three dudes walked up; two speaking French and the other, a Russian, also speaking French but with so heavy of a Russian accent it sounded like he was speaking Russian.

"Hey Sophia Where iz your friendz? I found my partzner and his boyzes I waz telling youzz aboutet" the Russian one said smiling with heavily accented English.

"They will be back soon. One is at the …" Four girls broke through the crowd surrounding Preston's new female companion whom he now knew her name was Sophia, all of them in their early twenties except one who looked to be maybe 18 or 19.

"Hey girl, this place is the bomb!"

"Aghhh! Girl, you have to try this one…"

"Sophia, who are your new friends?" they all talked at once. The three men smiled and whispered to each other.

Scent of a Woman

One of the French men said in French to his two friends, "Let's go and get a booth." The Russian then said,

"Comez with us wev have it tall." He was probably in his late 20's. He turned and walked away and the whole crew, guys, and girls, started to follow. Sophia grabbed Preston by the arm saying,

"Come on, you are with me." She was small with a large, little bottom protruding underneath the skirt. She had a young sweet smell like a flower that caught Preston's attention. *"I plan to use these guys to help me find the Cydonia Lounge,"* is what Preston was telling himself was the reason he let the small petite young lady overpower him and take him to the Russian and his Frenchman companions' booth.

The so-called store was a huge open warehouse with two dance floors. Aligning the walls were booths with mirror and glass counter tables. The upstairs section had glass transparent floors in places like beneath the tables in the booth. A cornucopia of fruit and nuts lay on the table offering every fruit from a watermelon to a grape. Expensive rum, whiskey, vodka, and cognac along with several brands of beer on ice decorated the table. One of the Frenchmen first pulled out some pink powder and then the other one had some snow-white powder with baby blue colored flakes. The girls started to giggle and smoked a blunt. At first, a couple of the girls and only one of the Frenchmen indulged while the Russian kept sniffing the powders. An hour and a half later after one of the bottles of whiskey, which happened to be Preston's favorite brand was gone, everyone in the booth was indulging with the powders. The guys talked about their short lives and flirted back and forth with the girl who had caught his eye. It was during the third hour, Preston started feeling good. Some Australian guy walked by with two girls and buddies and went up to one of the Frenchmen as they joined the party. He ordered some of the Pineapple and Strawberry and it blew Preston's mind. He sat in the Cloud 9 store until Sophia and her friends left for their hotel room with the other men—she said Preston could not follow. Sophia simply said,

"Goodbye. We have to leave now. Nice meeting you." She gave him a hug and then left. For a moment, Preston was heartbroken. All he remembered was the smell of her hair as it brushed against his cheek and the sexy butt twisting away from him—the last part of her he had seen. He felt an attachment to Sophia like he needed to protect her. He left the Cloud 9 store with Amanda's lustful moans, Tonka's panties, and Sophia's goodbye hug on his mind.

He walked up the street passing novelty smoke shops, fancy restaurants, sex shops, bars, a club called Fish, and then, finally, the Heaven store. He walked in through the old-school beads. Music from the 60s was playing at a lower volume than the Cloud 9 store. Soft cushions were everywhere and instead of an upstairs, there was a downstairs. He walked downstairs hoping to see Sophia since she helped with the pain of Amanda. Instead, he saw the menu: Codeine syrup, Opium, Ecstasy, Mushrooms, Peyote. He had had enough "fun" so he turned to leave to find his way to the surface.

As he was walking through the crowded streets, a huge arena-looking structure caught his attention. There was a huge picture of a female judge in a half bikini/half judge outfit holding a gavel. The woman on the picture was the little Asian woman Tonka who had placed her panties around Preston's eyes. The sign read: SPECIAL GUEST JUDGE TONKA, Preston had to go inside; there was no way he could resist. When he walked in, there was a huge hole cut into the ground with bleachers placed all around like a stadium. About 100 feet down in the middle of a dirt ground, little Tonka was holding a microphone and conducting a trial on what appeared to be patrons who broke the law while staying at Club Shindinki's Hotel and Casino. Some were accused of theft and one of rape. The jury was the audience who voted by touch-screen determining the guilt or innocence of the "detainees."

Scent of a Woman

Food and drinks were being served at extravagant prices. Large muscular men, built like professional football players or professional wrestlers, surrounded the ring. The whole show was quite entertaining until one man, the rapist, was found guilty of touching a little young lady inappropriately. He was dressed immaculately and had a smirk on his face the whole time. He even tried to slap Tonka on her exposed butt cheek. The convicted man was licking his lips at Tonka as she read his verdict.

"Guilty of all accusations!" Tonka said as forcefully as she could with such a sweet voice. She then gave the punishment.

"You are now sentenced to two ass beatings for your crime. One today and one tomorrow." Two of the large men started to walk toward the convicted man as he smiled at the spectacle of being judged by the supermodel Tonka.

"What are you talking about? This show has been really fun but now I demand you release me to the nearest British Embassy. I have full diplomatic immunity..." As the guilty man made his demands, one of the large men kicked him in his ass. A loud yelp came out as the British man quickly turned around and was as red as a beet in the face. He started to yell and point his finger at the much larger man's chest, yelling, "I'll sue you! I'll have you arrested! Do you know who I am? You will..." The crowd was going wild. By this time the second large man grabbed the convicted man by the back of his pants pulling them so far up the British man's butt crack, he ripped them. For the next 10 minutes, the two big men proceed to take turns beating the hell out of the British rapist with little resistance. They do not use their fist as much as the back of their hands to slap him around. Still, they managed to give him a bloody nose, two black eyes, a broken rib, and the anxiety of knowing he had another one coming tomorrow. The ass beatings were no less severe for the thieves. Each set of "Professional Ass Beaters" as they were called, had their own distinct style and technique for beating up the accused. Some used martial art moves, some street brawled, while others focused on wrestling power moves. Preston could not help but laugh at the sound the 6'4" 360 lb. fat Black thief made when a short stocky Ass Beater body slammed him. A loud splat and fart was heard and then shit flew everywhere out the too tight Hawaiian shorts he was wearing as they ripped at the seam. Because there was so much, they had to have an intermission to clean up a little after his trial.

The next person on trial, to Preston's surprise, was Fiske Braun. He looked scruffy like he had not been asleep in a few days. Preston was supposed to meet him three or four days ago—he had lost track of time.

"Mr. Braun here is accused of the minor crime of trespassing and assault," Tonka yelled into the mini-microphone. A large graviton screen above showed the view from a security camera of Fiske obviously inside a restricted zone snooping around. After a few seconds, it showed Fiske using some kind of weapon to subdue a guard to gain access to a locked secure zone. Once on the other side, a fog was released causing Fiske to pass out. It was probably some kind of an automatic defense system. Fiske fell for the same trap Preston had; immaculate security disguised by the illusion of incompetence. It causes the intruder to let his guard down. The crowd quickly found Fiske guilty, his punishment was "one swift kick to the ass" for trespassing, and 5 minutes alone in the center of "court" with the guard, he assaulted. The "swift kick to the ass" was to come now with the assault punishment set for tomorrow.

The crowd started to go wild as a deformed looking man jogged to the center of the pit. He had on a tank top and biker shorts. His upper body was that of a skinny kid but his legs were those of a bodybuilder on steroids. Bigfoot was his nickname and he was the deliverer of the one swift kick. Preston didn't know what to do at first, but he made his way

Scent of a Woman

to the front and jumped the guardrail and then started walking toward Tonka. She made eye contact with him and smiled as though she was happy to see him. She waved away the security guards and let Preston walk right up to her.

"Hey, what are you doing here?" she said surprised. She placed the microphone where it would not pick up her voice.

"Your lovers kidnapped me, remember."

"Nobody's my lover—it's all business…"

"… Look, the man right there is here looking for me." Preston pointed towards Fiske who was in a straitjacket- type device with duct tape over his mouth while his eyes were rolling around in his head.

"Please help us get out of here." Tonka paused for a second; she looked around at the crowd. She then softly said into the microphone,

"Due to new evidence, we have to postpone the ass kicking of Fiske Braun until tomorrow. I am taking a break." Tonka dropped the microphone and gavel and then just walked away. Her sexy, tight butt cheeks seemed to beacon Preston to follow her, as no woman could walk with such hip movement   naturally. First, three security guards appeared and then what seemed to be an entourage fell in line. Preston grabbed Fiske and followed. In his mind, this was it. Tonka was his only way out. They walked through a red-carpeted tunnel leading to the arena—probably a celebrity entrance. He took off the duct tape and straightjacket from Fiske. Fiske stared at Preston as if amazed and then finally he said,

"My God, you are the Mighty Ant."

"What? What have they done to you?" Preston asked as he noticed Fiske looked as though he had seen a ghost. Fiske started to cry like a baby. "What's wrong with you, snap out of it!" Preston yelled at Fiske as Fiske started to stare into space. Fiske then said,

"My biggest secret was I saw Prime Minister Vladimir Peter Chuikov and U.S. President Mary Lee fucking at my Castle Neutrality; I have it on micro-disc. She must have pussy- whipped him cause he mustered up a massive coalition to go fuck those niggers up... but now they know."

Preston was stunned by not only the information but also by Fiske's demeanor. It was so much different from the other times he had met with him. Fiske then just started to laugh.

"You know, they got you too, Mr. Ant. They said they had you a long time ago", Fiske giggled. A familiar smell hit Preston making him feel light headed. It was the Blueberry Armpit. Tonka was walking toward him with a huge green, blue, and purple cigarette with an orange tip burning. Preston then noticed another one of his favorite songs was playing in the background. She passed it to him and he could not resist. Preston's heart was racing as he looked into her eyes— he could still remember how her panties smelled so sweet. He felt he knew her on a deep level that no one else did. He took the hardest hit he could and passed out.

He awoke back in the room where he had first seen Getty. He was naked in the comfortable bed and Tonka was beside him with her back to him, tooted up, and totally nude. She was in a deep sleep; it seemed she had passed out also from the Blueberry Armpit, Preston thought. He felt hard as a rock. He could not resist rubbing the head of his penis up against Tonka's warm, hot exposed puss. It felt swollen to Preston— he could not believe it was really happening. He actually pinched himself and sure enough, it was real. Preston paused for a second and thought about a few things. His penis was right up against Tonka's puss with the head just starting to penetrate. Preston thought about Amanda and Willoford. He then thought about the *Theory of the Great Nothing* book he had read. His mind became clear and he felt free. He wondered if Tonka cared if he was touching her the way he was. Tonka moved her hips causing Preston to slide a full inch inside her.

Scent of a Woman

It was the best thing he had ever felt. He did not move for several minutes until he noticed somehow half his penis was inside her and she was slowly hunching back. Preston caught a subtle whiff of Tonka's woman juices and then lost all control. Tonka started to moan as Preston gave her all that he had. He rolled her over to look into her eyes. She opened her eyes smiled and then proceeded to make love to Preston. After his orgasm, he fell back on the bed when out the corner of his eye he saw Zessi Si coming into the room butt naked. He made love to her and Tonka again and then fell into a deep sleep.

When he awoke, he was in a lounge that looked like something from another world. Water was flowing across the roof, defying gravity. There were real animals separated by 99% transparent foot- thick glass making them part of the decor. A huge elephant with 9-foot tusk, a 30-foot python, and 700 lb gorilla seem as wise as any patron does. A black mane lion and eagle seemed to sway to the beat of slowed down rap songs. Images of Egyptian-looking pyramids decorated the walls, but upon closer observation, they were high-definition close-ups of the structure on Mars in the Cydonia region; actual photos taken by the late Mongoose and Wise Owl doing the Rail Gun experiment. Preston felt surreal as he was fully dressed in a nice suit and new shoes. He just stared at the walls for an hour. He could not believe the detailed hieroglyphs on the face. Only holding about 500 people, Preston actually recognized a few of the big-wigs present partying the night away after spending half a million dollars for an all-expense week vacation for two at club Shindinki Hotel and Casino including door pickup and return in an Areosport 3000 and two free escorts. Preston felt the same surreal feeling when Tonka walked up to him took him by the hand and walked him to a table with Getty seated beside Col. Brett and the Retired Judge. The Hawk person and Tyrone Honeycutt were also at the table. Tyrone looked as though he wanted to rip Preston apart while Hawk seemed rather unconcerned. The Retired

Judge and Col Brett eyes were dancing around in their head like Frisk Braun's were and how Preston felt his were. The heavy smell of Blueberry Armpit filled the air causing Preston to go into a dream-like state. Getty was dressed nicely, seated cross-legged. He had a black eye, which was swollen shut and his lip was busted up with stitches in it. Despite the scrapes and bruises, Getty looked like a White man to Preston now. Getty started with a serious look on his face.

"I always liked you Preston because of your integrity. I actually ignored your hating on me especially once I found out your wife was a whore." Preston knew then they had done something to him. Usually, the mention of Amanda did something to him. Now it seemed he had no emotions. Getty's voice continued as he pointed to the Retired Judge and Col. Brett.

"As you can see, I take care of people I like. You may know Clark Johnson and Ghost here. I personally made sure they were saved from the Great Elephant's insidious attack on Washington DC. I can assure you, he was out-voted by six to one yet… it was because of one damn woman, Summer. Your people killed her so where she died, the Great Elephant 'started his quest for her lost soul' at the expense of DC. I tried to stop the son of a bitch, but he kicked my ass… over a bitch." Getty was obviously upset at his old friend's actions.

"A dead bitch at that" the Retired Judge whom Preston now knew name was Clark Johnson added. He was obviously brainwashed.

"We must make sure nothing like this can ever happen again. One man must not have absolute power ever again," Getty continued after a pause. Col. Brett then started to talk sounding more like a robot then his normal self,

"Fiske Braun has informed us the Prime Minister of Russia fucked President Mary Lee at his Castle Neutrality…" Tyrone Honeycutt after taking a sip of a blue smoking drink interrupts Col Brett,

Scent of a Woman

"This Prime Minister, Vladimir Peter Chuikov, is upset his lover, President Mary Lee, was killed in the blast, so he has gathered a huge army of several nations against us."

"Over a dead bitch," the Retired Judge added looking disgusted. The Hawk's voice echoed inside Preston's head. "My friend, you have been reprogrammed for the good of society. It's called the Stanley Turds technique. We have been softening you up for some time, now we need to ask you a favor. I want you to put this over your eyes so we can further instruct you on what you need to do." Preston let them put goggles, earphones, and a breathing tube on him with no resistance. Preston last thought was he never would have imagined Col. Brett was the infamous pot grower called Ghost and a hydroponic setup was in his closet in Washington, DC, growing Blueberry Armpit along with his expensive chairs.

EPILOGUE
Moscow Russia December 5, 2021:

Vladimir Peter was frightened by what he had just read. Of course, he had partied at the "underground city" Club Shindinki Hotel and Casino, but never had he been invited to Cydonia Lounge. This was what most disturbed him. Was he, the Prime Minister of Russia and billionaire not an elite enough socialite to party on Mars? He was furious and could not sleep. He remembered his vacation to Africa. There were no free escorts for him. He paid $100,000 just for the Aerocar pick up and they sent an ugly Areovan packed full of millionaire Asians spending their cheap U.S. dollars. Just when he was getting comfortable, he actually witnessed the craziest thing he had ever seen. The Areovan flew over Israel and picked up some rich Jews and their Arab princess dates. The Areovan did not even take off; just waited a few minutes and then some rich Arabs who Vladimir Peter knew were the sworn enemies of the Jewish crew got on with some Jewish girls. It started out with some words being exchanged and then security came and "slapped the shit" out of the instigator. The big Black man with SECURITY written on his shirt then made everyone take a mandatory hit of marijuana called Blueberry Armpit. It was a quiet two- hour flight from Israel to the Congo Jungle and there were absolutely no more incidents.

Vladimir Peter took a sleeping aid and fell into a deep sleep, knowing in a few hours he would stomp out those threatening Russia's sovereignty with the World Constitution demands, while at the same time *"killing those Black niggers who hurt his baby President Mary Lee"* he thought to himself. So deep asleep he did not hear the small caliber gunfire that was muffled by the thick walls of the Kremlin.

Bear hovered the fully armed Areosport 3000 as Tyrone "Falcon" Honeycutt in an Angelskin suit hopped through a window with two other people. One led the way, the other two followed. Tyrone did not use his chug gun to subdue the guards but fired the plastic one that shot the wooden toothpick-like projectiles. Other times he just punched through their body. He had slain only about 16 men getting to the so-called most powerful man in the world's bedroom. *"The Wise Owl was right—this may be the best way to conduct war."* He thought. Prime Minister Vladimir Peter Chuikov door was unlocked and he was sleeping like a baby.

"Wake yo ass up!" Vladimir Peter felt himself being rudely awakened with someone hammer-punching him upside the head. Before he could focus his eyes to see who it was, he felt himself being kicked out his bed. "Wake yo ass up motherfucka!" the voice continued. Peter screams as he realizes it was not a dream.

"Help! Help! I am under attack! Intruder! Intruder!" he yelled in Russian.

"Shut yo bitch as up motherfucka! I come to beat your ass." A voice Vladimir Peter recognized. *"The American Preston Ross?"* he thought aloud. Finally, he focused, and he saw me dressed in a $20,000 leather and silk Bubba Wear outfit accessories and all. A chain with a medallion of an upside-down pyramid and an eye in the middle hung to my dick. Behind me, Fiske Braun had a cyber-camera filming it live, broadcasting on several cybervision channels. The Falcon watched the hallway firing a flurry of wood at the security units starting to converge on us.

"Yea ass hole it's me! For now, on you will call me The Mighty Ant, middle name Mighty." I took off the necklace Big Bubba Moody Jr. had given me. Then walk up to Vladimir Peter and started whaling away. I got the Russian Prime Minister in a headlock and started punching and talking shit to him. The Prime Minister after realizing millions were witnessing him getting his ass kicked bit me in the rib cage then started throwing blows in a windmill-style when I got up off him. One caught me nearly knocking me out. It was a lucky shot. It gave the bastard a little hope. Tyrone was laughing so loud witnessing the "two rich White boys" fighting who didn't really know how to fight it helped me shake off the effects of the haymaker blow. "*This is why The Falcon demanded to come,*" I thought angrily. Tyrone was laughing so hard he was screaming,

"I'm too weak to go on! Oh my God! ha ha ha I can't even breeth…ha ha ha! … I'm dying here, ha ha ha heee!" He sounded like he was crying. Fiske nearly was shot. Vladimir Peter had taken a lot more damage with an eye nearly closed, busted lip and nose.

"Oh you think it's a game, huh!" I yelled, lowered my head and then charged in fighting savagely really laying it on Vladimir Peter causing him to ball up like a bitch and then go into a defensive shell. Vladimir Peter fell to the ground, so I started to stomp him. I then went around the room picking up anything I could, breaking it over Peter's head and busting it open. I was fighting like the Gorilla, Prometheus. I then looked into the cyber-cam while holding the bloody unconscious Prime Minister by the hair and said,

"This could be you if you get out of line no matter who you are!" I feel my eyes dancing around in my head, but I feel more alive than ever.

The Day was canceled; all military forces were asked to stand down. All the world leaders realized they could be easily touched without civilians having to die for them. The World Constitution was signed and ratified within one year by every nation on Earth. This moved humans toward a second level of civilization, much more advanced than any seen before on Earth, eliminating homelessness, poverty, wars, famine, and most diseases.

THE END of Book Two.

www.ingramcontent.com/pod-product-compliance
Lightning Source LLC
Chambersburg PA
CBHW070049260626
47160CB00004B/1145